THE ICE HARVESTER

THE ICE HARVESTER

a novel

GP JOHNSTON

Copyright © 2018 GP Johnston

ISBN: 978-0-692-17560-6

All right reserved. Published by ALN International Publications, LLC

PART I

Ypres, Belgium. March 1915

That night, Henry Graham sensed that his death might be imminent. They marched through muddy fields in the dark, these men, passing soft rolling hills and outcroppings of pine forest and out again to acres of marshy farmland, their dark silhouettes moving under the glow of a fat crescent moon. The press reported that the war would be over by early spring, at the latest, and some of the men joked and chuckled with one another. They hoped to finally see some action before it all ended, their high spirits belying the recent rumors of chaos and carnage occurring up at the Front.

It was not until they were ten or so miles into the march that they came upon a darkened village that had been shelled to ruins. The men stopped and stared. There was practically nothing left. Only mounds of rubble and a large wooden cross from a church. One by one, they grew quiet.

Like the other new recruits in his battalion, Henry Graham did not know what to expect. Most of the men had never seen any action, except for the sergeant, a Swiss man who'd been serving with the French since the war started. As far as they knew, their orders were to join the rest of the battalion between a Canadian company and a French territorial company of Moroccans where they would wait it out as reserves. But orders often changed at a moment's notice, so it was really anybody's guess.

Further on, the sounds of artillery fire started and the night sky lit up with bright flashes. At first most of the men thought it was just thunder and lightning; but when the sergeant spat on the ground and looked up at the sky, they could all see it in his eyes—he was scared.

Nevertheless, they carried on, moving toward the sparks of light. They were very tired and the sixty pounds of equipment they carried on their backs weighed heavy on their bones.

Suddenly—

a terrible sound from above!

like a roaring wind—

Everyone in the line fell to the ground and covered their heads. There was an explosion followed by the metallic cling-clang of shrapnel falling around them. A couple of the men let out a terrified shout before they descended once again into silence.

Someone started laughing.

Graham was still on his belly when he finally took his hands off his head and looked up.

It was the Sergeant, standing over them. "It's all right, men," he boomed through his laughter. "You'll all get used to it. Soon, you'll be able to hear where they're going to burst."

What the hell am I doing here?

Realizing that the danger was over, the men rose. They

started to march again, everyone aware of their harsh new reality—some alive, breathing, walking the earth—might be moments away from their doom. Muffled prayers began to rise now from a few of the other men in the line, but most (Graham included) remained eerily silent.

Later they stopped to rest. Graham lit a cigarette and rested his back against the trench wall. A moment or two later, something scurried across his feet. He struck a match and shone the light on the ground: frogs, field mice and rats (the size of which he'd never seen before) scurried all around them, casting twisted shadows along the trench wall from the flickering flame.

"Christ all mighty," someone muttered.

"This war's the best thing ever to happen to the rats," the sergeant shouted. He gave them a wide-eyed grin. "They've been feeding off the dead, my Boys! Fattening themselves up. All they do is eat and fuck. Eat, eat, eat. Fuck, fuck, fuck. It's a glorious time to be a rat, my boys. A glorious time, I tell you!" He laughed loud and hard.

Another Legionnaire caught Graham's eye and they shared an uneasy look.

They barely had any time to rest before they were marching again. The drizzle turned to rain and came down hard for some time, before changing back to a steady drizzle.

The booming of the artillery and the flashes of light continued. It seemed as if it would never stop. At some point, the sergeant clicked his tongue and muttered out loud to himself: "The Germans are up to something. I can feel it in my bones. They're up to something, alright."

They carried on a long stretch of trench. Wooden planks lined the mud beneath them, making it easier to walk. The artillery noise grew louder, growing in frequency and intensity. Word came from down the line that they should watch out for sleeping men on the ground.

They turned down another line of trench. There were men already stationed here. Small hollows had been cut into the sides of the trench and there were some soldiers inside, sleeping

They finally made it to the reserve trench just before eleven. The men lined themselves up as the Company Commander, Capitaine Brousseau, inspected the troops. The Capitaine appeared to be in his early to mid-thirties; a tall, slim, and handsomely athletic looking fellow with a kindly air. He told the men they were going to be in for a long night. The Germans were up to something, he told them, and he felt the artillery fire was going to continue until dawn.

"They usually aim the shells toward the reserve and rear trenches, Men. I'm afraid we'll be getting the brunt of it."

Some of the men let out an audible groan.

"Nothing we can do about it," the Capitaine called out. "We'll just have to wait it out. Keep your heads down, and stay alert."

Some of the men were put on work detail, adding sandbags to the trenches, while smaller groups were put on sentry duty. The rest were told to try and get some sleep. Graham collapsed to the ground and rested his back against the trench wall.

A Legionnaire by the name of Callaway, a weary man in his forties, who'd been with the Legion long before the war started, sat down next to him. Calloway lit a cigarette and sneered. "Makes me fucking miss Algiers."

Graham lit a cigarette and rested his head against the hard clay. He looked up into the sky. The flashes of light continued. He heard another roar from above and instinctively covered his head. The shell fell about another twenty yards to the rear. An orange glow followed by the metallic clinging of shell casings falling everywhere.

Graham took a drag of his cigarette. Then he dug into the pocket of his great coat and pulled out a worn photograph.

Henry and Lillian.

Spring of 1909.

Standing beside the boat basin in Central Park.

"She's a real pretty one," Calloway said, looking over Graham's shoulder.

Graham tried to ignore him. His heart still ached to see her. Try as he might, he just couldn't seem to exorcise the immense pain that their love had caused. But the thought that he might be killed without ever seeing her again filled him with another kind of regret. He stared at that photograph. He started to compose a letter in his mind:

Dear Lillian:

There are many possible fates for this letter. The fate I am most hopeful for is that, by dumb luck, I manage to come out of this madness unscathed and return to you, envelope in hand, and look at your pretty face as you read.....

The memories came to him now. It pained him to think about it. He looked up into the night sky. Continuous flashes of artillery fire drew light on the black smoke, drifting like wisps of disembodied spirits in the night sky...

1909:

Six Years Earlier…

CHAPTER 1

Tarrytown, NY. February 1909

Before the war came, they were the wide-backed men, guiding the ice cakes upriver with long iron hooks. Hoisted block after block onto the roaring steam-powered conveyers running up the cliffs and into the white clapboard icehouses. Steam rose off their sweaty bodies and snow flurries twisted around them like gnats in the bitter wind. Their work coats were damp and the wool rested heavy on their bones while draught horses moved like demons in the mist.

That second week of February, a favorite gardener of the Harold family disappeared. An unexpected thaw made its way northward above the swelling waters of the Hudson River, and fell soft on the highlands of New York.

Within a few days, the ice thinned to the point where they couldn't harvest. They spent the days at Daly's Tavern drinking and singing union songs from the *Little Red Book*.

The *New York Times headline, February 12, 1909 read*:

Ice Famine Threatens Unless Cold Sets In.

They all got drunk, singing the songs of Joe Hill, Ralph Chaplin and T-Bone Slim. When the thaw lingered and their money started to run out, hunger set in. Some of the men started talking of revolution.

Some nights they sang.

Some nights they argued.

Some nights they brawled.

Still, they drank.

Eventually Graham spent all the money that he had left to spend. There were rumors of odd jobs in town, so he made his way up Tarrytown's muddy Main Street. Past "Squire" Elias Nann's Hat Store. Past the Pierson Greenhouses. Finally, he stopped at Sackett and Company Druggist.

The bell hanging on the hinge rang as the door slammed shut behind him. Inside, there was a musty odor mixed with the sickly sweet smell of syrup and chemicals. But for reasons he could not understand, the familiarity offered him an odd sense of comfort. He looked around and spotted a young soda jerk behind the marble counter, cleaning the surface with a rag.

Graham walked toward the back of the store. The wooden floorboards creaked beneath his feet. Mr. Sackett was the druggist, a slight man with a perfect Roman nose. He was standing behind the prescription counter. He straightened his bow tie, pushed his round spectacles up the bridge of his nose and crossed his arms over his chest, his eyes narrowing on the young man with a curious kind of suspicion. "What can I do for you, Son?"

"I was wondering if you had any work?"

"Sorry," Sackett said, shaking his head.

"Deliveries? Repairs? Whatever work you got. I'll do it."

"You're the third ice man who's come in here this week."

"That's because there's no work. Hasn't been work for a couple of weeks now."

"So I hear. Look, son, I wish I had something for you, but..."

"Guess I can wait out front in case you need me."

"No. I won't. And I don't need you out there bothering any respectable customers."

Graham acted like he didn't hear him. He bumped into a table display of Violet Glycerine soap and Willow Charcoal tablets on his way out, the small bell ringing again as the door swung shut behind him.

Outside, the air smelled of fresh cut lumber and thawed earth. Graham yawned, struck a match on the sole of one of his mud-caked boots and lit a cigarette. Maybe he should leave town and find work elsewhere. *What's the point in sticking around?*

After all, his pockets were empty. He knew there wouldn't be work tomorrow or the day after that. The thaw was likely to last the remainder of winter. He thought about jumping a freight train and heading out west. There was always talk of work out there. San Diego. More work than able-bodied men, they'd said.

An open topped motor car struggled to make its way through the mud on Main Street.

The noise from the car grew louder; its engine coughing

and sputtering.

Graham fiddled with his rolled up shirtsleeves, the cigarette dangling from the corner of his mouth as he watched the car approach.

The driver was a well-dressed, middle-aged man, and his companion looked to be his daughter, a young woman.

The car coughed one last time and let out a hiss of steam as the driver shut off the engine.

The driver was about to step out on the road, when he noticed the mud and piles of horse scat. "Excuse me, my dear," he said, crawling over his daughter. "It's probably best if I get out on your side."

Graham walked toward the man. "Here. Let me help you, Sir."

"No, no. I'm quite all right. Thank you." The man stepped out of the car and onto the sidewalk, balancing himself with his cane. He brushed off his suit with his free hand and gave Graham a friendly nod. "Lovely day today."

"Yessir."

"Nice to take a little break from the winter now and then, eh?"

Graham nodded.

"I assume the town druggists still sell gasoline?" The man asked.

"Think so. If not, you might try the Briscoe Motor Plant down the road. I can point you that way, if you want?"

Graham looked a little closer at the man. He was tall, rail-thin and quite pale; a gentleman with a thick mustache neatly trimmed over his thin lips. He wore an expensive-looking gray suit and perfectly enunciated every word he spoke.

Graham had no doubts that the man and his daughter were members of the elite society.

He hated them both.

The man thanked Graham for his assistance, shifted his weight on his cane and then limped into the druggist. The young woman remained in the car.

She had light strawberry-colored hair and wore a stylish navy blue dress that exposed a suggestive hint of the ankle; a white stone was pinned at the throat; and upon her head was a silk leghorn hat with a Peacock feather sticking out of the side. She was intently focused on the book in her hands.

Graham looked away and took a drag of his cigarette before glancing back. She was very pretty, he thought; but she seemed completely unaware of his presence. She covered a yawn and continued reading. He glanced back toward the druggist.

It was quiet, the only sound coming from the sparrows singing in the trees by the river.

A horse pulling a coal wagon clip-clopped up behind the parked motorcar and came to a stop. The driver walked around front, tied the reins to the green horse tie and patted the horse's neck. He whispered something and then reached deep into his pocket for a couple of sugar cubes to feed him.

Graham spoke: "What book is that you're reading?"

She didn't answer him.

He repeated himself.

She glanced up at Graham, hesitated a moment and then held up the book so he could see.

"*Lewis Rand*," he read the title. "Any good?"

"It's too early to say. I've just started it."

"I suppose you're in town to visit the Cornelius family?"

She tilted her head and gave him a curious look with the faintest semblance of a smile.

"Do you work for the druggist?"

He shook his head, no.

"I work for the Hudson Ice Company."

"Oh?"

"I'm an ice harvester, Miss."

She seemed unimpressed. "They say there's going to be a terrible ice famine. Is that true?"

"You don't have nothing to worry about, Miss. Someone of your station won't be inconvenienced."

"Well I suppose it makes life easier for you."

"Easier? What do you mean?"

"Less ice means less work, doesn't it?"

"Less work means less pay."

The young woman seemed uneasy again. "I'm sorry. I didn't mean to cause you any offense…"

She's like the rest of them. He was about to say something crass, but held back. He glanced over at the driver of the coal truck. It appeared he had mistaken their interaction as flirtation. He watched them now with growing amusement.

The young woman was about to say something else when the door to the druggist opened and her father reappeared, smiling and holding up the container of gas. "We're all set now, Lillian. All set, my love!"

The young woman straightened in her seat, trying to force

a smile.

"Do you think it will be enough to get us to Lindenhurst and then back to Manhattan?"

"I certainly hope so."

Seeing an opportunity, Graham stepped forward. "Here, Sir," he said. "Allow me."

The man obliged and gave Graham the container.

As Graham proceeded to fill the car up, the man broke into a long coughing fit. Graham stopped filling the car for a moment and looked in the man's direction. *He's sick. I've heard men with coughs like that not long before they died.*

Graham finished with the gas and then went around front to crank the drive shaft. After a few tries the car started. The man thanked him and gave him a nickel.

"Can't we drive some more?" Lillian asked her father.

"We're late to Lindenhurst as it is. Your mother will have my head if we keep Mrs. Cornelius waiting."

The man cleared his throat and straightened his back. He must have seen something in the way Graham looked at his daughter, because he smiled. "Good day to you, young fellow," he said, tapping the brim of his derby as the gears made a crunching noise and the car lurched forward and started to move.

The young woman held her chin up. She fixed her eyes straight ahead, avoiding Graham's gaze. But then she suddenly looked back. Graham saw the unmistakable twist of the corners of her lips, the crinkles at her eyes—the unmistakable markers of a smile. A smile, which, he could tell, she was trying very hard to control.

He watched them drive away.

CHAPTER 2

Dinner at the Lindenhurst estate that evening turned out to be a very pleasant affair. It was a small, intimate gathering, consisting only of Mr. and Mrs. Cornelius, Henry Vanderbilt, his wife and daughter, Mr. and Mrs. Harold along with their daughter Lillian, and Lillian's brother William who had come along with Lillian's parents.

"So you honestly feel that in this day and age women should not be allowed to vote?" Lillian asked when the issue of women's suffrage surfaced.

"Why trouble yourselves with something that's difficult for the fairer sex to understand," said Henry Vanderbilt. "After all, Lillian, women, by nature, are emotional. And emotion is the greatest deterrent in politics."

"Have you ever thought that, perhaps, we're only given to emotion when confronted with such faulty logic as yours, Henry?" Lillian smirked much to the amusement of the other guests.

When she felt it benefited her, Lillian Harold could come across as a helpless and attractive young woman incapable of reason. After all, this was what most men in her circles expected from her. Like most women her age, Lillian had been taught that intellect was a deterrent in finding a good husband. However, there were times when she allowed her intellect to come through. There was a growing fear about women intellectuals, or "trouble-makers" as they were often called. Women who encouraged their peers to utilize their intellect rather than waste it on mundane, simple tasks. It was taken as a sign of the decline of civilization for many in her circles. Yet her occasional strong opinions were seen by many men as a cute foible in Lillian's character. Many women resented her for this and gossiped about it behind her back. In truth, Lillian really didn't put much passion behind her own thoughts either way anymore. Her goal was to become the wife of Charlie Cornelius. And now, it seemed, her plans were coming to fruition. Each passing day brought them closer to a union.

"What's wrong, Vanderbilt?" Lillian said. "Do you not have a rebuttal?"

Again, more laughter. Lillian placed her hand on Charlie's forearm under the dining room table. He tensed up.

She released her grip and looked down at her dinner plate. Her confidence shaken, she remained unusually silent the rest of the evening. For reasons Lillian could not fully understand, Charlie had become increasingly distant toward her over the past year. She worried that he had taken a mistress, though she doubted that could be the case. She rarely saw Charlie show much interest in any of the other girls. In the past, she simply dismissed his behavior as a masculine indifference to affection; but lately Charlie's peculiar behavior had started to bother her more and more.

Following dinner, the men went to the hunting room to play billiards and smoke cigars, while the women headed toward the parlor where they drank tea and gossiped about anyone and everyone who was not present at the dinner.

As the evening came to an end and everyone made their way toward their respective rooms, Lillian decided to go for a walk along the grounds. She needed to clear her head. She was also in dire need of a cigarette (a secret, dirty habit of hers that would shock her fellow guests). When she was sure she was far enough away from the mansion, she reached under her dress and pulled a silver cigarette case from her garter. She opened the case, selected a cigarette, lit it and blew a plume of smoke up toward the night sky. It was very clear out. *Which planet is that below the moon? Saturn?* She thought it might be Saturn this time of year, but it had been quite a long time since she'd really stopped and thought about the night sky. She took another puff, trying to remember the names of the constellations. Despite the day's earlier thaw, it was surprisingly cold. She wrapped her free arm around her waist to try and keep warm.

Then she heard footsteps coming from behind.

"Lillian?" Charlie called out. "Are you out here?"

Lillian quickly tossed away her cigarette. She took hold of her dress, trying to flutter away the smoke.

"I'm over here!" Lillian called out. Her heart pounded in her chest.

Charlie's silhouette was approaching past the low-hanging branches of the Great Weeping Birch. He came closer now.

"Is everything okay?" He asked.

She nodded.

"Are you sure? It's freezing out here."

She shrugged.

"Something is wrong, Lillian. I can tell."

At first she did not answer him. Finally, she said: "Tonight at dinner, when I placed my hand on your arm—you tensed up."

Charlie gave her a look. "I did no such thing."

"Yes you did."

"Lillian..." He hesitated. "Lillian, for God's sake, it's all in your head. We've had this discussion before. Let's not go down this path again."

"It's about Roger, isn't it?"

"Roger? The gardener?" He gave her a dismissive look. "Of course not."

"Then why have you been so distant? Everyone asks why we haven't moved to the next step of our engagement, and I have no idea what to tell them."

"Come on, Lillian; it's cold out here. Let's go inside."

"Answer me, Charlie. It's the least you can do. If you love me, like you say you do, you can at least answer me."

She waited for Charlie to answer. She studied his face and a horrible thought ran through her mind. She started to panic. "Surely you don't believe them, Charlie? Please don't tell me you believe those horrid rumors about me?"

"Of course not. It's just that..."

She gave him a piercing look. “It’s just what? What are you implying?”

“It’s just that you aren’t a school girl anymore, Lillian. You’re a woman. When you talk to men, men like that gardener…you give them the wrong impression.”

“And what is that impression?”

Charlie said nothing.

“Oh. I see. So you think I gave him the impression that I wanted him to make mad, passionate love to me?”

“There were already rumors about you and him. Yet you continued to see him and have long conversations. Did you want the reputation of a ruined woman?”

“How dare you, Charlie!”

“You left yourself an open target in spending time with him, Lillian. What’s more, these rumors affect my reputation as well, as if….as if I’m some kind of cuckold.”

“Roger was no more than a dear friend. Nothing more. Mother had no right”—

“You’re angry at your mother for forcing him to leave; but what do you propose she should have done under the circumstances? Let the rumors continue? Allow your family’s reputation to be ruined?”

“Why are you being so cruel, Charlie?”

“Because I love you. And I care about you. But I can’t marry you while this gossip is circling about. To rush into marriage now would probably only exacerbate the talk. We have to play it as if we’re unaware and not bothered by it. We need to keep things exactly as they are for now.”

"Charlie--" her voice cracked. "Please don't tell me you think I'm a woman of questionable morals?"

"Like I said, Lillian, you need to be careful of the impression you give to men. I know it's just you being friendly. But I don't want our future to be filled with scandalous rumors because of who my wife chooses to have as a friend."

She watched him as he walked away. *There's a part of him that believes these rumors*, she thought. She had seen the hurt look in his eyes. Her heart ached, her body trembled and, as she opened her mouth, the only sound that came out was a soft whimper as she said his name.

I'm going to kill myself.

Without looking back at her, he called: "Please come inside, Lillian. You'll catch your death out here."

CHAPTER 3

Later the next day, a line of trolley cars clanged their bells as they rounded the corner, weaving through the red-bricked textile mills and past the waiting motor cars and horse-drawn trucks.

With the workday finally done, the town was a bustle of activity. Tired mill workers spoke in a Babel of languages. The child laborers, small and frail, all of them laughing now, called out to one another as they raced across the cobblestones of lower Main Street. The city was a feast of sound and smell: the crushing grind of the motor cars' shifting gears, the smell of smoked sausage, fish and cabbage, the clip clopping of horse hooves, the singsong shouts of the street vendors and fishmongers.

Graham moved through the crowd. He hopped a trolley, which lumbered out past the mills, through the tenement homes and then out into the dimming sunlight past the town limits.

It was still mostly farm country here. Graham could smell the wet fields.

Tall, ancient trees: oaks, elms, maples, and hemlock

all cut down and uprooted where rows of new clapboard houses were being built. Every now and then, men with rods surveyed the lands for new houses. Progress had come to Tarrytown.

He finally reached his stop and stepped off the trolley toward Norwood Street. Eventually he came to a new clapboard boarding house owned by Pietro and Maria Botto. There were bare grapevines staked at the side of the house beside a picnic table and a few small, recently planted trees in the front yard. Graham walked up the front steps, opened the door and stepped inside.

The main room was filled with people. Lights flickered with the unsteady pulse of newly installed electricity. The air inside was choking with the smell of burning tobacco, cedar and simmering meat and tomato. Everyone greeted one another with a nod and a handshake. Here and there, people spoke to one another, very few in English. Indeed, there were barely any American-born people inside.

A minute or two later, a large man stepped out from the hallway, looming over everyone. He was missing an eye. Graham recognized him right away. It was Big Bill Haywood.

Haywood made small talk with those at the threshold before excusing himself to circle the room, moving from person to person until he was sure he'd spoken with everyone.

Someone clinked a glass with a spoon and everyone took a seat.

Haywood stood in the middle of the room. He looked around at his small audience, as if measuring them up. A few more murmurs; a throat cleared here and there.

"Fellow workers," Haywood began. "I am here today, because some of you have expressed an interest in forming a union. I want you all to know that the International Workers stand united with you. After all, we all believe in the same thing. We believe in the need to confederate the workers of this country, who, for too long have been slaves to their capitalist masters. By joining the IWW, you are joining your brothers and sisters throughout the world to be part of a working-class movement, a movement that will emancipate the working-class from the slave bondage of capitalism."

Haywood paused. The large man conveyed a calm assuredness. A soft smile began to creep from the corners of his mouth. He told them that the working-class would be in possession of the economic power, the means of life. In control of the machinery of production and distribution, without bowing down to those capitalist masters.

A man cleared his throat and stood up, looking around the room with a sheepish expression on his face; he said in a thick Slavic accent: "That's all fine to say, Mr. Haywood. And what you say…it's very nice to think we can change things if we strike. But the truth is the mill owners control the police and the judges. We can be arrested or killed and no one can do anything about it. And who will really care? Most of us…we are foreigners. They despise us."

Haywood nodded. "You are right about the corporate masters. They are better armed. But let me speak plainly and from the heart: I don't think it matters who they control or how powerful they may seem. Because the truth is this: if the workers of the world want to win, all we have to do is recognize our own solidarity. We have nothing to do but fold our arms and the world will stop. The workers are more powerful with our hands in our pockets than all the weapons and wealth and power of the capitalists."

"As long as the workers keep their hands in their pockets," continued Haywood, "the capitalists cannot put theirs there. When the workers absolutely refuse to move, lying absolutely silent, they are more powerful than all the weapons that the other side has for attack."

A woman jumped up from her seat and started applauding. Others joined her.

A few people started to sing: *the Internationale.* Everyone else in the room joined in.

A couple minutes later, there was a ruckus outside. Before Graham and the others could figure out what was happening, the front door was kicked in and a rock crashed through one of the windows. Then the back door shot open. Men whose faces were covered with bandanas came running in, carrying clubs and black jacks. Graham knew who they were right away: Pinkertons. Union Breakers. Hired by the employers. Someone screamed as they began beating anyone in their path.

Some tried to fight back or escape, but they were outnumbered. There was no way out. Someone hit Graham in the side of the head and he stumbled. He shook it off, turned and swung, hitting the Pinkerton square in the face. The man staggered and Graham grabbed him by the throat, pushing him against the wall before letting him fall to the ground and making a run for it. Someone took a torch and lit the curtains on fire. The flames began to spread to the walls and the house filled with black smoke.

Outside, Graham saw two men beating someone down. Graham recognized the man from earlier, a small Italian immigrant.

One of the Pinkertons hit the Italian in the face repeatedly, though his companion told him that the man had had enough. But the one Pinkerton wouldn't stop. He grabbed the man and lifted him up from the ground so that he was back on his knees. The Italian was swaying back and forth barely conscious, blood running out his nostrils, his mouth.

The Pinkerton yelled: "We're sick and tired of you goddamned foreigners coming into our country and agitating, spreading your destructive views. You don't like it here—you can get the hell out!"

Graham watched in horror as another man appeared from around the corner with a red-hot branding iron. "All right," said the man, who was evidently in charge. "Let's do it."

The larger Pinkerton bent down in the beaten man's face. "You boys don't want to love this great country of ours? We're gonna make you love it."

Suddenly, two of the men yanked him up so he was standing. They tore off the man's clothes then threw him back down on the ground. Someone grabbed his head up by the hair and shoved an American flag in his face.

"Kiss the flag! Kiss it!"

The man mustered what little strength was left in him and kissed the flag. The men laughed. The larger Pinkerton took the branding iron and approached him from behind. Graham picked up a brick near the home's foundation and strode toward them.

Before the Pinkerton realized he was in any danger, Graham hit him in the back of the head with the brick. The man stumbled and turned around, confused. The Pinkerton reached behind his head and looked at his hand, now covered in blood. He sneered at Graham and came toward him, a bit off balance. Graham swung again, this time hitting the man in the temple. The man's knees buckled. He collapsed to the ground, a pool of black blood expanding around his head.

The two Pinkertons looked at their friend and then at Graham. He raised his hand.

"You boys want the same?" Graham said.

The two Pinkertons looked at each other again before glancing down at their wounded friend.

"Is he dead?" Graham asked, trying to catch his breath.

"Not yet, but he will be if we don't find a doctor," said one of them. They quickly ran back toward the front yard, presumably to get reinforcements.

The Italian was lying on his back, groaning.

Gurgling sounds rose in the Pinkerton's throat. His legs, arms and mouth were twitching. *What've I done?* thought Graham. *Sweet Jesus, what've I done?*

"You better go, Comrade."

Graham looked over. It was the Italian.

"Run and don't look back. They'll be coming for you."

Graham nodded.

The Pinkerton's arms and legs stopped moving and the man let out a death rattle. Graham knew right away that the man was dead.

"Go!" Cried the foreigner. "And don't stop until you are miles away from here!"

Graham looked and saw a group of Pinkertons rounding the corner of the house, some with guns. Graham ran off as fast as he could, shots ringing out behind him as he ran into the deep, dark, night.

CHAPTER 4

He ran until he couldn't run anymore. Through woods, down roads, across open fields, he ran under the light of a full moon. He heard the sounds of police blowing their whistles now, dogs barking, men calling to one another. They were all looking for him. He moved from place to place, not staying anywhere too long, using the night as his cover.

So far he had managed to stay one step ahead of them. The sky turned a deep shade of blue as dawn broke. He knew he needed a place where he could keep more or less out of sight, somewhere they wouldn't think to look for him.

And so he ran down along the railroad tracks and back up the high cliffs along the Hudson River, ran down another road, finally heading toward the Cornelius Estate, Lindenhurst.

A high rock wall surrounded the estate. Graham jumped up and grabbed hold of the top with his fingers to pull his body up. Through the bare trees and up the sloping property, he could see the mansion's façade of yellow and white limestone. The mansion's miniarettes rose tall over the bare trees in the growing light of the new day. He glanced to his left and right to make sure that no one was watching. *This is crazy. The guards might shoot, thinking you've come to kill Cornelius.* But Graham knew he had no other choice. He could hear the sounds of dogs barking up the road, men calling out to one another, making their way in his direction. The search hadn't slowed one bit. He hoisted his body over and jumped down to the other side.

He was cold, wet and tired, walking up the deep sloping property of the estate, his boots trudging in the mud, the thawed wet earth. The trees' bare branches swayed in the bitter, westerly breeze coming off the Hudson. It felt like winter again.

At one point, he spotted one of Cornelius' guards walking in the distance, his rifle slung up on his shoulder. Graham hurriedly took cover behind a Norwegian Spruce.

The guard stood there for some time. He lit a cigarette. Every now and then he looked around, smoking the stub down to his fingers before finally tossing it and walking away. Graham had gotten lucky. Next time he had to be more careful.

He got up and brushed the pine needles from his hands.

The sun continued to rise as the sky to the east turned the color of blood.

He headed further west, trudged up a bit of sloping ground before heading down and cutting through a thicker cover of woods to help keep him out of sight.

He stopped at the edge of the woods beside a small clearing. The smell of pines and soggy earth. Ten yards beyond the clearing was a small half-frozen lake. He figured this was a good spot to wait it out for at least a day. Maybe two. He just needed enough time for the police to think he was long gone and out of town. Then he would have to leave at night, very late so no one could see him.

And so he waited. He slept for a bit, resting his back on a tree trunk. When he woke up, he was shivering. At one point, he took out his knife and whittled a stick to bide the time, looking around every couple of minutes, making sure that no one was coming. He was dying for a cigarette, but couldn't risk someone spotting the glow of lit tobacco.

Every little sound, a bird tramping on a leaf, an acorn falling, caused him to sit up with a start. His heart was still racing. *It'll probably be the death penalty if the cops find me.*

A little past noon, he thought he saw something moving through the trees. He moved forward in a squat and ducked behind an oak tree before looking out.

It was the woman he'd seen in town a couple of days before. Lillian.

She stood against a tree at the edge of the small, half-frozen lake, nervously looking around to make sure she was alone. She started to unbutton her coat. Slowly, the young woman began lifting her dress up, exposing her ankles, her calves, even her knees.

Reaching under her dress with her left hand, she took out a silver cigarette case and then let her dress fall back down. She opened the case, took out a cigarette, looked around again and then lit it. Graham watched her. He'd never seen a respectable woman smoke a cigarette. She had deep, sorrowful eyes.

When she finished smoking, she tossed her cigarette away. She walked around, picking up rocks and putting them into the pockets of her coat. A few minutes later, Graham saw someone else coming down the hill; it looked to be a maid. The maid approached Lillian. They talked for a couple of minutes, though Graham could not make out the conversation. A minute or two passed and then Lillian, much to Graham's surprise, started walking out on the ice, heading toward the center of the lake. *Is she out of her mind?*

"Miss! The thaw's made the ice too thin. Please come away from there," the maid pleaded.

Graham couldn't believe she hadn't fallen through yet.

Lillian seemed indifferent to the danger she was in. "You should go now," she said to her maid. "They might hold you responsible if you're here."

"Miss, please"—

Lillian stood at the edge of a large circle where the ice had fully melted. She stood there for a moment, looking down into the dark water. The maid called again, her voice desperate. Lillian looked up at the gray wintry sky. She took a deep breath and stepped forward. Gone; disappearing into the dark, freezing water.

The maid screamed and ran back toward the mansion, calling for help. *Sonofabitch,* Graham thought. He could run. But where the hell was he going to run to now in broad daylight? He looked toward the lake. If he didn't get over there now, he knew she would die. *Save someone to make up for killing someone?*

"Damnit!"

He ran out to the lake, just barely making it to the circle of water. He lay on his stomach near the edge and reached down. The freezing water stung his arm. He couldn't feel her anywhere near him. *She's going to die and I'm going to go to jail.* All of the sudden, he heard the ice cracking underneath him. He made a move to get up, but before he even knew what had happened—he was underwater.

The cold sent shockwaves through his body. It felt like he was being stabbed by millions of knives. He tried to find an opening to get his head above water level but he could not seem to find the spot where he'd fallen in.

Then he saw a shadow at the bottom. He swam down and took hold of Lillian around her waist. She tried to resist, but he tightened his grip and swam up. Despite the thaw, the ice above them was still solid. Try as he might, he couldn't break through.

He could hear the muffled sounds of men shouting as the guards and laborers came rushing down the sloping grounds toward the lake.

He started pounding on the ice with his fists, searching for a spot where he might be able to get through for air. There wasn't much time. He needed to breathe. *So this is how it will all end?*

Men pounded on the ice above them with rifle butts, shovels and spades. Graham's strength was fading. He was about to let go of Lillian when a spade suddenly broke through.

Dim sunlight appeared and the next thing Graham knew his head was out of the water. He coughed and gasped for air.

The men were barking orders to one another. Someone pulled Lillian away from Graham and gently laid her on the ground to tend to her.

Two others grabbed Graham by the shirt and pulled him out of the water. Shivering, he let out a hoarse wheezing and a gurgling noise from somewhere in his lungs.

They brought him to the edge of the lake and laid him down a few feet from Lillian. Surrounded by strange faces, convinced they'd turn him into the police—he stood to fight.

"Get off me, you sons of bitches!"

A man whispered in his ear: "It's all right, Son. Just take it easy. It's all right."

But the guards were shouting all at once, asking his name and where he came from.

One of the guards screamed in his face: "Are you an anarchist? How did you get on this property? Did you come here to harm Mr. Cornelius?"

He started to cough out water.

"Who are you?" The guard barked again.

Then he heard her voice.

"I know him," she said, her voice weak and hoarse. "He was standing outside the druggist when I went into town the other day."

Graham looked toward Lillian as someone picked her up and ran her back to the house.

"And what do we do with him?" One of the guards asked, jutting his chin at Graham.

"Here," the man who'd whispered earlier said, trying to lift him up. He signaled over to one of the other men. "Help me carry him up to the house."

"To the house?"

"He's not going to the house," one of the guards said. "He's going to jail."

"Go on," the man ordered. "He could die if we don't get him warm soon. Get him up to the house right now!"

The two men hoisted Graham's arms around each of their shoulders and carried him up to the mansion. They were nearing the west portico of the estate when someone opened the door and led them inside. It was warm inside the mansion, a home like nothing he'd ever seen.

A guard appeared in front of him. Graham was woozy, but he looked him in the eye and asked: "You going to call the cops?"

The guard sneered, raised his arm and swung the black jack. The blow hit Graham on the side of the head. He was knocked out cold.

CHAPTER 5

Graham came to in a small bedroom with beige walls. There was a metal-framed bed and a small writing table and chair in the corner. The rest of the room was empty. A loud racket of clanging pots and pans and cutlery came from the scullery just outside. He could smell roasting lamb and cranberries floating up from under the door.

He wasn't sure how long he'd been unconscious. He went to get up but felt dizzy and weak so he lay back down.

A little while later, someone knocked. He didn't answer. Another knock, then the door opened and a scullery maid came hurrying into the room.

The maid was followed by three men. Graham recognized one of them as Lillian's father. The second man was tall and thin, athletic with a well-trimmed mustache probably somewhere in his late twenties, possibly early thirties. He was dressed in a suit and his hair was quite dark, parted down the middle and held in place with pomade. Graham thought he looked like a Dandy. The third man, however, was shorter and stout, with round spectacles. He carried a black, leather doctor's bag.

"How are you feeling, son?" Lillian's father asked.

Graham didn't answer.

"Is this the man you and Lillian saw by the druggist?" the younger gentleman asked.

"Yes, I believe so." Mr. Harold looked at Graham. "It was you who filled my car with gasoline the other day, isn't that so?"

"It's all right to answer," said the young man. "We aren't the police." He smiled and grabbed a chair, pulling it up toward the edge of the bed to sit down.

"My name is Charlie Cornelius," the young man said, extending his hand.

Graham thought he had really done it this time. Maybe, if he seemed penitent enough, they might just let him go. "Mr. Cornelius…I'm sorry I was on your property, I didn't even realize"—

"There, there, Sport. You needn't apologize. And please, my name's Charlie. As far as we're all concerned, whatever brought you here was a miracle. A case of Divine Intervention, my mother would say. If it weren't for you, my Lily might no longer be with us."

Graham looked around the room. He wasn't sure what to make of all this. Was this man with the warm-hearted smile really Charlie Cornelius? Son of Andrew Cornelius? Was this all some kind of trick? A way of stalling until the police arrived?

That Pinkerton is dead. There is nothing I can do to change what I've done.

"Lillian tells us that she went to retrieve some jewelry that she spotted on the ice and fell through. Can you tell me…did you see…what I mean to ask: is that how it truly happened?" Charlie Cornelius asked.

Graham didn't answer.

"My friend, I assure you, you are free to speak."

"Why are you asking me? Is she known to lie?" Graham finally spoke.

A silence. Glances darted around in the room.

Charlie cleared his throat. "Well…I suppose we can talk more later. For now, though, I simply thank you for your bravery."

Cornelius pointed out the shorter man and introduced him as Dr. Lippincott. He asked Graham if it would be all right if the doctor looked him over.

The doctor pulled the sheets back a bit and took Graham's wrist to check his pulse. He pulled a stethoscope from out of his black leather medical bag and put it against his chest. Mr. Harold turned his head and started coughing.

"Are you all right?" Charlie asked.

Mr. Harold nodded; but this coughing fit lasted for quite some time. By the time it finally stopped, his face was crimson and he looked exhausted. Graham didn't need to be a doctor to know it was consumption.

As the doctor continued to examine Graham, his facial expression became grim. He looked at the maid. "Would you mind excusing us?"

The maid hurried out without a word.

"His lungs are filled with fluid, and his body is still showing signs of hypothermia." He frowned, put the stethoscope back in his bag. "He needs to be watched closely in case things worsen."

Charlie looked at Graham. "My friend, tell me where you live. I'm sure your family must be very worried about you by now."

"I don't have family."

"No?"

"I've been living down at the Sisters of Mercy for the ice season."

"Well I suppose the nuns should know where you are, so they don't go and give your bed to someone else. I can send one of my footmen down there to tell them you're here."

"I'd rather you didn't."

"No?" Charlie and the other two men looked at one another. "Very well, then. Do you have a name?"

Graham didn't answer him.

"For God's sake, man. We're not here to do you any harm. I just want to know your name."

"Henry." *Henry Flanagan.* "Henry Graham, sir. My name is Henry Graham." Charlie walked over to the door, opened it and stuck his head out to call for the scullery maid. When she came into the room, he asked her, "who decided to put this man down here?"

"I think it was Mrs. Cornelius, Sir," she said.

Charlie scowled and shook his head. "It's too cold and damp. He should be upstairs in one of the guest rooms. Send for someone to carry him up to the Northeast Room, and make sure someone stays with him to make sure he's kept warm."

Charlie looked at Graham. "Listen, Sport. You need to fight hard to recover. More good fortune has come into your life today than you could have ever imagined. It certainly would be a shame if you decided to pass along before you could enjoy it."

At that, Charlie smiled again.

Graham wasn't quite sure whether he could trust Charlie, but his friendliness had helped put him at ease.

A moment or two later, the three men stepped out and spoke to one another in hushed tones. Graham strained to hear.

"It truly could have just been an accident like she says," Charlie said.

"Perhaps; but she's tried this kind of thing before..."

Mr. Harold's response was too muffled for Graham to make out the words.

The doctor joined in: "In my opinion, I would most certainly agree to the new European treatment for your daughter."

"The poor girl. Surely there must be another way."

"The alternatives are far worse," the doctor said.

The men became gravely quiet. Charlie Cornelius stuck his head in the room and looked at Graham again. "Go on, Pal. Get some sleep."

He closed the door.

CHAPTER 6

Lillian Harold was resting in her room when a knock sounded at the door and her brother William entered. She was not yet certain whether she should be grateful that her life had been spared. Earlier, as she plunged into the dark waters, she found herself overcome with regret. *Have I made a mistake,* she had thought to herself over and over again as she sank to the bottom. Still, she felt both a slight tinge of relief and sinking disappointment when she felt Graham's arms wrap around her and carry her up to the top.

Her heart was still aching over Charlie. Try as she might, she could not convince herself that she could ever make him love her the way that she loved him. And now he had been affected by the terrible rumors about her. Even if she had not done anything sordid or immoral, she was still wracked with guilt.

William sat beside her bed and took her hand. "Lillian? Are you awake?"

Lillian couldn't bear to look at him.

"Lillian?"

"I'm fine, William," she said. "Just leave me be."

"Do you want to talk?"

"No."

Her brother let out a tired sigh.

"I want to know what happened today out on the lake."

"Why do you need me to tell you? Haven't you all been talking about it endlessly, already, William?"

"Everyone says it was an accident."

She rolled over and turned her back to him. "Good night, William."

"He does still love you, Lillian."

A silence.

William scowled. "I swear to you, Lillian."

"I don't think Charlie will ever love me. How could he love a woman of such questionable morals? In his eyes I'm ruined."

"That's enough, Lillian. He doesn't believe those rumors. He's told me so. Many times."

"I wish I could believe you, William. Truly, I do. But that is a lie."

"Think of all the years you two have known one another. I can't recall a time that there was ever any doubt that the two of you would be together."

In spite of her mood, she felt sudden nostalgia. Memories from their childhood crept in: ice skating, moving furniture from one room to the next to drive the servants crazy, swimming in the lake at Lindenhurst, sneaking out late at night to meet in Central Park to watch a meteor shower (where they stole their first kiss), family births, illnesses, deaths—they had seen and shared so much together. More than anyone else outside of their immediate families.

They said nothing for a moment or two. Then Lillian said, "How is that man, doing?"

"What man?"

"The one who saved me."

"I suppose it depends how he fairs tonight," William said. He looked around the room. "I heard you were speaking with him in town a couple of days ago."

"Do you think I invited him here?"

"No." William hesitated, careful not to set off his sister's anger. "I suspect the ice harvester followed you here, Lillian; or else he was here to harm one of us. I don't like it. I don't like it at all. If you ask me, I think the Cornelius family is mad to allow him to stay here."

"What do you suppose they should do with him then, William?"

"There are infirmaries in town."

"He saved my life."

"Maybe. But it still doesn't answer what he was doing on these grounds. Everyone of our stature is in danger these days, Lillian. You know that. They're all out to kill us."

"If he planned to harm any of us, don't you think it odd that he would risk his life to save me?"

William scowled. "Still, you need to be more careful about who you talk to. Men like him will get the wrong idea."

"Well, you fool, let's suppose he is here because I gave him the wrong impression. Had I not, you'd be crying over my corpse. Good night, William. I'm tired and I need to sleep."

Ypres Belgium. March, 1915

Graham continued to look at the photograph. It offered him what little comfort there was to be found in his current position.

"She's a real pretty one," Calloway repeated, still looking over Graham's shoulder.

Graham tried to ignore him.

Calloway nodded toward the picture. "That your girl back home, Graham?"

"No." Graham put the picture back into his coat pocket.

"I hope you aren't one of them fools who joined the Legion over a woman." Calloway let out a spiteful laugh. He shook his head and continued: "I'll tell you, Graham, men'll go and do some crazy things when it comes to a girl. And all for what? That little Daisy's den between their legs?" Another shell roared above them. The two men covered their heads again, listened for the explosion and saw another bright orange ball rise up. Calloway looked very nervous. "That one seemed a bit closer. Don't you think, Graham?"

Graham removed his helmet for a moment and rubbed his head. His hair was soaked with sweat. He barely heard what

Calloway was saying. *What the hell am I doing here, Lillian?*

"As for me," Calloway continued, "I'm ready to fight the good fight. Kill some of these Hun sons-of-bitches. You hear what they did to those priests, Graham? Hung 'em up in the bell tower and rang the bells with their heads."

Graham shot him a look. Half the stories they'd heard were pure propaganda. He wondered if Calloway truly believed them, or whether he just needed to lend some kind of nobility to their efforts.

"I'm a Catholic, just so you know. At least, I was brought up Catholic. Not sure Saint Peter would consider me a model worshipper. But I still take offense to them murdering priests." Calloway hesitated a moment, shook his head, and suddenly changed direction. "I was hoping they'd have us in France. The French girls are real nice, Graham. And if you can't find a nice French girl, there's always the brothels. You know they got separate brothels for the enlisted and for officers? The way you tell is they got a red lamp in the window if the brothel's for the enlisted, and they got a blue lamp if it's for the officers. Don't that just beat all? The British insisted on it. The officers get the pick of the litter. Classist bullshit. Even during a war. Guess they don't want us putting our member into the same places as their gentry class."

Graham wanted to tell Calloway to shut the hell up. But the man didn't seem to care whether or not Graham was listening. Calloway's relentless blabber was simply a means of quieting his nerves.

I need to get out of here. I need to get back to New York.

At least one more time, I need to see you.

Calloway looked around. "You know if the Belgian girls are like the French girls, Graham?"

"Guess if you live long enough, you can find out."

Calloway laughed. "You know what, Graham? I think a nice girl might be just what you need. Go find yourself a girl who gives you lots of attention, and you'll forget about that one you're carrying around in your pocket." Calloway craned his neck and looked around. "We should ask the sergeant if he knows anything about Belgian girls. Where is that crazy sonofabitch?"

The sky was beginning to turn a dark shade of blue. Dawn had started to break. A call to "attention" was ordered. As the sun rose from the east, the men had their rifles inspected. Around eight o'clock in the morning, the artillery bombardment suddenly stopped. The men looked at each other and smiled. They started to laugh and hug, happy to have made it through their first night unscathed.

"Don't get your hopes up, men," the Sergeant called out. "We got a little agreement with the enemy. We don't shell him and he don't shell us at breakfast time. It'll all start back up before you've had time to shit out your rations."

An hour or so later, the Germans began shelling again. The frequency and intensity of the shelling seemed to have gotten worse. A young Legionnaire caught Graham's gaze. He couldn't have been any older than sixteen. His lip trembled.

"You'll be all right," Graham said to him. "Just keep your head down and you'll be fine."

Throughout the day, the shelling weighed heavy on their nerves. Each terrifying whistle caused Graham's body to tense and his eyes to flinch as he waited for the inevitable explosion. Some men were already starting to whimper. To their right, a command of French colonial troops. To their left, a brigade of Canadians. The Legion was told that they had new orders. They would be a support line now in case the Germans decided to launch an attack. But after each period of intense shelling, there was always a rest. Whether the Germans had cancelled their attack or were just trying to break the morale—no one could say.

Later that afternoon, the shelling started again. The intensity of the shelling was greater than ever. Word came down the line again to prepare for an attack. A Legionnaire asked Graham for a light for his cigarette. The soldier nodded thanks, and began walking down the trench. A distant whistle grew into a monstrous roar and the shell flew into the trench with a great explosion. Before the smoking soldier even realized he was in any danger, he was vaporized into a wet, pink mist. The soldier next to Graham started to weep. The shelling continued, more ferocious than ever. Graham looked down and saw that his hands were trembling. He could not make them stop.

Finally, the shelling stopped again. Rats were screaming and the wounded cried out for help. In the background he could hear it…

At first, he thought it was just his imagination, but then he realized the sound he heard was real. Among the horrors around him—

There was the sweet song of the sparrows.

I will live through this, Lillian. I will return to New York.

CHAPTER 7

Tarrytown, NY 1909

Graham awoke the next morning in the northeast bedroom. It was small, but it was the nicest room he'd ever been in. There were light frescoes painted at the edges of the ceiling and the furniture was built of a gilded walnut. There was a mirror over a chest of drawers and at the foot of the bed there was a table and two chairs beside the white marble hearth. He could hear the sparrows just outside his window.

A little later, a chambermaid came into the room and squatted down in front of the hearth to prod the fire. Graham said hello and she turned around with a start. The maid looked to be in her early twenties with brown hair, hazel eyes and soft freckles on her cheeks.

She put the poker back beside the white marble mantle. "You're quite the talk around here, Dearie. That was a real brave thing you did."

Graham grimaced. She told him her name was Colleen Callahan and that she'd come over from Liverpool five years ago when she was fifteen to work for the Cornelius family.

At one point, Graham asked her how the Cornelius' treated her, and she told him they were quite kind to the help. She must have seen his distaste, because she said: "What? Are you disappointed?" A mischievous grin broke out. "You're one of those agitator types, ain't ya?"

"How's Lillian?" he asked.

"Miss Harold, you mean?" The chambermaid went over and started brushing the curtains. "She'll be fine." She shook her head and sighed. "Terrible accident. Terrible."

"Is that what they're calling it?"

The maid shot him a look. "Hush your mouth. I don't know what happened out there, but my advice to you is to be quiet about it if you know what's good for you."

"She looks like she's carrying the weight of the world."

"Miss Harold…she's sometimes given to black moods. But her melancholy—it'll all pass."

They were quiet for a minute or two.

"So what are their plans?" Graham asked. "Are they going to turn me over to the police?"

"To the police?" She laughed. "You saved Miss Harold's life, for Heaven's sake! Why would they turn you over to the police?"

They must not know what happened at the Botto house.

There was a sudden knock at the door and the chamber maid jumped with a start. She rushed across the room and opened the door.

"Is he awake?" A woman's voice came from the hallway.

"He is," said the maid.

"We would like to see him."

Mrs. Cornelius came hurrying into the room in a dark red dress. She was in her early fifties and her hair was jet black with only a few strands of gray. She still maintained the fashionably plump figure that was in style during her youth.

She was followed by a thinner woman, her face aged. It looked as if Mrs. Cornelius' cheer was somewhat irksome to her.

Mrs. Cornelius stopped just before reaching the bed, then turned and looked back at the door, exasperated. "What are you waiting for? Come in, Alice! Come in!"

A tall, skinny girl walked slowly into the room. Around seventeen or eighteen. Her thin face, pronounced chin and bird-like nose distracted from her pretty blue eyes. She gave Graham only the slightest glance before retreating toward a far corner of the room, where she stood fidgeting.

Mrs. Cornelius clasped her hands, her eyes glistening with happy tears. "And you must be Henry! It is such a pleasure." She patted the back of his hand. "I am Alva Cornelius, Charlie's mother. This is Sarah Harold, Lillian's mother and…and the mute creature in the corner is my daughter Alice."

Graham looked at the girl and nodded. She shifted with unease, but the slightest traces of a smile formed at the corners of her mouth. He saw that her teeth were horribly crooked and bucked, and she quickly closed her mouth to cover them. "It's"—she cleared her throat—"it's very nice to meet you, too."

"I wanted to thank you and to welcome you to our home," Mrs. Cornelius continued. "But obviously there are no words to express our truest feelings of gratitude. Mrs. Harold is here to thank you as well, but as you can imagine—this day's been a little overwhelming for her. She's still not in the best of spirits."

Sarah Harold looked at Graham for a moment and then nodded, forcing a crooked smile. "I don't know how we will ever be able to repay you, Mr. Graham."

"Alice? Don't you wish to welcome Henry into our home?" She waited for Alice to speak. "Alice?" When her daughter still did not speak, Mrs. Cornelius let out a sigh and rolled her eyes. Quickly changing her demeanor, she smiled again at Graham. "Henry, your being where you were, when you were… Let me ask you, Henry, do you believe that our lives are predetermined by the Creator?"

"Not really sure, Maam."

"If it weren't simply God's guiding hand—what else could have brought you to Lindenhurst?"

His body became tense. He glanced at the chambermaid, but she had not raised her head since Mrs. Cornelius entered the room. Graham cleared his throat. "What brought me here?"

"I mean, surely there must have been a reason," Alva Cornelius said. "You didn't just wake up one morning and find yourself here, did you?"

Graham cleared his throat. "I don't know. I suppose it was just such a nice day that I decided to go for a walk. Eventually I found myself down along the train tracks by the river. I crossed your land as a short cut to get back to the road. I'm sorry for being on your property, Mrs. Cornelius. For trespassing and such. But I just wanted to get back home. Just so happened that when I was cutting across—I saw that young woman—Miss Harold?— fall through the ice."

Mrs. Cornelius smiled, patted his hand again. "Henry, of course you don't really know why you came to Lindenhurst. You see, it was the hand of God guiding you to us because it is not Lillian's time to return home to the gates of Heaven. Thanks to you, and the guiding, merciful hand of our Lord, she's still with us."

Graham glanced up at Alice Cornelius who was looking around the room, yawning.

"Well, Henry," Alva finally said, rising from her seat. "I know you need your rest."

At this, Mrs. Cornelius looked at Mrs. Harold and nodded that it was time for them to go. Then she looked at her daughter. "Come now, Alice. Hurry up. We need to prepare for our return to Manhattan."

Mrs. Harold said: "Again, Henry, I do not know how we will every repay you."

"It is so good to have you as a guest here, Henry," Mrs. Cornelius chimed in. "I do so hope to see you out and about today."

Much to his surprise, Mrs. Cornelius looked at Graham again and smiled, her face taking on a look of earnest compassion and warmth toward him. These people were not as he had always imagined.

CHAPTER 8

Graham got out of bed and found a note on the nightstand and a set of fresh folded clothes on the chair beside the fireplace. The note was from Andrew Cornelius; it was short and to the point; if he was feeling up to it, and able to move about—Mr. Cornelius would like to speak with him this morning.

Graham put the note down. He walked across the room and looked outside the Eastern-facing window at the grassy knolls and the pines, hemlock, bare oak and linden resting under a gray winter's sky pregnant with snow. He saw some workers moving about near the stable house just to the north and through the bare trees. He could make out the grand conservatory on the far northern end of the grounds.

Graham got dressed and stepped into the hallway, walking past a series of closed doors.

Further down the hall, he eventually came to a monumental room, which took up two stories and had an open timbered ceiling pierced by two skylights. The walls were covered from floor to ceiling with gilded framed works of art. At the east end of the room was a musician's gallery and to the west, overlooking the Hudson River, was a great stained glass window. Slats of colored light shone down through that stained glass and rested on the striped oak and walnut floor. There was a small fire crackling in the fireplace and a rocking chair and armchair in front of the marble mantle.

He slowly walked around the room, glancing indiscriminately at the paintings.

"So you must be the hero."

Graham turned. He saw a man smiling but eyeing him with suspicion.

"My name is William Harold," the man said, coming forward. "I understand you're a friend of my sister?"

"Your sister?"

William Harold smirked. "My sister…Lillian? Lillian Harold?"

"I don't know that I'd say friends..."

"Pretty girl, our Lillian. Wouldn't you agree?"

There was a cold breeze of disdain in William Harold's voice. Graham knew right away that he didn't like him.

"Surely you agree?" William said, a devilish smirk still on his lips.

"She's pretty enough, I suppose"

"Pretty enough?" His eyes narrowed on Graham. "What do you mean by that?"

"Just that she's pretty. Nothing more."

"I heard you wouldn't stop staring at her in town."

Graham locked eyes with him now. He'd be damned if he was going to back down from this dandy. "We talked a bit. That's all. I didn't stare."

"That so? And yet you followed her all the way back to Lindenhurst?"

"Who says I followed her?"

"Come-on, now, Henry. Don't play me for a fool. It's embarrassing for both of us." He chuckled. "I suppose I should believe, like Mrs. Cornelius, that you were just sent here by God?"

"You can believe whatever you want to believe."

An uneasy silence took hold. William came closer.

"Do you like art, Henry?" He asked, his tone now cordial.

"Guess so," Graham said.

"Do you have a favorite artist?"

"Not really."

"Most of these works are Corot, Courbet, Bouguereau. Are you familiar with their works?"

Graham shook his head, no.

William shot him a conspiratorial grin. "Well, let's just say, they're very popular among the *newer* moneyed families."

A man's voice came from behind. "You bastard!"

They both turned to find Charlie Cornelius and Lillian Harold. Graham nodded politely toward Lillian but she acted as if she didn't even notice him. Charlie, on the other hand, gave him a wide, earnest smile.

"Hello, again, Henry." Charlie came over and shook Graham's hand. "How are you feeling, today?"

"Much better. A little sore and groggy; but other than that fine. Except for my head. I can thank one of your guards for that."

"One of our guards? Why on earth would one of our guards hit you on the head?"

"Suppose you'll have to ask him that question."

"I certainly will," Charlie said, pausing for a moment before changing the topic. "Well, I suppose we're forever in your debt, sport." He looked at Lillian and smiled. "Good thing for Lily you were here when you were."

"You don't owe me anything," said Graham.

Charlie smiled again, put his arm around his shoulder and began leading him out of the room. "We're going down for breakfast; it'd be swell if you joined us."

"I got a note from Mr. Cornelius. Says he wants to speak to me."

"I'm sure he can wait," said Charlie.

Graham hesitated.

"Oh for God's sake, man. Don't tell me you're like all the others terrified of the old man?"

"I'm not afraid of him," he quickly answered, annoyed. "I just figured"—

"Come-on, friend. If he was in a hurry to see you, he'd let you know. Believe me. He's probably holed himself in to stare at ledgers. You need food to regain your strength. I'll take you to him after breakfast."

They brought him downstairs to the dining room. Charlie's sister Alice was already sitting at the table eating alone. When she saw Graham, she blushed and looked down at her plate.

The conversations that morning were dominated by

Charlie, William and Lillian, as they chatted about people Graham didn't know. Only now and then did they look up and ask Alice or Graham for their opinion. Graham glanced at Lillian. She was nothing like the person who tried to drown herself only a day before. *Strange. Everyone is pretending as if nothing ever happened.*

Lillian hardly paid Graham any notice. She was preoccupied with Charlie and her brother. In fact, it seemed as if Alice and Graham were practically invisible to them.

So Graham talked with poor Alice. At first it seemed like she couldn't utter more than a few sentences. Eventually, however, Graham put her at ease. And when she began talking about the plot of a book she was reading which was greatly influenced by Darwin's *Origin of the Species* she lost herself completely.

Unlike everyone else, it seemed to Alice that Graham didn't find her boring at all. He listened intently to what she had to say. Graham got the impression that no one had ever asked Alice her thoughts or opinions on anything until now.

At one point, Graham said: "You know what, Alice? You might be one of the smartest people I ever met in my life; and I'm including old guys who've seen a ton."

Alice blushed, a smile forming at the corners of her mouth, exposing those crooked teeth. She quickly closed her mouth to cover them. Even so, her face beamed and, for the remainder of breakfast, she stole quick glances at Graham whenever she could.

CHAPTER 9

After breakfast, Graham walked toward the conservatory.

Snow flurries circled in the cold wind, stinging his cheeks as he trudged up the crisp frozen ground. Eventually, he came to the conservatory—an enormous glass building which stretched hundreds of feet from east to west. At its center was a pavilion topped by a Moorish dome. The front of the building was glass and wood. Graham entered through the ornamental doorway and he felt a blast of moist tropical heat hit him as soon he entered. Inside, he could smell orchids, orange jasmine and ginger lily.

In the center hall there was a garden filled with ferns and palms around an ornate fountain.

Graham came to a billiard room. He took one of the billiards, pushed it softly against the far end of the table and watched it roll slowly back.

He found a sitting room further to the east. Also empty.

He walked past the seed room, the potting room, and eventually the apartments where the landscape workers stayed. But he still didn't see anyone.

"Hello?" he called out.

"In here," a man called out from one of the potting rooms.

Graham walked inside, peered into the dim light and spotted Mr. Cornelius far back in the room. Cornelius was a shorter, stout man who was slightly bald. His sleeves were rolled up, and he was standing beside one of his gardeners, planting bulbs into some potted soil.

"Ah, Henry!" Mr. Cornelius walked toward him, wiping some of the dirt from his hands on a rag. "It's an honor. How're you feeling?"

Cornelius told the gardener he could finish without him. He led Graham past some grape vines and popped a grape into his mouth. "My little hobby," he said, gesturing around. "Something about working with plants, digging one's hands in the dirt with the knowledge that the end result will be something of beauty is the only thing that gives me any peace, Henry. I know you'll find this hard to believe, considering the things that have been written about me, but…stripped down bare, I suppose I'm a very simple man."

They came to an office where a small fire was burning in the hearth. Mr. Cornelius sat behind an ornate maple desk. The room smelt of smoke and cedar. The fire crackled and a small group of orange embers floated up the flu. Directly behind Mr. Cornelius was an intricately carved maple bookcase holding a collection of black leather-bound ledgers. An ornate Tiffany electric lamp sat on the desk. Cornelius smiled at Graham and asked him to take a seat.

"And your lungs, son? How do the lungs feel?"

"They're all right."

Cornelius turned and looked out the window for a moment. “The reason I’ve called you here is because last night, before my wife and I were ready to retire, we got to talking with the Harolds and my son Charlie about ways in which we could repay you. Of course, the first impulse was to just give you a lump sum of money.”

“Sir, that really isn’t necessary.”

Cornelius held up his hand. “No, no. Hear me out, Henry. Hear me out.” He paused. “But then we thought some more—what would be the greatest way to honor you? And, after some deliberation…I’ve decided to give you a position, a management position mind you, one in which I can show you the game of the Street.”

“The street?”

“Wall Street, son.”

Graham didn’t say anything.

“You look white as a sheet.”

“I don’t know if I’m fit for that sort of thing.”

“Balderdash!”

“I don’t have much in the way of schooling, Sir.”

“Let me tell you a little something about my father, Henry: the man could hardly read, but no one can say that he wasn’t a businessman. My father started from scratch, ferrying people back and forth from Weehawken to Manhattan when he was fourteen years old. He saved every penny and purchased a bigger ferry to take more passengers, and continued saving every penny thereafter until he got older and moved on to steamships.

"When the textile mills started getting built up and railroads connected the steamships from Boston to New York, he saw an opportunity and he jumped, taking a position of management on the Stonington Railroad. And what do you think he did next? He cut the fares on the competitors' price and drove down the stock price on Stonington, allowing him to take over the presidency. And did his lack of education stop him? No. And why? Because he had common sense, son; he worked hard; and he had enough courage to take risks.

"He might've seemed crass and ignorant to a lot of the old money families—but he didn't give a damn what they thought of him. What he cared about was acquiring wealth. He used the tools God had given him and got everything he ever desired. He believed that he could do it and he did.

"If you ask me, I believe every man in this country could be a millionaire if only he just put his mind to it and got off his rump. So few men actually utilize the gifts God gave 'em, Henry. As for you my boy, I suspect you've always sensed you were a cut above the rest of the chaff out there. Am I right?"

Graham looked uneasy. "With all due respect, Sir, I don't believe anyone's got the right to think they're any better than anyone else."

"No one's born any better. You're right. Not in God's eyes, at least. What I'm talking about is confidence, son. A sense that you're destined for better things. Confidence! It's the most important gift. You're destined for more than working as some damned ice harvester."

"It's an honest living."

"I'm not saying it isn't. I know there's things you've probably read or heard about me that might make you think different...but I make an honest living, too."

Silence.

"You're uncertain about giving the Street a try."

"Yes."

"What harm could there be in it? You'll make more money than you could ever imagine, son."

"I know that."

Cornelius gave him a knowing smile. "So you don't want to join with the enemy, is that it? Look. I know there are foreign agitators who like to go about influencing the working class. You get these Italians, Jews, what have you—spreading anarchy and socialism, preying on the ignorance of people and everything goes to hell. The poor saps working for me don't realize: if they unionize it costs me money. If it costs me money, it costs jobs, it costs livelihoods, it costs a man the food he puts on the table for his family. If it becomes too expensive for me to run my plants in New York and New Jersey, I'll move them to Pennsylvania. Do you realize how many out of work coal miners are out that way? And if it becomes too expensive in Pennsylvania, I'll move it further out west. Heck, those railroad Chinamen will work for next to nothing. Why would I pay my workers more when I can pay someone less to do the same job?"

"I'm afraid I see things a little differently, Sir."

"It's like a cancer spreading across the country, Henry. The workers, even clever men like yourself, believe these rabble-rousers over me. Yet I'm the man who puts the bread on their table! I'm not just in this for myself, Henry. It's easy to paint me as the villain because I'm rich. But the truth is, what's good for me, is good for everyone else."

Graham crossed his arms over his chest.

"I treat the people who work for me very well. Take a look at how some of my competitors treat their employees. I pay good wages, help with housing, built schools for the children of my workers, provide better working conditions. Because I treat those who work for me well, I think it's fair that I should expect loyalty."

Cornelius paused, seemed to recompose himself and then smiled. "I can see that I've talked too much. It's a weakness of mine, Henry. I sometimes go off. Nevertheless, what do you say, son? Will you come and work for me?"

"As tempting as your offer is, Mr. Cornelius, I can't."

Cornelius paused and leaned forward as if he was about to bring Graham in on a secret. "There's a cancer spreading in this great nation of ours, trying to destroy everything great men have worked so hard to achieve. These agitators really don't care about the workers, Henry. What they want is to usurp my power. Socialist, anarchists, unionists—whatever they're calling themselves—they want the power so they can rule the country. And do you know what kind of rulers they'll be? Tyrants, Henry. Tyrants! Say goodbye to liberty, erase everything this country stands for."

Graham didn't say anything.

Cornelius grimaced. "Look Henry. I sent my footman to

get your things at that boarding house where you've been living, and he showed me this." He held up a little red book and waved it. "I see you have one of those little Red Song Books."

Graham still didn't say a word.

"You a socialist, son?"

"I'm not political, Sir."

"Balderdash!"

"You've all been kind. And I really appreciate your letting me stay here and all"—

"You hear what happened the other night? Those socialists had a rally and one of them went and killed a man. The poor fella had a wife and a few kids." Cornelius eyed Graham.

Graham's heart sunk. He was quiet for a moment. "They know who did it?"

Cornelius shrugged. "Heard they're still looking for him. I think they have a reward out." Cornelius paused, "You all right, son? You look white as a ghost. Damn. I've lost my train of thought…oh yes. I remember now. What I'm trying to say is that you're better than the rest of that rabble, Henry. Don't turn down an opportunity that you'll regret for the rest of your life."

Graham looked down at his feet.

"Whatever the reasons you were here at Lindenhurst, my boy, don't matter to me. Whether you came on my property, as you claim, to get back home or not—it doesn't matter. But know, we all feel indebted to you and that you are welcome to stay as long as you want and you will not need to worry about money ever again if you choose to work for me. Of that, you can be assured."

Graham sat there a moment. "I'm sorry, Mr. Cornelius."

Cornelius frowned. He looked truly hurt and surprised. "I'm sorry too, Henry. Sorry indeed. And I think you'll be very sorry someday. Nevertheless, I'll honor your decision. But why don't you mull things over for a while. Will you do that? After all, this is your future we're talking about. Think it over, and if you change your mind—you can always let me know."

"I will need to leave very soon," Graham said, then regretted it. He knew Lindenhurst was probably one of the safest places for him right now.

"I have to get back to New York before the snow starts," Cornelius said. He walked Graham to the door. "Just be patient and wait until you hear from me, son."

CHAPTER 10

Everyone had returned to Manhattan except for Graham, Alice Cornelius and a skeleton crew of servants who stayed on at Lindenhurst.

For the next couple of weeks, he continued to regain his strength.

Every evening, Graham would come downstairs to the servants' dining hall to have coffee with the servants. They would sit in the room next to the scullery and talk over the clangs of pots and pans. Mostly, though, he talked to Colleen Callahan, the chambermaid. She filled him in on the comings and goings of life in the mansion. She enjoyed working here, she said, and she liked the entire Cornelius family, especially Mr. Cornelius. She spoke of him in such a glowing manner and seemed to know so much about his business dealings that Graham eventually said: "You sure do know an awful lot about Mr. Cornelius. Is he that close to the other help as well?"

Colleen's face turned red. "I don't honestly know."

He nodded, and then he said: "I think I"ll be leaving Lindenhurst soon."

"Why? There's no need to go, Henry. It gets very lonely here whenever everyone's gone back to Manhattan. And, if you must know, I do enjoy your company so much." She smiled at him. Their eyes locked for moment. She blushed. "Besides, didn't Mr. Cornelius ask you to stay until you hear from him?"

"It's been a while. I suspect he may have even forgotten he has a guest here who's overstayed his welcome."

"Oh, Dearie, he's just busy. He hasn't forgotten you. He'll send for you when he's ready. Trust me, I know."

"No. It's best if I leave."

She hesitated. "What's the matter? Don't you enjoy my company?"

"No, I do."

"So then why would you want to go?" She asked, pouting.

He didn't say anything. Colleen glanced toward the door and grimaced. Alice made her way into the scullery to join them.

Graham and Alice had started to strike up a friendship. And as the days passed, Colleen noticed that it seemed as if Alice wanted to grow closer to Graham.

Alice interrupted the conversation between Graham and Colleen, unaware of her ill manners. She told Graham she wanted to confide to him something she'd overheard. Colleen frowned and turned and pretended to be busy, clanging pots and pans while Graham and Alice conversed.

Alice looked around. "There are suspicions about how Lillian fell through the ice."

"Do they think I had something to do with it?" Graham asked.

Alice shook her head, no. "They think she might have been trying to take her own life." She spoke in a whisper. "It wouldn't be the first time that she'd tried something like this. She tried once before. She keeps her wrists covered for a reason, you know."

Silence.

"The Harolds are planning on bringing her to Europe come April. There are doctors over there who've got this new method of helping people's nerves. They call it the talking cure. Charlie and Mr. Harold were suspect. But the doctor told them that there's been surprising success and that the alternatives are far worse."

He took a sip of his coffee. There was something bothering him that he had been meaning to ask.

"Today while I was walking the grounds, I saw a man come to the front door of the estate."

"Oh?"

"He was wearing a gray suit with a black armband? A brown derby. Do you know who he was?"

Alice shrugged and shook her head, no.

"It was a Detective," Colleen Callahan, the chamber maid, chimed in.

"What did he want?" Graham's heart started to pound in his chest.

"That man that was murdered a couple of weeks ago had a young daughter. They were looking to raise money for the man's family."

"Oh that's dreadful," said Alice. "Have they caught the killer?"

"Not yet. He said that the manhunt's spread through nearly the entire state and they'll not give up until they catch him."

"Was he a foreigner?"

"They don't know. A couple of witnesses said they thought he was an American."

At some point, they'll find me here. Someone will recognize me.

"I was telling Colleen that I think I should be leaving Lindenhurst very soon."

"What for?"

"I've over-stayed my welcome. Your father must have forgotten that I'm here."

"I told Henry, he's just busy," Colleen chimed in, coming over to the table where they were sitting. "Trust me, Henry, he hasn't forgotten you."

"She would know, Henry," Alice said, smirking. "She's my father's favorite servant."

Colleen looked down.

Graham shook his head. "I should leave this place."

"Where would you even go? You'll be working for my father soon anyway," Alice said.

"No I won't."

"No?"

"I turned down his offer."

"You turned down my father?"

"Yes."

Alice beamed. "I've never heard of anyone saying 'no' to anyone in my family before."

"Well, I did."

At this revelation, Alice's pupils grew to saucers. Graham saw Colleen shoot an irritated glance in Alice's direction, but he didn't give it much thought.

He eventually agreed to wait it out a little longer. Until it was warm enough to sleep outside before he'd leave.

"If I don't hear anything from him soon, I'm leaving," Graham said. "No matter what."

But that night, as he was drifting off to sleep in his bed, he heard someone come into the room. It was dark, but he could tell the visitor was a woman.

"Alice?"

She shushed him and put her finger to his lips. He realized it was Colleen.

He could hear the ruffling sound of her taking off her dress. She slipped under the covers and pushed herself against him. Her skin felt soft and she kissed the sides of his face, and then kissed his neck and his chest. She let her fingers drift down his stomach and further down still where her hands could feel that he was ready. She climbed on top of him and guided him inside of her and started moving her hips. She groaned softly, at first, and she leaned over him and gently kissed his lips. Her breath was soft and sweet. "Now will you stay?" she whispered.

"Yes," he said.

"Do you promise?"

"Yes. I promise. I'll stay."

"Good," she said. She started moving her hips again and her groans grew louder until she bit into his shoulder. When they were finished, they lay there, heads on the pillow, their noses touching, smiling softly at one another, catching their breath.

She turned, locked her eyes on his and stroked his cheek. "You know, Henry. You should rethink Mr. Cornelius' offer."

"I won't work for the enemy."

"The enemy? Mr. Cornelius isn't the enemy."

"Tell that to the strikers in Pittsburgh who got beaten by his guards a couple of months ago."

"You should look at this opportunity in a new light, Henry. Look at a position with Mr. Cornelius as opportunity to make more of a difference as an insider rather than an outsider agitating for strikes."

He thought about it a moment. What she said made sense. Nevertheless, he dismissed it. "I've already made my decision."

She smiled. "You're a stubborn mule, aren't you?"

She came to him nightly after that, though she never slept in his bed. She'd lay with him for a little while in a post-coital embrace and then she would leave in a hurry before anyone downstairs realized she was gone.

During the day, she was very busy but she still always managed to find him out whenever she had a second to spare. Graham could tell that she was growing increasingly fond of him.

Graham, however—he was growing increasingly restless. He was ready to move on, and starting to think about heading west again. He spent most days in quiet introspection, wandering the snow-covered grounds of the estate and walking along the banks of the Hudson River. He was finding it increasingly difficult to push away the great pangs of guilt over killing that man. And if it wasn't the guilt, it was the constant wondering about when they would find him. He questioned his decision to turn down Cornelius' job offer. After all, working closely with Cornelius might be the best place for him to hide. Maybe he had let an opportunity slip through his fingers that would never come again. While Alice saw his refusal as an act of bravery and remaining to true to one's self, he thought more about what Colleen had been trying to convince him of—that the opportunity could make more of a difference than agitating for strikes.

As the days passed, his mood turned darker. Sometimes he would stand on the cliffs at the banks of the river and look northward. From here, he could see the shadowy outlines of the ice harvesters, working in the freezing mist. He watched them attach the scraper to draught horses. Watched the horse-drawn shine sleigh following behind the scraper and spraying formaldehyde on the ice to clean up the horse waste. The horse-drawn cutters came next. The entire river was cut. Sectioned off. Some of the men took their pry bars to task, guiding the ice cakes along with the river current. Toward the steam powered conveyor. Up into the white, clapboard ice house high above.

From the cliffs, high above, he watched them working.

CHAPTER 11

Days passed and then it was April. Buds started to appear on the skeletal branches of Tarrytown. The weather was more inviting. Alice had long-since been summoned back to Manhattan by her mother, and Colleen's feelings for Graham had continued to evolve. She was no longer keeping her relationship with him a secret. It was starting to make him feel uneasy. Although she was a pretty girl and nice to be around—Graham wasn't certain of his feelings for her. In any case, he would have to leave here very soon and go on the run.

There were times, too, when he even felt something akin to resentment toward her.

On that gloomy day in April, when the air smelled of rain, Colleen insisted that they go for a walk after lunch. As they were making their way back toward the mansion, Graham noticed the look on Colleen's face. There was a Cadillac with an enclosed back parked in front of the mansion. The driver was standing just outside the car.

"Mr. Graham?" the driver called out. "Mr. Cornelius has called for you to come to Manhattan."

"I need to go in and get my things."

"That's already been taken care of, Mr. Graham."

Graham looked at Colleen. There was something about the sadness in her eyes that made him recoil. It wasn't fair; but he did. And now that he was finally summoned by Cornelius, he knew there was no way she could prevent him from leaving.

He was secretly glad to be called away.

"It wasn't supposed to be like this, Henry."

"What do you mean?"

"I didn't want to feel this way about you," she said, trying to put on a brave face, but the poor girl looked like she was on the verge of tears. "Just promise you won't forget about me?"

"Don't be ridiculous. I won't forget you."

"Promise me."

"I promise."

She blushed and looked down at her feet.

He lifted her chin, so that their eyes met. "I'll write you in a day or two."

"How long do you think you'll be gone?"

"I don't know. Not long I suppose."

He smiled. The driver was watching, so he turned his back and walked to the car, relieved to be free.

CHAPTER 12

The New York Central barreled south, rattling and clanking on the tracks. Graham walked up the aisle to his seat, followed by one of the Cornelius family's footmen, carrying Graham's gummy sack. The footman put the sack on a rack above, and then took a seat behind him.

Graham gazed out the window at the passing scenery, at the new buds at the edges of branches and the patches of grass under the grayness of that day. Small drops of rain streaked the windows as they sped south.

My God, he thought, how long had it been since he'd last stepped foot in New York City? It must have been nearly eleven, twelve years now? Not since he'd left the tenements. He thought about his mother and his heart grew heavy.

The last time he saw her, she had gone days without eating or sleeping. Even the men who used to come to pay to sleep with her said she'd lost her looks.

He remembered that day. He was a few blocks away with friends when someone came and got him to let him know he was urgently needed at home.

He ran back and, when he got to his tenement building,

he found his mother outside, naked. She was standing in the middle of the street yelling and screaming incoherently. A crowd had gathered in shock. They kept their distance, as if they'd cornered a wild animal and were worried it might lunge toward them.

His mother didn't seem to recognize him. She was covered in blood after slashing her arms and chest with the butcher knife that she held in her right hand. He watched in horror as she tried to hack off her breast. There were shocked gasps and a few screams.

Graham ran up from behind and wrapped his arms around his mother, holding her tight. She was crying and kicking. He was surprised at how hard it was to hold her frail body. Eventually a couple of policemen came running over and helped Graham restrain the poor woman. Finally she dropped the knife, too tired to go on. Blood ran down her face; her arms; her chest. One of the policeman called out for something to cover the woman's nakedness. A street peddler came over with a burlap bag.

A little later, a horse-drawn paddy wagon came and took his mother to the hospital. They fixed her wounds and they kept her there to try and fix her mind.

But her mind was unfixable, the doctor said.

Ravaged by syphilis.

"The mother you may have once known," the doctor told Graham, "is gone now, I'm afraid. And it would be better for you to think of her as if she were, in fact, dead so that you can move on with your life."

Soon thereafter, Henry Graham left Manhattan.

He was not yet fifteen years old.

He worked in the mines of Idaho, and later in Wilkes-Barre Pennsylvania. Took a brief apprenticeship as a coach builder in Ohio. Then back east to Paterson, New Jersey to one of the silk mills before getting fired and blacklisted for trying to organize a union. He left and headed west again to Boulder, Colorado to work the mines for a year or two and then returned to the east once again. This time to Tarrytown where he managed to land some work this past winter as an ice harvester.

He still thought about her every now and then, his mother; but the thoughts were fleeting and they came at rarer intervals. Still, he questioned whether or not he should have heeded the doctor's advice and leave Manhattan. After all, it was akin to running away. *I let my mother die alone in an asylum. I should have been there for her, I should have stayed to take care of her. But now she is gone. Gone forever. And I am left with nothing but the lingering ghost of regret.*

The train arrived at Grand Central and Graham stepped out onto the platform and walked with the crowd to the street. Slanting sheets of rain fell as the footman led Graham through the throngs to a motor car. A middle-aged man in the back nodded as he opened the door for Graham.

Graham moved over to make room for the footman.

"Quite all right, sir," the footman said. "I see a transom over there. I'll take that back. It's been a pleasure making your acquaintance."

At that, the footman disappeared into the crowd, as the driver pulled the motor car out into the street and began driving uptown.

"I trust your ride on the train was agreeable?" The man asked.

Graham nodded.

"I've been asked to take you to get a new suit."

"A suit?"

The man nodded, smiling slightly. "For tonight's dinner. Mrs. Cornelius has arranged some entertainment this evening in your honor."

Graham gave him a puzzled look. The man gave the driver directions, then eased himself back into his seat, crossed his arms over his chest and stared straight ahead. He did not speak another word for the remainder of the drive.

CHAPTER 13

Mrs. Cornelius scowled at the dinner placement cards on her desk, just waiting to be filled out. Deciding who should sit where—it was always a tortuous task. The position at which one sat at the dinner table always meant something. It was nearly impossible to have a dinner party in these circles without insulting someone. Mrs. Cornelius thought that by recruiting her daughter Alice as well as Mrs. Harold and her daughter Lillian, that it might make the dreaded task a little more bearable. But it seems they were all at just as much of a loss as Mrs. Cornelius.

"Do we put Henry up toward the front?" Mrs. Cornelius asked.

"Well, this dinner is being held in his honor," Mrs. Harold began, "So I would think it would only make sense."

"Yes, but then who do I have sit near him? Who wants to sit with an ice harvester?"

"Well, he isn't just an ice harvester, Alva. He saved my daughter's life."

"I know that, but he didn't save the Vanderbilt child, or the Goulds, or the Morgans' child."

Mrs. Harold scowled.

Meanwhile, Lillian was sitting in a Louis XIV armchair. She was in another one of her inexplicable black moods. She looked about the room with a detached air of boredom. She'd heard about enough of Mrs. Cornelius' thoughts, and she felt her mother wasn't making things any better. Finally, in hopes of putting an end to the damned discussion, Lillian spoke up.

"I think I might like to sit with him," she said.

Mrs. Cornelius and Mrs. Harold gave Lillian a puzzled stare.

"Seeing as how he saved my life. Charlie and Alice should be somewhere close by—putting all of us together would not insult any of the older guests."

Mrs. Cornelius and Mrs. Harold looked at one another, pondering this suggestion. Lillian had made a breakthrough.

Lillian continued: "Then if you have Alice at the tail end of the table, you can place the Count of Montenegro beside her, which, I'm fairly certain you had planned on doing anyway." Lillian gave Mrs. Cornelius a knowing smile. "No one will take offense at being placed on the other side of the Count."

Mrs. Cornelius smiled. "Why, Lillian, you're a natural."

Lillian forced a smile. Try as she might, when moods like this took over, she could not make herself feel happy. The only thing that could remotely break through the black void was spending time with Charlie.

"But what of the other side?" Mrs. Cornelius asked.

"Will Mr. Segal be in attendance?"

"He will."

"Put Mr. Segal on the other side," said Mrs. Harold. "He's a Jew, and he so dreadfully wants to be accepted into this circle that he'd be willing to overlook anything."

"I can sit on the other side of Henry," Alice chimed in.

Mrs. Cornelius ignored her daughter. "Lillian, you'll make the most wonderful hostess one day."

Lillian looked toward the window at the muted gray sky and rain streaking the glass.

Mrs. Cornelius glared at her daughter. "And you, Alice! You need to pay attention. There is a man here who's interested in your hand. A genuine Aristocrat from Europe. You'll need to know these kinds of things should you become his wife."

Alice said nothing.

Mrs. Cornelius sighed. "Alice?"

"Yes, mother?"

"Did you hear what I just said?"

"Yes, mother."

"Well, how come you haven't said anything? You sit there, sullen and brooding and never say a word. This is why some people say you are a dumb mute."

Alice stared blankly at her mother and then looked down at her shoes.

"I say, Alice, how do you expect to charm a man like the Count when you are so clueless to the world that's going on around you?"

"I don't know, mother."

"Oh Alva," Mrs. Harold chimed in. "She'll come around in her own time."

"She's nearly eighteen years old," said Mrs. Cornelius. "I thought perhaps she would have grown out of this by now."

Lillian glanced over at Alice. If she sank into the seat any deeper she'd make herself disappear completely.

"Alice?" Mrs. Cornelius enquired.

When Alice did not answer, Mrs. Cornelius raised her voice. "Alice?"

Alice looked up with a slight start, but still she said nothing.

Mrs. Cornelius shook her head. "Alice, you really must develop your manners. It irks me to no end."

"Yes, Mother."

A silence fell over the room. Mrs. Cornelius waited for Alice to speak, but they both stared without uttering another word. Finally, Mrs. Cornelius simply sighed. She looked back down at the dinner placements and spoke to Mrs. Harold: "Are you aware that Mrs. Astor refused my invitation again?"

Mrs. Harold clicked her tongue in disapproval. "I wouldn't let it get to you, Alva. She refuses everyone."

"Not everyone. I know for a fact that she attended the Newbold's invitation just the other week. I'm sure if your family offered an invitation she wouldn't refuse, either. I can't stand her air of superiority. As if we aren't worthy of her presence because her family has had money longer than ours? As if this makes her somehow or other superior? After all, the Astors are descended from a pork butcher! Yet, she acts as if she were from a royal line. I swear to you, this is the last time the Astors will receive an invitation from me. And this time I really mean it."

Mrs. Harold shook her head. "You mustn't take it so personally, Alva."

"I don't take it personally. I could care less about her presence. I'm simply bothered by her rudeness. Incorrigible. That's what that Mrs. Astor is."

Lillian took a deep breath and rose from her chair. She walked softly to the window and looked out into the late afternoon. Below her, a black motor car idled outside the front of the Cornelius Brownstone. A group of servants had hurried out into the rain, carrying umbrellas.

Her heart started to race with the expectation of seeing Charlie. But she was taken by surprise when she saw Henry Graham—the ice harvester—emerge.

She'd almost forgotten what he looked like.

He appeared somewhat unsure what all the commotion was around him. He looked up at the townhouse, as if it was a tourist attraction. His eyes drifted past one window to the next until he found the window where Lillian was standing. He didn't acknowledge that he had seen her, but she knew that he had. He stood there with his eyes fixed on her before the servants hurriedly ushered him out of the rain and inside the brownstone.

Lillian remained at the window. She could hear her mother and Mrs. Cornelius still blathering away, their words rising into an incomprehensible babel of nonsense. She wondered what it must be like for women of Graham's class. Women so untouched by the anxiety of living up to strict social norms. Women of her own social class, thought Lillian, were dull and self-absorbed and simple. She looked back down. Graham was gone. *What are the lives of those people actually like?*

Henry Graham will be a welcome guest tonight, she thought. Something much different from the same old clap trap.

She felt her mood lift ever so slightly.

CHAPTER 14

One by one, the guests arrived, some of the most fashionable family couples of 5th Avenue. The Vanderbilts, the Goulds, the Whitneys, the Carnegies, the Morgans, the Flagers, the Frisks...one after the other they came. Graham felt overwhelmed. He'd heard most of their names before, but it always seemed to him as if these people weren't really humans. More like mythological creatures. Yet, here they were, and what's more—here he was among them.

Mrs. Cornelius, dressed in a large blue gown, brought each of her guests over to Graham and introduced them. She kept referring to him as Lillian's guardian angel. Mrs. Cornelius had treated Graham with such grace this evening that he now felt guilty for once telling Colleen Callahan that her lifestyle was one of wretched excess. Tonight, however, he found her to be a warm and welcoming hostess.

Nevertheless, he was nervous. He felt terribly out of place. He could feel small streams of sweat dripping from his temples and down the sides of his face.

Charlie remained standing by Graham, strategically positioned by his mother to jump in whenever there were any lapses in conversation.

Graham had met most of the guests when Lillian's brother William approached.

"Ah Henry, you remember my pal William Harold, I'm sure," Charlie said.

William shook Graham's hand, unsmiling. His palm felt soft and moist.

"So," William said, looking around, "I imagine this must be a little overwhelming for you."

"Not really."

"I understand you're originally from Manhattan, Henry?"

Graham shuffled his feet and cleared his throat. "A long time ago."

"Ages, I'm sure. And your family? They still live in Manhattan?"

Graham's face remained impassive. "No. I have no family left here."

His distaste for Lillian's brother was continuing to grow toward hate.

"I was under the impression that at least your mother was still living here?"

"No. She died a long time ago."

"Shame."

"That's a dreadful business," Charlie chimed in. "I'm sorry to hear that, Henry."

William opened his mouth to say something else, when Alice suddenly appeared.

"Hello, Henry!" She took his hand, excitedly, her teeth

jutting out of her mouth. "I knew I'd see you again!"

Before she could say anything else, Charlie cut her off. "Well, well, well. Look who it is!"

The three men watched in awe as Lillian entered the drawing room with her mother and father. She wore a light, blue gown with a ruby necklace. Mrs. Cornelius directed the Harolds to meet with Graham. Alice's smile quickly morphed into a frown, as she was pushed aside. Mrs. Cornelius reintroduced Mr. and Mrs. Harold first, and then gently putting her hand on Lillian's gloved wrist, said: "And obviously you remember Lillian?"

She extended her hand.

"Of course I remember." Graham was unable to contain his admiration. He thought Lillian looked remarkably beautiful. He smiled and tried to lock eyes with her, but she wouldn't entirely meet his gaze.

"How could anyone forget you, Lillian!" Mrs. Cornelius interjected.

Graham smiled, embarrassed.

When all the guests had arrived, Mrs. Cornelius called for everyone's attention: "Shall we all commence into the dining room?"

As they left the drawing room, Graham felt a hand on his shoulder. It was William. William nodded his head toward his sister. "Why don't you put your eyes back in your head, pal. Just because you're dining with us, doesn't give you the right to lust after my sister. Stick with the servant girls and the whores."

Graham glared at him.

"Don't think I didn't see the way you were looking at her. I'm very perceptive."

William seemed unimpressed with Graham's silent threat, and continued: "I know you were on the Cornelius property for no good; and I know you're lying about your intentions. You followed my sister to Lindenhurst."

"That so?"

Charlie suddenly appeared at the door. "Come-on you two! Please don't leave me alone with these people!"

William laughed. Graham feigned a smile, but he was so angry that he had a hard time keeping his composure.

Everyone took their respective seats at the dining table. Graham sat toward the end beside Charlie Cornelius, and Mr. Gabriel Segal on his other side. Lillian Harold sat on the other side of Charlie, beside her mother, who was next to Mrs. Cornelius at the head of the long table, opposite Mr. Cornelius. William sat opposite Charlie and beside Mrs. Vanderbilt (who also sat near the end of the table beside Mrs. Cornelius), and his father sat on the other side of him. Alice Cornelius sat between Mr. Segal and the Count of Montenegro, because Mrs. Cornelius was fiercely determined he would marry her daughter and finally give a title to their family. Beside the Count sat Mr. Gould, and across from Mr. Gould was his wife. Each spoke to one's standing in society.

Mrs. Cornelius smiled quietly at her unsurpassable hosting skills.

Mr. Segal gently touched the crook of Graham's arm.

"Looks like they put the Jew and the Catholic right next to each other," he whispered to Graham. "All we need is a Negro and we could start our own secret society."

Graham looked at him. He was small, with thinning red hair and ruddy face. It took him a moment to realize that Mr. Segal's remarks were an attempt at humor. He managed to laugh nervously and nod.

Graham's heart was beating wildly. Despite the fact that he'd had nothing to eat since boarding the train in Tarrytown, his nerves had made him lose his appetite. The only person who seemed just as uncomfortable was the Count of Montenegro, sitting beside Alice Cornelius. Alice sat like a mute at the table, sipping her soup, shyly. Meanwhile the Count sat beside her, his eyes somewhat glazed. Every now and then, however, Alice would glance toward Graham, and when he caught her gaze, she would give him a small smile.

The table erupted in conversation. Graham sat silently, unable to distinguish one conversation from the next. At some point, he realized that someone was speaking directly to him. He looked up from his plate and saw that all eyes were now on him.

Graham said, "I'm sorry. What was the question?"

"I understand you spent some time living in the tenements. Are they as bad as they say?" It was Mr. Vanderbilt.

"Well," Graham began, then stopped to clear his throat. "Well, they're nothing like this place, that's for sure."

The guests at the table laughed. Graham managed a smile. A servant came to take away his first course, and he realized he'd hardly eaten anything.

Mr. Vanderbilt smiled. "I know that at least, which is why I'm so interested. I've read of the terrible conditions, and I was just curious…I mean, to hear it from someone who actually lived in one of them—are they as bad as the papers say?"

Before he could answer, Mrs. Frisk said to her husband, "my dear, do you remember when your mother invited Mr. Riis over for tea? Tens of people sleeping in one room, I remember him saying. I could not even imagine."

"I certainly do remember," said Mr. Frisk. Frisk looked over at Graham. "Have things in the tenement improved since then, Son?"

"Since when?"

"Since Mr. Riis took his conochromes," Mrs. Cornelius explained. She looked at her guest around the table. "I must say, fashion really came together for that cause. It was because of us that good old Roosevelt set about making reforms. But I should think things must be much better now."

"Lord knows they could not have gotten worse!" Exclaimed Mrs. Gould.

"Here. Here," Mr. Harold piped in.

"Have they, though, Henry?" Mr. Vanderbilt said.

"Well, it's been a while since I lived in the city. I don't know if they're any better. But they were very hot in the summer. Most of the time, people just sleep on the roof. When I was a kid, we'd sleep out on the stoop at night."

"You should have seen how many boys they had in the room at St Dominic's," Lillian chimed in. "If St Dominic's is an improvement from the tenements, the tenements should be outlawed."

Graham turned to Lillian as she spoke. He was impressed by how sure of herself she was.

"Do you all remember the heat wave that struck about fourteen years ago?" Graham asked. The guests nodded. "Drunkards and derelicts would lie dead in the streets. Horses would drop dead, too. They'd begin decomposing in the hot sun, and explode."

"Explode?" Mrs. Vanderbilt repeated.

"From the buildup of gases," Mr. Harold explained.

"There was guts and piss everywhere. The stench in the streets was unbearable."

A silence fell upon the table. Graham wondered whether he'd crossed a line. He wanted to rise from his seat and disappear into the night.

Mr. Harold cleared his throat and rose from his seat, holding his glass. "I would like to make a toast," he began. "There are no words to express my gratitude to this young man, in whose honor this dinner is being held. He showed incredible courage and gave no second thought to risking his own life in order to save my Lily. For that, I will be eternally grateful. So tonight, I raise my glass Henry, whose future, I suspect, now shines greatly upon him."

"Hear, hear," someone said.

"Please join me in welcoming Henry to our table with us tonight, and forever in our circles."

The guests smiled and offered a chorus of good wishes.

For the remainder of the meal, Graham couldn't relax. Here were the people that the papers wrote about, followed their lives and doings and parties, the very pillars of society. Here they were living and breathing just like him.

Yet, what struck him oddest of all, was that they seemed far more fascinated by him than anyone else at dinner.

When the meal was over, and the guests began to leave, Graham headed straight up the stairs to bed.

Mr. Cornelius called out from the bottom of the stairs: "Good night, Henry."

"Good night, Sir."

"Did you enjoy the dinner?"

"It was like nothing I've experienced before, Sir. Thank you. It's something I'm never going to forget."

"I'm sure there will be many more like it."

Graham gave Mr. Cornelius a questioning look.

"Sleep on everything we talked about at Lindenhurst. You're a smart young man, and I have no reason to think you'll make the wrong decision."

Cornelius smiled again and bid him goodnight. He turned and, rather than climbing the stairs to his bedroom, headed down the hall toward the servant's quarters with an expectant gleam in his eye and a light spring in his step.

CHAPTER 15

The next morning Lillian Harold woke to find a note on her bedside from Charlie. It said to be ready by eleven for the walk they had planned in the park. Lillian was a bundle of giddy nerves. She pressed the note to her nose, breathed in.

She'd been looking forward to this walk with Charlie since Mrs. Cornelius suggested it at last night's dinner. While she was happy to find herself sitting beside him last night, there was hardly a chance for the two of them to speak. Most of the conversation revolved around that ice harvester. At first, she was intrigued as everyone else; but her curiosity eventually gave way to a kind of frustration as he seemed to be keeping her from having a good conversation with Charlie. It was hard enough to get Charlie to pay attention to her to begin with, let alone with the additional distraction of last night's dinner guest.

Even though he often set off one of her black moods, Charlie was also the only thing in her life that could make her happy. In all the time they had known each other, Charlie rarely spoke more than a few words of affection. On a few occasions, Lillian confided this to her mother; but her mother simply gave her a reassuring smile and told her not to worry. "Young men are generally oblivious to the true feelings of women," her mother told her. "You simply need to be patient until Charlie figures things out. Once he does, all he'll be able to think about will be you, Lillian."

When they were together and he was showing her attention, her dark mood would almost always dissipate. Charlie could always make her laugh and she found his kindness and compassion to others to be without equal. When she had told him about her visit to St Dominic's orphanage and the conditions she observed there, he donated a vast sum of money, created a board of directors to make sure that the orphanage's conditions were kept up to his liking, and even stopped by now and then to play baseball with the children.

What made her feel best of all, was when she attended various social functions with Charlie. There was no question that he could always command a room from the very moment he walked in; in fact, women practically swooned the moment he entered. But when Lillian was beside him, walking arm in arm, it felt as if it highlighted her own beauty. It would be a lie to say she did not enjoy the jealous glares and whispers that came from the other girls at these parties.

They had known one another since childhood, Charlie and Lillian. In fact, Lillian had known Charlie all of her life. Owing to the fact that Charlie was a few years older than Lillian, she had always looked up to him and admired him. No one dared put a hand against her or speak an ill word to her when Charlie was near. She still remembered the time when she was five years old and Charlie was eight. The Harolds had hired a nanny who was a wretched woman. She scolded Lillian incessantly. Her brother William would cower in the corner whenever the nanny went on one of her tirades. One summer, while they stayed with the Cornelius' up in Newport, Charlie could hear the nanny yelling at Lillian, telling her that she was a horrid child. Charlie stood in front of Lillian and confronted the nanny. He told her that if she spoke another word against Lillian, he would throw her out of the window. That nanny stood there in dumbfounded silence. She told him to mind his manners.

"Very well," he said. He then took Lillian's hand and lead her out of the room. He sought out Lillian's parents. Once he found Mr. Harold, he demanded that they sack the nanny immediately, and if they did not, Lillian should come and live with his family where she would be safe.

"Well, then," Mr. Harold said to Charlie. "It seems the matter is settled. Thank you, Charlie."

That was the last Lillian or William ever saw of the nanny. To this day, whenever Charlie was near, she felt safe. It was mostly when Charlie was away that her moods became exceptionally dark. The truth of it was: in her mind, she wasn't sure if she was worthy of a man like Charlie Cornelius.

The morning hours dragged on. Lillian paced back and forth in her room. Eventually she decided it might be best to wait for Charlie in the drawing room. She saw herself sitting in the easy chair until the footman brought Charlie in and she rose slowly as his eyes lit up at the sight of her face.

Today's walk, she was certain, would mark the next stage of their courtship, the final step before their engagement and their marriage.

The bell at the door finally rang. Lillian straightened up. Her heart was pounding and she could feel her face going flush. She took a deep breath. Let it out. A moment or two later, a knock sounded on the drawing room door and Lillian bid them to enter.

The footman entered. Lillian stood up slowly, just as she imagined, moving toward the door with all the grace she could muster. Then her smile suddenly twisted as her eyes narrowed in confusion.

"Hello?" she said, looking past Graham who pinched at the edges of his derby hat.

"Will there be anything else?" The footman asked.

Lillian shook her head, no, and waited for him to leave.

"Is Charlie running late?" she asked Graham.

"He's gone off with your brother, I'm afraid. He said to tell you that he's sorry."

"So he's off with William?"

Graham nodded.

"Did they say why or where?"

Graham shook his head. "He just asked if I would come here and accompany you on a walk through the park in his stead."

"The two of them are inseparable." Lillian forced a smile; but there was no hiding her hurt. "I think it's very odd they are so close. Something unsavory about their friendship. Don't you agree, Mr. Graham?"

"You'd know better than me."

"Is it a nice day today, Mr. Graham?"

"Couldn't ask for a nicer bit of weather."

"I suppose it would be a shame to waste such a day."

Graham smiled. "It would."

"All right then…" She grabbed a purple bonnet, then made a gesture toward the door. "To blazes with Charlie Cornelius. You'll do just fine, Mr. Graham."

The trees of Central Park were starting to green. The crocus and daffodils had broken the soil and the grass sprouted like a wave. It was one of the first genuinely nice days of spring and the park was bustling with people. Couples strolled together; women dressed in their bonnets, and hoop skirts, some strolling with parasols.

Most of the conversation was carried by Lillian. Graham listened intently to her small talk.

"And how about Alice Cornelius last night?" Lillian said. "Did you see the look on her face? The poor girl. Her mother can be so dreadful toward her. She has it in her head that Alice should marry the Count. She so dreadfully wants a title in the family and the count dreadfully needs money, so I guess you could say it's a fair arrangement."

"She's very smart," said Henry.

"Alice?" She gave him a look. "Most people have the opposite impression."

"At Lindenhurst, she read all day every day in their library."

"But what good will that do her?"

"I suppose it'll make her even smarter."

"Like I say, what good will it do her? It's not as though she will be able to put it to much use."

Lillian chuckled. She noticed the polite smile on Graham's face and realized he probably found little interest in such gossip. "And how about you, Mr. Graham? Did you have a good time last night?"

"I did."

"Probably a little overwhelming? Being surrounded by so many strangers?"

"A little."

"Well, you did a fine job. You charmed everyone at the table, I will say that."

He gave her a look.

"What? You don't believe me? It's the truth. On the way back in the cab, my mother made s comment about the fact that she would feel terribly intimidated if she'd come from your circumstances, and suddenly found herself in such society. She felt you carried yourself with such composure that she could easily have mistaken your station."

Graham looked at her out of the corner of his eye. "She said that?"

"She said given the proper education, she felt no one would ever know where you had come from, that you were once one of them."

"One of them?"

Lillian suddenly broke into laughter and gave him a playful touch on the hand.

"Well, I don't think your brother would agree with your

mother. That's for sure."

"Why would you think that?"

"Your brother's got it out for me."

"That's ludicrous. He doesn't even know you."

"Some men hate for the sake of hating."

"William isn't like that. He's not like that at all."

Graham made a face. A passerby almost bumped into him.

"Truly, he's not, Henry—may I call you Henry? Perhaps he takes a little getting used to, but he's not what you think. He's actually a hoot. You'll see."

They came upon a stand renting rowboats to take out on the pond. Graham reached his hand into his pants pocket. *Even with the clothes that I am wearing, the mansion where I am staying—my pockets are still empty.*

"Here," Lillian said, digging into her small purse.

Graham looked down at his shoes as Lillian handed the man a nickel, and he told them to choose whichever one they liked.

Graham helped Lillian climb into the boat. He took off his jacket and his shoes, rolling up his pants and stepped into the water to push the boat off. He quickly climbed in, and the sudden addition of his weight caused the boat to rock from side to side. Lillian let out a playful screech.

"If I fall in you'll have to save me!"

An uneasy silence fell over them.

It seemed they had both done whatever they could to avoid discussing it, that day at Lindenhurst. Lillian acted as if nothing had ever happened; as if the darkness that had made her decide life was no longer worth living no longer clung to her. For the most part, she seemed quite happy, although once or twice he thought he detected a weariness in her eyes. Nevertheless, he rolled up his sleeves and started to row out to the center of the pond.

As for Lillian, she felt surprisingly at ease with Graham. She took note of the broadness of his shoulders, the laborer's width of his back. So different than the men in her circles who worked behind desks or lived lives of leisure. She wondered if his new life in society would cause him to lose his physique.

Graham looked at her and smiled, oblivious to what the young woman was thinking. He offered her a cigarette and she scoffed.

"Do you think I'm a woman of questionable morals?"

"I'm sorry," he said, putting a cigarette in his mouth and the pack back in his jacket pocket. "I didn't mean to cause you any offense, I saw you"—

"Do you know a lot of girls who smoke, Henry?"

"Seems to be more and more common these days."

"Well not in my circles."

There was something about the way in which he smoked that she found attractive. It suddenly occurred to Lillian that she couldn't take her eyes off of him. What's more, her mood was now surprisingly light. *But he certainly isn't any Charlie Cornelius,* she thought. *No one can compare with Charlie.*

A little later they brought the boat back in. There was photographer who offered to take their picture for a quarter.

Graham refused; but Lillian insisted.

"I'll be leaving for Europe soon, Henry, and I don't know when I'll be coming back. What if we never see one another again? This photograph might be the only memory we'll have of our time together."

The photographer had them stand side by side, mistaking them for a couple.

"So I understand Mr. Cornelius may be getting you a job in finance?" Lillian asked, while the photographer fumbled about.

Graham noticed a policeman standing over to the side. Was he eying him with suspicion? He turned his gaze back to Lillian, his heart racing.

"Henry? Did you hear what I said?"

"I'm not going to work for Cornelius," he said.

"Why not?"

"Because I won't help him smash strikes and make money off the sweat of the workers."

"Oh, please, Henry. I don't see how you turning down Mr. Cornelius helps anyone. It doesn't change the conditions of labor; it doesn't help the workers get more wages, and it certainly doesn't help you. I think it's foolish to lose such an opportunity."

He hesitated. The policeman was still looking in their direction.

"Just give it a try, Henry. What is there to lose? Besides, I could use a strong man like you to row me out on a boat on days like this."

"You paid for the boat."

"Yes, but you rowed. So it seems we've settled."

Graham squinted into the sun. The policeman turned and walked away, much to his relief. Lillian smiled at him and something totally unexpected happened—he wanted nothing more than to kiss her.

"Besides, finance can be very lucrative, Henry. You might even pave your way into society. We could move in the same circles. Imagine that!"

"I don't think you want me running around in your social circles."

"I don't see why not," she said. "In fact, I think I should very much like it if I saw you again." She turned her head and looked off. Then she looked at him again, her eyes radiating. "In fact, I would like that very much"

The flash suddenly popped. A big bright flash of white. The image of the two of them, Henry Graham and Lillian Harold.

Standing outside the boathouse.

Spring 1909.

Captured forever.

Ypres, Belgium. April 1915

Graham put the photo back in his coat pocket.

The intensity of the shelling through the night had Graham doubtful that he would survive this war. But deserters were shot, he knew. Shot and killed in disgrace as cowards.

On Thursday, Graham and Calloway were put on Sentry duty. A few minutes later, there were some small explosions. Calloway elbowed Graham in the ribs and pointed in the direction of the French colonials. Two separate clouds of smoke floated just above No Man's Land. A soft breeze pushed the clouds of smoke together until finally merging into one. A stunned and baffled silence seemed to permeate the battlefield.

"What the hell's going on?" Calloway asked.

There was a faint smell wafting in the air that reminded Graham of pineapples and peppers. "I don't know, Calloway" Graham said, watching in silence as the cloud slowly approached the French colonial trenches. "I have no fucking idea."

A volley of rifle fire rang out as the smoke cloud drifted closer and closer, until it fell down into the Algerian trenches. The rifle fire continued. Then, one by one, the shots began to cease. Soon, there was no one firing.

The silence terrified him.

A few moments later, the Algerians came screaming as they retreated from their trench. Their brass buttons had turned green and their eyes were rolling back in their heads. A thick white, glue-like substance was gushing out from their mouths and it took Graham a few seconds for his mind to comprehend the horror. The chemicals were disintegrating the men's lungs inside their chests. The men were literally coughing their lungs out.

Graham and the other men looked at one another. The Germans were coming across No Man's Land now. They were wearing gas masks, holding their rifles forward, shooting toward the cloudy mist.

"Fix bayonets, my Men!" The Capitaine shouted.

They rose up on the fire step and began firing at the Germans as they crossed. Every now and then one of the Germans would fall and disappear into the gas cloud.

Soon the Germans took the French Colonial trench and the Moroccans were forced to flee.

Word was soon passed down the line that someone in the Canadian company recognized it was Chlorine gas.

"Piss in your handkerchief and hold it to your mouth!" They were ordered. "The piss'll help neutralize it!"

The men took out their handkerchief, opened their zippers, pissed on them, and then put them to their mouths.

The cloud was settling in parts of the reserve trench. Calloway came running over, grabbed Graham by the shoulder, coughing and gasping. "They've broken the line! They've broken the line!"

Graham looked around for an officer, someone to tell them what to do; but it was utter chaos. The men held their ground, waiting for some kind of order or command. They watched the direction of the trench line that led toward where the Moroccans had retreated in case the Germans headed their way or in case they started another advance.

It looked as if the Germans were moving in the opposite direction toward the woods, and someone gave the order to fire at anything they saw moving. The smoke began to dissipate and some of it drifted in their direction. Some of the men began to panic when they felt their throats starting to burn. Fear had kept Graham in place, mindlessly awaiting orders that seemed to never come. Finally, he could not take it anymore. He hurried down the trench calling out for the Lieutenant, the Sergeant, the Capitaine. But there was no answer.

"The Lieutenant's dead."

Graham looked down. A soldier was sitting on the ground, shaking. "He was just standing there and I heard a shot. I thought he tripped but when I went to help him up his brains started to come out."

Graham bent down, wiped the blood and fleshy goo off the soldier and realized it had come from the Lieutenant. Graham could not find any officers. The men cowered, getting ready to run.

Graham had a feeling the Germans might run from the overtaken trench in their direction. "Grab your grenades!"

Graham shouted. "Throw 'em toward the Moroccan trenches."

Some of the men did as he ordered, and a quick burst of explosions sounded. Graham heard some screams and shouts from a number of Germans and saw detached limbs flying through the air.

"Let's go!" he shouted, not looking to see if anyone was following him. He ran down the trench toward the Canadian line, now struggling to fight off the German advance. He began firing wildly. The gas cloud had thinned and was now only up to his ankles. He kept on firing. The few Germans who were still in the trench turned to face him. A volley of shots came from behind Graham and he knew he was not alone. His throat started to burn, felt like it was starting to close up, but he managed to shout to the men to turn and reverse.

On the way back, he spotted the Capitaine, his head bandaged with some blood dripping down the side of his face. Graham put his hand on the officer's shoulder, and then the officer turned to face him. Like everyone else, he was wide-eyed and frightened. Upon seeing Graham, however, the Captitaine seemed to snap out of his paralysis.

"We can't stay here much longer," Graham shouted. "We're done for if we stay back in our trench."

The Capitaine nodded.

"What do you want us to do?"

"We've lost communication with the rear," the Capitaine said. His voice rang with certainty. "Tell the men to sit tight for now. Just sit tight and hold the line!"

The word was passed down. They remained where they

were, sharing the trench with the Canadians.

They finally managed to turn back the German advance. At dusk, artillery fire started up behind them, shelling the German lines. By seven o'clock that night, the artillery fire grew fiercer and they began shelling open targets.

An order was delivered by a runner and the Capitaine told the men to get ready to counterattack. The Capitaine looked at Graham. "I think it's best if we send the men in the direction of that farmhouse to the left. What do you think?"

Graham managed to force a smile. "Your guess is as good as mine."

The Capitaine put his hand on Graham's shoulder. "Good luck to you."

The men stepped on the fire step. Waited. The Capitaine blew a whistle and the men leapt over the top of the trench. They fired their rifles, tears coming from their eyes.

It seemed to Graham like some kind of hallucination. He saw the men falling all around him, heard the rat tat tat of machine gun fire from the German trenches, saw the way the bodies of men would lurch and jerk spasmodically before falling to the ground. The men let out primordial screams as they pushed forward, jumping over the large craters; as if they were all possessed by mad demons.

Finally, Graham reached the farmhouse. There were three other men inside, waiting for the others, but time passed and no one else arrived. Graham could hear someone in No Man's Land screaming, crying, calling out for help and after a while he realized it was the Sergeant. The men looked at one another.

"It'll be suicide to get to him," one of the men said.

"He's done for anyway," another nodded.

Graham held his rifle close. Stared straight ahead, trying to block out the sound of the Sergeant's cries.

Night fell, and the artillery fired again. But then it stopped, and there was the sound of rifle fire somewhere in the distance. Graham thought it was coming from the woods. The brunt of the battle was now turning in that direction. The screaming started again.

"Fucking die already!" One of the men shouted, covering his ears.

Graham got up.

"What the fuck are you doing?" Someone asked.

"I can't take it anymore," said Graham.

Graham ran out into the night, fell to the ground and started to crawl in the direction of the Sergeant. He came to a shell hole and peeked his head inside. The Sergeant's face was twisted with anguish. He was waist deep in yellow-crusted water and mud. The hand of another man was floating above the water, still holding his rifle, but the rest of him was submerged.

The Sergeant looked up and saw Graham but he did not seem to recognize him. He stared off into the distance. "I've made a mistake, I'm afraid," he said. "Yes, yes, I've had enough now and I'm ready to come home."

Graham winced. He rolled down into the shell hole and grabbed the Sergeant around the waist. He felt something warm, and soft coming out of his shirt. The Sergeant let out a scream. Graham took some morphine tablets out of his pocket, gave them to him. "Here. Chew on these."

Graham crawled out of the hole. He tried to pull the Sergeant out. Suddenly the roaring whistle of an artillery shell cut through the air and Graham watched as it came crashing down upon the farmhouse. A bright orange explosion tore through the night, illuminating everything in a red-orange glow. Graham knew there was no way anyone inside could have survived. He took the Sergeant by the arm and finally managed to pull him out.

"Can you walk?" Graham asked.

The Sergeant shook his head, no. Some of the Sergeant's innards were pushing out of his shirt. Graham lifted him up on his back and started running in a squat. He headed back toward the trench, only thirty yards away when three flares whizzed into the night sky and illuminated his surroundings. Graham's instincts took over, and he started to run as fast as he could in a zigzag. He heard the rat-tat tat, and rifle fire and felt a thud in his back and felt the Sergeant's life go out completely. Graham spotted the opening in their barbed wire and ran toward it in a straight line but he felt his leg go out from under him and knew right away that he had been shot.

Graham grunted as he hit the ground, dropping his rifle. He had to get in that trench or another bullet would most certainly kill him. He reached forward, dragged his body, took hold of the edge of one of the sandbags. He felt a bullet cut through the front tip of his boot as he went over the trench and fell hard into the mud.

Graham lay in the muddy trench gasping, trying to catch his breath, his throat still burning from the remnants of lingering Chlorine gas. A few men made their way toward him. He recognized one as Calloway. They were about to pass him over for dead when Graham mustered up enough strength to grab Calloway by the pants leg. He jumped with a start, looked down.

"Jesus!" Calloway cried. He looked down at Graham's leg. "Looks like they got you good."

Graham said nothing at first. "Where's everybody else?"

"Just us two…don't know what's happened to everybody else."

The other Legionaire yelled out for a stretcher bearer. Graham worried that he might bleed out. He was shivering with cold. Finally, two medics arrived with a stretcher.

He felt himself growing weak and grabbed Calloway's sleeve. "I don't wanna die."

"You ain't gonna die," said Calloway.

"I can't die."

"Didn't you hear what I said? I said you ain't gonna die."

But Graham could see the grim expression on Calloway's face.

Graham reached into his pocket for the morphine tablets, and then remembered he had given them to the Sergeant; instead he felt the photograph in his pocket. He grabbed Calloway and pulled him close. He wanted to give him a message; but a sharp pain came over him and he grabbed at the sides of the stretcher as his body became rigid and he screamed in pain. The two medics hurried him down the trench on a stretcher and loaded him into an ambulance.

The ambulance struggled to move forward in the mud, but finally made it out. They pulled in front of a farm house that was now a make-shift hospital. There were wounded men laying on stretchers out front. The two medics unloaded him from the ambulance and a nurse met them out front and rushed them inside. Graham was barely conscious. As the medics went past the nurse into the operating room, she happened to glance at the wounded man's face.

"Henry?" she said. She stood there for a moment, shocked. She hurried after them, calling out his name. "Henry! Henry!"

CHAPTER 16

The day in Central Park had gone by too fast. Graham walked with hurried steps from the Harold Brownstone, down along Fifth Avenue, Lillian on his mind. He was tempted to smile and wish the best to everyone he passed on the street. He would have liked to stay out with her until the sun went down and the stars came out.

The only thing that had hampered this day was that policeman, staring at him. Graham wasn't sure if the police had a description of him, or even possibly a photograph that they might have obtained somehow. Perhaps it was just paranoia; but there seemed no other explanation as to why a policeman would be staring at him with such suspicion (the look was one of suspicion, Graham had not doubt).

Yet, the policeman simply turned and walked away. Why? It had to have something to do with the way Graham was dressed, the company he was keeping. After all, who could imagine someone like him hiding amongst the circles of the fashionable society? Perhaps, there was no safer way for him to evade capture than staying on this path. Working for Cornelius. In addition, maybe what both Lillian and Colleen had said was true: he could do more to affect change by being on the inside rather than agitating from the outside. His decision was made. He will ask to see Mr. Cornelius and tell him he has changed his mind.

The butler came to the door to let him inside. Graham did not have to ask to see Mr. Cornelius. Mr. Cornelius, it turned out, wanted to see Graham.

Graham was led into Mr. Cornelius' office, where, as usual, Cornelius was hard at work poring over his ledgers. He offered Graham a seat and a cigar. Graham took the seat and politely refused the cigar.

There was a few seconds of silence before Mr. Cornelius spoke.

"What did you do with yourself today, Henry?"

"Nothing much, Sir," he answered in a clipped tone.

Mr. Cornelius gave him an odd look. "Are your activities none of my business? I apologize if I'm being too intrusive."

"No, no." He cleared his throat. "I actually took a walk with Miss Harold in the park."

Mr. Cornelius looked up from his ledgers. "Lillian?"

"Yessir."

"Wasn't Charlie supposed to be with her today?"

"Charlie asked if I would go in his place."

Mr. Cornelius raised his eyebrows. "And what was it that kept Charlie so busy?"

"I don't know, Sir."

"Was he with William?"

Silence.

Cornelius frowned. "You don't need to answer, son." He leaned forward conspiratorially. "Between you and me, I don't care for that William character. Something distrustful about him."

Graham did not say anything.

"You aren't so fond of him, either; are you?"

"I don't have an opinion."

"No need to be diplomatic here, son. The young man is an asshole."

Graham laughed.

"I would think Charlie would be much better off gallivanting with a young man such as yourself. William's a rather sour influence." Cornelius paused. "Charlie's going to lose that girl. He doesn't give her the time and respect that a young woman like that comes to expect. You, on the other hand…well, I wouldn't be surprised if she's home right now thinking about you."

Another silence.

"And if you ask me," Cornelius continued, "if she were to run off with someone else, Charlie would have no one to blame but himself. He's very lucky you're not a rich man. Otherwise…" Cornelius paused, eyed Graham. "Then again, a hard-working fella like you…well, it's only a matter of time before you start making money of your own. With the right breaks, and the right amount of hard work…hell, son, you could be a millionaire. That'll be enough to get a girl like Lillian."

Graham gave him a hard look.

"Do you remember meeting Mr. Frisk last night? He was quite impressed with you. He agrees that you're someone I could show the ropes in playing the game on the Street. Sky's the limit as to the amount of money you could earn." Cornelius shrugged. "Nevertheless, I know you've made your decision and I respect that. However, I would like to at least give you some money. Something to help you out as you venture into your future, Henry.

Graham sat back in his chair. "If you don't mind, Sir, and it's not too late—I think that I would like to come and work for you."

Cornelius looked at Graham. "Is that so?"

"Yessir."

"Well, son. I'm pleased to hear that. But I think you should know something: I treat those who work for me well, and I think it's fair that I should expect loyalty. For the laborer, I expect them to discourage unionizing. And I'm going to expect a much higher level of loyalty from you than I would of anyone else."

"I don't quite understand what you're trying to say, Sir."

"I need you to give me your utmost loyalty."

"In other words, you want me to turn my back on what I believe?"

"I don't give a damn about anything you believe. I just need to know: are you with me, or are you against me?"

Graham hesitated a moment.

"If you're not going to be with me, we can shake hands and wish one another the best."

"Okay. I'm with you, Sir."

Cornelius eyed him. "Are you sure about that?"

"Yessir. I am."

Cornelius smiled. "Well then, son. It seems the beautiful face of fortune is shining down on you and your future."

Graham went upstairs to his room. He looked at the photograph of Lillian. Although he tried to convince himself working for Cornelius would be the safest way to evade capture, deep down he knew this was also a way to see her again. He told himself nothing good could come from getting closer to Lillian. After all, she was Charlie Cornelius' girl. But what did he owe Charlie? They weren't friends. They just met. But what would a girl of Lillian's station ever see in someone like himself? He reminded himself, too, of Lillian's behavior at Lindenhurst, the fact that she'd tried to take her own life. The fact that Alice told him she'd tried it once before and they were sending her off to Europe to "get her mind right." *She's trouble,* he told himself. *It would be best if you never see her again.*

Still, try as he might, he could not stop thinking about her, wanting to see her, to touch her, to be with her in ways she might not be happy about him thinking. It seemed as if he'd lost control of himself. All that seemed to matter now was Lillian Harold.

CHAPTER 17

They were somewhere in the middle of the Atlantic Ocean, between the new world and the old. Lillian was having a bit of an argument with her mother. She wasn't keen on the idea of Europe or this "talking cure" as they called it. Psychoanalysis?

She didn't tell her mother the truth—she was worried that Charlie might find someone else in her absence.

Instead, Lillian complained incessantly about her past days overseas learning Latin, philosophy, literature and art—and all for what? To make her a better conversationalist? She reminded her mother that the only intelligence a woman offered a man in conversation should never be more than regurgitation of facts, rather than opinions. "I suppose, Mother, you find it acceptable that a woman's views don't really matter in the end," Lillian said. "Here we are in the twentieth Century and a woman still can't vote."

Mrs. Harold was visibly annoyed. Ever since her accident at Lindenhurst, Lillian was developing a significant disdain for their way of life.

Lillian, of course, understood that there were certain mores set out for her as a young woman and she'd always abided by them.

More or less.

But it seemed like this life provided no more than idle gossip over tea in parlor rooms. And if it wasn't gossip, it was planning or attending parties with some kind of philanthropic element to make their excesses appear less wretched.

Her mother scoffed. "How dare you make such an assumption, Lillian! Our lives are not meaningless! These meaningless parties creates jobs; food needs to be bought, decorations purchased, gowns and suits designed and created. All of this money trickles down to the lowest workers of society. It is good for society and it is good for the country on a whole. So don't talk to me about frivolous activities, Lillian. You can be such a horrid little creature!"

Lillian screamed and clenched fists. Mrs. Harold, however, remained perfectly calm. To dsstrangers, Lillian always appeared poised and calm; but for those who knew her best—namely her mother and father—her black moods could morph into rage. "I feel pity for the man who will one day marry you and have to deal with your tantrums, Lillian."

"How dare you say something like that to me!" Lillian's eyes began to well with tears. "You should go to hell, Mother!"

Her mother could see how much her remark stung her. "Lillian," she said softly. "I'm sorry. I should not have said that."

Lillian grabbed her fur coat without a word and charged out of the cabin, making damned sure that she slammed the door shut as hard and as loud as she could.

A bitterly cold wind blew off the ocean and across the deck. Lillian wrapped her fur coat tightly across her chest and watched the high waves crashing against the side of the steamer, the icy ocean mist lingering in the air, stinging her cheeks. Looking down into those waters, she contemplated jumping. As she walked along the deck of the ship, Lillian felt her anger starting to fade. She contemplated that maybe her anger over her lack of independence was a paradoxical expression of her desire to be closer to Charlie and become his wife.

She was ready to go back inside. As she turned a corner, she spotted her father sitting alone in one of the wooden deck chairs. Lillian was closer to her father than her mother. She shared her father's curiosity. The two were like kindred spirits, which was one more thing that had always annoyed her mother.

But seeing her father alone out here in this cold, a foreign worry in his gaze, gave her pause. She'd been in denial before; but she realized now that her father was much sicker than he'd been letting on.

Mr. Harold turned his head, and, when he saw that it was his daughter, a smile appeared on his face. He sat up straight, once again a dignified gentleman.

"How long have you been standing there?"

"Not long." Lillian came over and took a seat on the deck chair beside her father. "It's freezing out here."

"The cold salty air is good for my lungs."

"Is it?"

He smiled. "I don't know, really. But it keeps me out of the watchful eye of your mother, so it must do some good."

"You're incorrigible."

He laughed and fell into a bit of coughing.

Lillian tried to appear stoic, but her heart was aching. She was going to have to prepare for the fact that her father would not be around forever.

"How are you feeling, Lillian?" her father asked.

"I'm fine."

"I was about to come inside, but I heard you and your mother arguing."

"I would rather not talk about it. She's a wretched woman."

"You have an artist's temperament, Lillian. You always have."

Lillian smiled in spite of herself. "Charlie's said that to me once."

"Did you get to spend much time with Charlie in New York?"

"Time with Charlie? You should probably talk to William. Charlie seems to prefer his company over mine. It's very odd, father. Those two seem so inseparable. It's as if he is in love with William, don't you think?"

Mr. Harold gave her a reassuring smile. Maybe she was being a little ridiculous in her jealousy of her brother's friendship with Charlie.

"So you're not sure how Charlie feels about you?"

"I don't know. It's hard to describe. It's like one minute he's giving me all his attention, like I'm the only woman in the world. And the next minute it's like I don't even exist. It's so confusing."

"Maybe that's why you're sweet on him in the first place."

"It's not. I tell you it's not."

"Either way, it's just the way young men act, Lillian. Like fools. I've no doubt he's incredibly fond of you. Even I've noticed the way his face lights up when he speaks of you"—

"If you ask me, Mrs. Cornelius wants us to marry more than he does!"

"Now you're just being ridiculous. Besides, there is plenty of time for marriage. Plenty of time to find out if he is the man that you want to spend the rest of your life with."

"I know that he is. I've no doubt." She forced a smile. "I've known since we were children. We've courted for too long not to become husband and wife."

Mr. Harold looked up at the sky and squinted. "Lillian, you must remember that despite what you think, you're still young. Anything could happen. So many things in your life will change that you'll look back one day and wonder how you could have ever thought such ridiculous things. I know you're not happy about going to Vienna to meet with this doctor, but maybe it's a good thing. Time away from Charlie might help you learn whether or not you truly do love him." He took her hand in his. "I only want you to marry someone who loves you back with the same passion, someone you know you'll be happy sharing your life with. Too many people in our circles have married out of convenience, like they were forging some kind of business deal. They've all wound up miserable in the end. I don't need to tell you that some people are actually going so far as to file for divorce.

Divorce! That was unheard of when I was your age. I don't want you to have to ever face that kind of scandal, Lillian."

Lillian looked at her father now. "And you and mother? Why did you marry?"

Mr. Harold smiled. "I loved your mother very much."

"And do you still?"

"Yes. Though we fight all the time, I do still love her as much as I did when we first started courting."

"And what about mother?"

"What about her?"

"Did she love you?"

"I like to think so. In her own way. There was another boy. Before me. I don't know why they never married; I suspect your mother still wishes they had. But so it goes, Lillian. There isn't much I can do to change that. One can't force the heart to feel something it can't."

Lillian had long suspected there was little love in her parents' marriage. But she'd also suspected that her father, at one time, had loved her mother and tried to make her happy. On more than one occasion she'd seen her father try and express some kind of affection only to watch her mother turn a cold shoulder to him, or express some kind of indifference –even frustration—in distracting her from some task at hand.

Try as she might, Lillian couldn't remember the last time they sat down to dinner when her mother hadn't given her father some kind of criticism. There was always a hint of her growing dissatisfaction with the fact that her husband seemed unable to provide the kinds of luxuries for his family that her friends' husbands provided.

"I suppose you need to make sure that the man you are going to marry is the man you are certain brings you happiness."

Lillian looked at her father. "I do think Charlie is that man. I have no doubt that I love him more than anything."

"I know that will make your mother happy. God knows if you marry Charlie you'll never be in want of anything." He paused, smiled. "As for Charlie's distracted nature… he'll come around."

"Are you sure?"

"I was a young man once, too. I know how these things work."

They sat quietly, the two of them, Lillian and her father. Neither one of them spoke. At one point, Mr. Harold mentioned he had spent some time with Henry at the dinner. He said he found him to be a pleasant young man. "Andrew tells me that there was a chambermaid at Lindenhurst and a romance had blossomed."

"Really?" Lillian said. "I'm surprised. He didn't mention that to me."

Mr. Harold was quiet a moment, as if carefully measuring his words. "You know, Lillian, I do feel the need to tell you that you need to be a little more aware of what impression you might give to a young man like Mr. Graham."

Lillian took on a wounded expression. "What are you implying?"

"Just be careful. That's all."

"Careful?"

"You remember you and the gardener..."

"We were nothing more than friends!"

Mr. Harold could hear the shrillness in her voice. "I know you are a virtuous girl and will remain so until your wedding day. I'm just saying it for the good of your own name as well as the good of the family name. No sense in adding any fodder to the gossip mill, eh."

Again, they were quiet.

She moved closer to her father. He seemed frailer, weaker than she ever remembered. She looked out at the ocean now. *He's ill,* she thought. *And there's nothing I can do to stop it. It is in God's hands.* And so they sat out in the cold, Lillian and her father, much longer than either of them should have. But they were together.

CHAPTER 18

Graham began working under Mr. Cornelius' tutelage the very next week, learning what his mentor called, "the game of speculation."

The very first day, when Graham was brought to the offices, Cornelius sat down across from him at a large, polished oak table and asked him what level of education he had.

"I left school when I was eleven, Sir."

Mr. Cornelius' expression was blank. "Can you read, son?"

"A bit. Yessir."

"Can you add? Subtract?"

"Yessir."

Mr. Cornelius gave him a warm smile. "You're a little intimidated by our business circles, aren't you?"

"Suppose. A little bit, maybe," said Graham.

Cornelius smiled. "Let me tell you this, Henry: the best schools only rarely produce the best men. From what I've seen, the streets teach the most important lessons; so long as that individual has the capacity to learn them." He leaned forward, his eyes radiating a warm friendliness. "And I think you have that capacity son. I wouldn't be giving you this opportunity if I didn't."

On Wall Street, Mr. Cornelius was known for being slightly eccentric. Despite the fact that he had grown up in a moneyed family—he preferred to surround himself with self-made men, like his father. His inner-circle consisted of a former dairy farmer, a former Vermont peddler, an Italian immigrant who he'd seen fight on the docks of Jersey City; and now a former ice harvester.

What most surprised Graham about Cornelius was that he was a man of both remarkable generosity and excessive appetites. He loved to spend money on the best of everything. The best home, the best yacht. If he saw someone with something that impressed him he had to have it—only bigger and better. He wore only the very best suits, drank the best liquor.

More than anything else, however, Cornelius had a voracious appetite for chorus girls. He'd even undertaken plans to build his own theatre on Broadway. Just to cut out the middle man, he said, and have ready access to all the girls.

At first, Graham was uncertain of his feelings toward Cornelius. However, he had shown him nothing but kindness since they'd met. And he was, in his way, quite entertaining. Still, he was so obsessed with money and the power it brought him that sometimes it seemed to Graham there was little more to the man than a gluttonous appetite and greed.

On Sundays, it was different. Cornelius would appear at church with his wife and Alice and sometimes Charlie if he wasn't off on an adventure somewhere. Afterwards he would return to his brownstone on 5th Avenue.

"Sunday is my day of rest, my boy," Cornelius told Graham after summoning him to his brownstone one Sunday. "It is the only day I don't seek out the carnal pleasures from one of my mistresses."

At that point, a door opened and a number of downtrodden figures filed into his study. Graham was told to ask each individual how much money they needed, take a record of it and report it back to Cornelius. Graham did this, and then reported to Cornelius' office and watched in disbelief as Cornelius wrote each and every check.

"You do not utter a word of this to anyone, Henry," Cornelius said. "Not a word."

"I would think you should let this be known, Sir. It might help your reputation"—

"To blazes with my reputation, Henry. What good is doing this, if I use it to serve my own purposes?"

Graham was amazed at Cornelius' generosity. Despite all his faults, he was starting to believe that he was not the evil monster he had always imagined.

But among the businessclass, Cornelius was known, more than anything, as a swindler. He was an expert at watering stocks, of manipulating markets, paying off politicians and judges and anyone else who could somehow benefit him. He was known as a crook and much worse; but he was also greatly respected because, as Mr. Cornelius said to Graham: "they would all be doing the same thing if they could; they would be milking the Street by every tit, if they knew a way."

At first, Graham was ignorant of the fact that many of

the tricks of the trade Mr. Cornelius was teaching him were illegal. He just thought that was how business operated. It wasn't until he ran into another speculator who filled him in of Mr. Cornelius' reputation. No sooner had the man decried Cornelius' methods did he lean in, and hold out a couple hundred dollars, whispering: "tell me how he does what he does, young fella, so I might be able to do the same?"

Nevertheless, as time went on, Graham became greatly enamored with Mr. Cornelius despite his short-comings. He admired his intellect, his savvy and his work ethic. The respect was returned by Cornelius, as Graham had quickly proved himself to be an exceptional understudy.

Within a few months' time, Graham began making more money than he could have ever imagined. His previous life as an ice harvester was beginning to grow foggier and foggier each day.

He began buying himself new suits at Brooks Brothers, dining at some of the nicer restaurants in town. At night, he would go to his apartment and read voraciously to become more cultured for his new circles.

In short, Henry Graham was growing into another man completely.

Still, the memory of that Pinkerton kept him up many nights. Every policeman and every stranger he saw waiting outside his apartment building made his muscles tense up, his heart start to pound with anxiety. He would try and convince himself that enough time had passed that they had probably stopped looking for him; but it was to no avail. Not a day went by when he didn't have at least one moment of panic that today would be his last as a free man.

And if it wasn't the paranoia of his capture, it was the guilt of having killed a man. A mortal sin. There were times, it's true, when he'd find himself standing in front of a church, trying to muster the courage to go inside and confess to a priest. But it had been so long since he'd last gone to confession and he'd accumulated so many other sins that he felt he was a hopeless case, unworthy of absolution.

So he kept the secret to himself, never telling anyone. And the secret weighed heavy on his soul, driving him mad inside.

CHAPTER 19

It took some time, but Lillian began to make progress with her "talking cure". She told the doctor her deepest thoughts and secrets, like a penitent confessing to the priest. The doctor felt her anxiety was the culmination of three different things: her fear of Charlie's abandonment, menstruation-linked depression, and the fact that she masturbated to excess.

During the spring of 1910, the doctor deemed Lillian well enough to leave Vienna with her mother and father for a short time. They joined Mrs. Cornelius, Mr. and Mrs. Stuyvesant Fish and Mr. and Mrs. Vanderbilt at the Cornelius' villa in Florence. The guest of honor that evening was the young Count from Montenegro, whose fortunes had continued to diminish since the dinner held for Henry Graham. His interest in marrying Alice Cornelius was increasing by the day.

The Count was a man in his late thirties. Dark black hair, parted straight down the middle. He had dark bags under his eyes and he wore an upturned mustache.

At dinner that evening, Mrs. Cornelius arranged it so the Count was placed next to Alice, who didn't speak a word throughout the evening.

When the dinner was complete, the men went into the billiards room, while the women went to the other side of the villa to a parlor. Dreading the inane chatter, Lillian took it upon herself to ask Alice if she'd like to join her outside for a walk in one of the gardens.

Lillian's family had been friendly with the Cornelius' for as long as she could remember. Lillian felt a little bad that, in all that time, she had never really been able to get to know Alice. Though Alice suffered from a debilitating shyness and odd manner that turned most people away—Lillian still felt it somewhat wrong to keep the same distance.

As for Alice's odd manner, there was no one more flustered by it than Mrs. Cornelius. Her awkward skinny physique, the blank expression—she had taken it upon herself to mold her daughter into something more admirable, more fitting of the name "Cornelius". In fact, she had taken over every aspect of the poor girl's life. As for Alice, she went along with her mother's wishes with such a detached indifference that the whispers that the girl was a bit "dim" only increased within the circles of society.

It was cool that night as they walked slowly through the garden. Lillian and Alice wrapped their shawls around their shoulders. The newly blooming flowers of spring sat still in the darkness as they made their way through the paths of herbs and plants and closed flowers. Their breath rose up, caught in the light of one of the flickering gas lamps that lined the path of the garden. They stopped in front of an ornate stone fountain, still dry due to the cold weather.

Lillian looked around to check for passersby. She bent over and lifted her dress, exposing her ankles.

"My God, Lillian! What are you doing?" Alice asked.

Lillian said nothing and reached further under her dress to pull out a silver cigarette case. She looked at Alice and smirked. "You won't tell anyone now, will you?"

Alice shook her head.

"I don't see why it's all right for men to smoke but it is considered unseemly for women. Especially when one considers all of the medicinal goods that comes from smoking. Do you agree, Alice?"

Lillian held the silver cigarette case toward Alice, offering a cigarette. Alice looked at the silver case for a moment before shaking her head, no.

"Don't worry. I won't tell anyone."

Alice looked around. Finally, she reached over and took a cigarette. Lillian lit the cigarette for her and Alice took quick puffs without inhaling. Great plumes of smoke rose in the air and circled her face.

A few seconds passed without either of them saying a word.

"So what do you think of the Count?" Lillian asked.

Alice shrugged, puffing on her cigarette like a fish sucking air. Lillian thought Alice looked even more ridiculous at the moment.

"So you don't like him?" Lillian asked.

"Oh. He seems nice I suppose."

"But he doesn't melt your heart?"

Again, Alice shrugged, looked blankly at Lillian. "He

seems nice."

"I believe there's nothing more that your mother would like than for you to marry the Count."

"I know."

"Just think," Lillian said. "That would make you a Countess!"

Alice said nothing, puffed on her cigarette, looked at it and said, "I think I am done with this." She looked around for some place to put it out. "Mamma would be very pleased by me being a Countess I should think so, yes."

"And you wouldn't?"

Alice shrugged again. "I suppose it would be nice."

Lillian was now regretting having asked Alice to join her in the garden.

"You don't love him, is that what you're saying?"

Alice gave Lillian a look. "I don't even know him. How can I love him?"

"Yes, but…I think that most times if someone is going to fall in love with someone they know right away. There is at least something there, some kind of attraction."

"He is nice," Alice said again.

"Tell me, Alice, do you think it's most important to love the man you marry? Or do you think the love will one day grow?"

Alice shrugged and did not say anything. Lillian sighed, looked up at the brightness of stars over the villa. She used to be able to name nearly every star up in the sky. She was fascinated with space, the universe as a whole, actually. She would read book after book, regaling Charlie with her vast knowledge of the cosmos. Most men would have dismissed her, laughed at her odd curiosity—but Charlie, on the contrary, encouraged her, praised her for her intellect. They'd shared their first kiss under the stars. But as they got older and their circles began to grow more judgmental, Charlie became justifiably concerned about her intellect outshining his in public settings. So she now kept it well hidden. Most of the time. Even alone with Charlie—where it was perfectly acceptable for her to express her opinions, she'd started silencing herself, focusing instead on what was expected of a young woman in order to move closer to her marriage with Charlie.

And now, as she stared up into the cosmos, that vast never ending forever—it suddenly occurred to her that she'd forgotten the names of half of those stars.

"Do you think you will marry my brother?" Alice asked.

At this, Lillian's face suddenly brightened. "I would certainly like to someday. Why? Has he said anything to you?"

"He tells me nothing."

Lillian frowned. "Has he ever said anything to you ever? About me? Ever?"

"I suppose that he has," said Alice.

Lillian's patience was reaching an end. She looked at this buck-toothed creature standing before her, thought about just shaking her until some kind of sense rattled around in her brain.

Alice looked down and studied her feet for a moment or two. "I'm sure he does like you, Lillian. I'm sure he does very much."

Her words didn't seem to carry much weight, but Lillian forced a smile.

"We should probably go back inside now," said Lillian.

Alice nodded. Then she said, "Do you think we will ever see Henry again?"

"Henry?" She struggled to understand. "Henry Vanderbilt?"

"Henry Graham," Alice said matter-of-factly.

"Henry Graham?" Lillian thought it over a little more. "You mean the ice harvester?"

Alice nodded her head yes.

"What about him?"

"I was just wondering if we will see him again, that's all."

"Possibly," said Lillian. "I understand your father has given him a job."

Alice shook her head. "No, no. My father offered him a job, but he refused."

"Well, he obviously changed his mind."

Alice looked surprised. She was quiet a moment. Finally, she said: "Well, I'm sure he'll do very well. But if my father thinks he'll be able to get Henry to turn his back on his principles he will be sadly mistaken."

"Time will only tell, Alice. Do you remember what Mr. Gould once told us over dinner? He said that he could pay half the working class to kill the other half."

"Maybe he can. But he could never pay Henry enough to do that. Never."

Lillian grinned. "Why, Alice Cornelius! Are you smitten with that man?"

"Don't be ridiculous."

"You are, though, aren't you?"

Alice looked hurt. "Don't tease me, Lillian."

"I'm sorry."

But she noticed Alice's eyes lit up when she mentioned the ice harvester's name. She was prey to the same emotions as everyone else, which would be the source of much sadness in her life. *If the poor girl were simply dim, or an utter imbecile… life might be easier for her*, Lillian thought. *Look at her. She's an awkward mess.* Lillian tightened the shawl around her shoulders. "Do I smell like smoke?" She leaned into Alice. Alice shook her head. They went inside.

"Lillian?" Alice called behind her, as they walked down the hallway, her voice echoing off the marble.

Lillian stopped. Turned and looked at her.

"Is it true?"

"Is what true, Alice?"

"That you are seeing a doctor to make your mind right?"

Lillian shot Alice a look. The poor girl was an absolutely hopeless case.

She turned her back on the girl, her future sister-in-law, and walked down the hall without another word.

CHAPTER 20

One night in October, Charlie invited Graham to come and join him for dinner at Rector's for his birthday. The restaurant was full. When Graham showed up in one of his new suits, he was sure William Harold shot him a sneer of disgust.

"Henry, I am glad you've decided to come!" Charlie said, rising from the table and shaking his friends' hand.

Most of the young men seemed indifferent to Graham's presence, nodding before resuming their conversation about a long contested game of badminton.

"You play badminton, Henry?" one of the young men asked.

Graham shook his head no.

"Never?"

"Never."

"Well you look like an athletic fellow," the young man said. "I imagine you'll pick up on it pretty quickly."

The young men drank champagne and dined on oysters, talking about this girl or that girl. Names Graham did not recognize. That is until someone mentioned Lillian.

"So, Charlie," someone asked. "When will you propose?"

Charlie laughed. "I'm not ready quite ready to be anchored yet."

"Watch out," they said. "Lillian's awfully pretty. Somebody else might come along and try and steal her away from you."

"Someone else, eh?" Charlie smirked. "Who would that be? You?"

The man laughed. "That just might be!"

William pushed his glass of champagne forward, "To be honest, Charlie, I think Henry is the one you should watch. He's been looking to steal Lillian's virtue since he first saw her in Tarrytown."

"You scoundrel!" Charlie shouted, laughing and giving Graham a playful shove. "That's what we get for putting you under my father's wing."

"You work for Charlie's father?" One of the men asked, chuckling.

Graham nodded his head yes.

"Now that's a scoundrel if ever there was one," said the one young man. "Do you like young chorus girls as well, Henry?"

"Who doesn't like chorus girls? Why don't you just ask him if he likes breathing?" Someone cracked to a round of laughter.

"Your mother was a chorus girl, wasn't she, Henry?" William asked, his eyes narrowing.

The table grew silent. Graham could see that William was very drunk.

"No," said Graham. "No, she wasn't."

"So what I've heard is wrong?" William paused, looked up at the ceiling. "Oh yes. That's right…I remember now how she made her living…"

"Come-on," Charlie said. "What kind of talk is this?"

"Here, here," someone said.

William started to laugh. "For all you know, anyone in this city might be your father. Maybe, just maybe…you might be a Cornelius after all."

"That's enough, William," Charlie glared at him.

"I think maybe I should leave now," Graham said, rising from the table.

Charlie took hold of his arm, and led him away from the table. "No. Stay. William's drunk, that's all."

Graham glared at William out of the corner of his eye. "I should leave before I hit him."

"He's not a bad guy once you get to know him, Henry. Really he's not. He's just a snob. A snob to me, too, if you must know."

"He's an asshole is what he is."

Charlie laughed. "That, too. But he's also Lillian's brother, so I deal with it. I'll talk to him when he's sober. But there's more to William than you think, Henry. He'll come around to you one of these days. If you knew him as long as I have, you'd understand." Charlie turned to the table, "I think you owe Henry an apology, William."

William smirked. "I am sorry, Henry…"

"Apology accepted," said Graham.

Still smirking, William quickly added: "Sorry that you had

to watch your mother fuck strangers for money."

Graham grabbed William by the shirt and struck him hard on the face. William fell to the floor. His nose was bleeding.

"Good God, man!" One of Charlie's friends said to Graham. "Take it outside, at least."

William managed to get back up to his feet. "Listen here, bastard. I'll destroy you. I promise you that. I will destroy you."

Graham took a step toward William to hit him again, but Charlie put his hand on Graham's chest. "Go on, Henry. It's best if you leave."

Graham hurried out of the restaurant. He wandered the city streets, wondering if the evening had cost him everything. It was very late when he headed back to his apartment building.

He suddenly stopped in his tracks.

There was a strange car idling in front of his building. A man was sitting in the front seat. He spotted Graham and made a move to get out of the car.

Graham's heart sunk.

This is it, he thought. *They've found me.*

CHAPTER 21

He was about to make a run for it, when the man called out his name.

"Mr.Graham? Mr. Henry Graham?" the man called out.

Graham stood there, keeping his distance. It seemed the man was alone.

"Are you Henry Graham?"

Graham didn't say anything.

"Listen, pal, I don't have time for any games. Mr. Cornelius wants me to bring you to him."

Graham felt a rush of relief. He got into the car, and was driven down to the piers at Chelsea.

Cornelius was waiting with seven other men. The men looked familiar to Graham. They were city and state politicians as well as a few business acquaintances.

"Ah, Henry!" Cornelius called out as soon as he saw him. "Finally! I thought we were going to have to leave without you."

The men came aboard Cornelius' new yacht, which still smelled of fresh paint. As they were ferried across the river, the men went into the saloon for some drinks and cigars. Inside, the wood was solid white pine and every panel was carved with an exquisite high relief.

It wasn't long before they docked in Jersey City. Cornelius led the men through the marina to the door of what seemed like an ordinary, non-descript building.

The door seemed to open automatically. They took a set of stairs and came to another door, which also opened automatically. The other men were whispering and laughing, like young boys. Graham got the impression that they were all in on some kind of secret. A fog horn cried out in the night.

They entered the apartment and were led into a red room. Heavy velvet curtains shut out any light from outside. There were no visible lights, yet the room was fully illuminated. Paintings hung on the walls. Graham assumed they were worth a lot of money. They were mostly bucolic scenes, young girls shepherding or playing in the fields. The furniture was ornately carved, and the indirect lighting cast a glow of soft light over all of the fine ornaments in the room.

Another door suddenly opened and nine chorus girls came hurriedly in, pushing one another forward and giggling.

Cornelius walked over and started opening bottles of champagne, firing the corks across the room while the girls clapped their hands and laughed. The men were ecstatic. Cornelius began pouring champagne, the frothy bubbles pouring over the sides of the glass. He started handing the glasses to his friends and then the chorus girls.

Cornelius sidled up to Graham and put his hand on his shoulder. "Of course, you don't speak a word of this place to anyone."

Graham nodded.

"I heard about what happened this evening, and I figured you could use a good time."

Graham frowned. "Guess that'll be the last time I'm invited to dinner."

Cornelius dismissed him with a wave of the hand. "Quite the contrary. I imagine most of those men have wanted to punch William in the face for quite some time." He smiled, hesitated. "However, my boy, next time you challenge a man to a fight, ask him to step outside rather than fixing him right then and there."

"I'm sorry, Sir," Graham said, looking down.

"It's over now, son, and Charlie said William had it coming."

"Speaking of Charlie—is he coming tonight?"

Cornelius rolled his eyes. "Charlie sees this as debauchery. Lillian should count herself lucky. He's incredibly faithful to her and I imagine he'll be an incredibly faithful to her." Cornelius hesitated for a moment. "Does Charlie say what his intentions are with Lillian?"

"A little, Sir. He says he's going to marry her at some point. That he knows she won't wait forever."

"Probably best then to not interfere with him and his ridiculous adventures." Cornelius looked around. "Charlie's not much when it comes to business, Henry. He has the ability; but he lacks the passion. I've seen many men who never reached their full potential because their wives were a distraction. They like what the money can buy them, but they don't like the number of hours their husbands must put in to provide such luxuries." Cornelius smiled and winked at one of the girls and then gave his attention back to Graham. "Lillian is the kind of young woman who'll require a lot of attention, Henry. Probably more than most, considering her moods."

"I don't know her well enough to say one way or the other. I just know they're both pretty sweet on one another."

Cornelius grunted, patted Graham on the back. He walked up behind one of the girls and wrapped his arms around her, kissing her neck while she squealed and playfully tried to break free.

The night wore on. Cornelius continued to open bottle after bottle of champagne and later Lobster Newburg was brought in from DelMonicos across the river.

Everyone grew louder, more foolish with every glass of champagne.

"Would you girls like to go to the upstairs room now?" Cornelius announced.

Both the girls and the men gave a rousing response.

And so Cornelius led them up another set of stairs. This room was brightly lit and the walls were painted a deep forest green. Palms and flowers decorated the room and a waterfall cascaded down against a back wall. The ceilings were incredibly high. There was a tall ladder placed at the center of the room. Above their heads was a net fastened up on the walls and a trapeze hanging from the ceiling.

"Go on girls!" Cornelius shouted, the other men laughing and cheering. "Go on!"

The girls climbed up the ladder. They swung from the trapeze until their arms grew tired and then they let themselves fall to the net. Cornelius and his friends stood under the netting and pushed the girls up and caught them as they came back down, and then pushed them back up again. Like kids, the men clapped as each girl swung above them. Graham stood alone in the corner of the room, drinking.

"Let Lucy have a turn," Cornelius called up. Graham looked at one of the girls. She was the prettiest of the bunch. He thought she looked remarkably familiar. A little later, Cornelius came over to Graham.

"Have you ever seen a more beautiful girl?"

"I think I know her."

"You think you do, but you don't. Her face is everywhere, Henry. She's on beer trays, cigarette and tobacco cards, celluloid pin backs, cigar labels, playing cards, not to mention the pages of every Manhattan magazine and newspaper."

"Is that so?"

"Yep, she was the calendar girl for Swift's Pompeian face cream and Coca-Cola." Cornelius looked up and saw Lucy nervously standing on top of the ladder. "Go on, my little dolly," Cornelius called. "It's alright."

Lucy climbed up the ladder. She was remarkably thin with long Chestnut hair. She took hold of the trapeze, looked around from here to there.

"It's all right, dearie," one of the girls called to her. "The net'll catch you if you fall."

Lucy stepped back, took a deep breath and let herself go,

hanging by her arms and swinging back and forth. The men below clapped and shouted with delight.

Her arms finally grew tired and everyone shouted at her to let go. The men rushed under and pushed her up. She was much smaller than the other girls and she let out a shriek each time she was pushed up. She clapped her hands. "Let me go again! Let me go again!"

"Of course!" shouted Cornelius. "Girls, step aside and let Lucy go again!"

One of the girls decided to strip down to her underwear and then the rest of them followed. Throughout the night, Graham noticed girls leaving the room with some of the men.

Later that night Lucy came over to him.

"You're the quiet one, aren't you?" she said.

He shook his head. "I'm just tired."

She took his hand. "Mr. Cornelius says you work too hard."

Graham looked across the room. Cornelius caught his gaze and smiled at him. He shouted across the room: "You've earned it, my boy!"

Graham looked at the girl. "I'm very drunk."

She laughed. "That's all right, Dearie. We all are."

She took his hand and led him down a hallway. They walked into an unoccupied bedroom and she smiled coyly at him and closed the door.

CHAPTER 22

That fall, Lillian, finally finished with her talking cure and met her parents in Paris before traveling with them to visit her aunt and uncle on the French Riviera.

She loved Paris in the fall, the trees lining the main boulevard, the fierceness of the orange and red colors of the changing leaves. She loved, too, the kind of freedom and respect the city gave to a young woman like herself. In Paris her opinions were actually regarded by men as well as women.

Despite this new freedom, she still felt a kind of longing for the traditional...to be the wife of Charlie Cornelius. So much so, that she often found herself practicing her signature in her notebooks, signing her name as: *Lillian Cornelius*, working on just the right loops and slants so that the last name looked appropriately regal . She missed Charlie very much and she wrote him every day. His responses, however, were less than consistent. Nearly two months had gone by since she'd received any correspondence from him. She wondered if there weren't a stack of letters waiting for her back in Paris, though she knew better. In her last few letters, she had written the address of her uncle just so Charlie could reach her. She was starting to worry maybe he had found someone else.

Graham's letters, on the other hand, came as regularly as clockwork. Lillian looked forward to them mostly because he always mentioned Charlie. Lillian had learned that Henry and Charlie were now good friends (much to the dismay of her brother). So, she took it upon herself to start a correspondence with him. Rather than expressing her desire to learn what Charlie was up to, she used the guise that their day together had left a lasting impression on her. And perhaps it really did. For the first time since she could remember, she pondered the possibility that there were other men besides Charlie. Her Austrian doctor brought this to her attention. Since their correspondence had started, it was not uncommon for her thoughts of Charlie to meander toward Henry.

Lillian walked down the stairs and into her uncle's study where her father was sleeping. His health had not improved, and they had come to the Riviera hoping the warmth and salty air of the Mediterranean might relieve his lungs.

Lillian noticed a painting of a young girl. The girl was sitting on a chair beside a birdcage, looking at a canary with a somewhat melancholy expression. She appeared to be at the beginnings of puberty; but what struck Lillian was her remarkable beauty.

Someone called her name.

It was her uncle. "Ah! I was wondering where you had wandered, Lillian."

The uncle frowned at his brother-in-law sleeping in the

chair. Then he did his best to appear cheerful. "There is some mail here for you."

He held up the envelope and she hurried to him, certain that the letter was from Charlie. But when she looked at the envelope, she immediately recognized Graham's handwriting.

"Is everything all right?" He asked..

She nodded, looked at the envelope and then forced a smile, pointing toward the painting on the wall.. "I was admiring this. Where did you get it?"

"James Beckwith painted this girl a couple of years ago. Your aunt bought it. Apparently, she is the future of American beauty."

"She is a very beautiful," she said. "She has such dark, sad eyes."

"I suppose," said her uncle. "Seems the fashion these days is skinny little girls, rather than the full figured women from my youth."

They made small talk and eventually her uncle left the room. Lillian walked over to the chaise lounge and sat down. She looked at the envelope, sighed and opened it up, wondering what Graham would have to report.

But unlike Graham's earlier letters, Charlie was mentioned only briefly, something about his birthday at Rector's and some "nasty business" breaking out between her brother and himself; but if she heard anything about this incident, to not think any less of him, because it was a matter of dignity and honor and "everything is swell now".

But what struck her most, what sent a jolt to her heart was the way in which he finished his letter:

Lillian, please know that my intentions with you are true. Seeing as how I don't know when, or if, I will see you again, I will write with total honesty. I know you plan to marry Charlie, and I would never step in the way, as Charlie and I have become the best of pals and I want only for you to be happy. I know my station in life is a much lower than people like yourself and Charlie. But please know this, Lillian: I am going to be rich. I've seen enough in the short time working for Mr. Cornelius to know what can be accomplished. I may not have an immediate plan. But I do have a goal, and Mr. Cornelius says that the best plans are those that are formed along the way. I trust you are having a nice time in the Riviera. I hope the weather is fine. It's starting to get cold in New York. I cannot wait until I receive my next letter from you.

Warmest Regards,

Henry Graham

Perhaps, Lillian thought, she was reading too much into his words; perhaps it was nothing more than the kind of posturing he exhibited that first day they met in Tarrytown. Or was this meant as a request for her not to rush into marrying Charlie? Regardless, for the first time, she realized the true depth of Henry's feelings and felt anxiety bubbling up in her stomach. Deep down, she realized her own feelings toward Graham might be a little more complicated than she would like. It was her fault. She should never have begun the correspondence. She took the letter and walked over to the hearth. She swore to herself that she must never write him back, convincing herself that it was best for them both if she became nothing more than a memory to him. She tossed the letter into the fire and watched it burn.

PART II

CHAPTER 23

The wedding of Alice Cornelius and the Count of Montenegro was held at Lindenhurst on the Twenty-eighth of September, 1913. By all accounts, it was a beautiful affair. The three hundred guests were all treated to a grand spectacle, the likes of which could only be planned by Alva Cornelius.

The parlor floor and the library were lavishly decorated with flowers. Guests meandered through Japanese lilies and pink and garlands of white roses on the ceiling and walls. Every alcove and niche of the mansion was filled with exotic palms and the sweet aroma of flowers.

The ceremony had been held in the East Indian Room. The gifts to the bride and groom were displayed on the second floor of the mansion and guests were invited to line up to view them. Henry Graham followed the others more out of politeness than interest. The jewels, the gifts—they meant nothing to him. He only wished to see Lillian Harold.

They had not seen one another in more than four years, not since that day in Central Park. She had long since stopped responding to his letters. Why? He still did not know. Graham was determined to impress her. For the past three weeks, he had rehearsed everything over and over again in his mind. There was gossip that Charlie would soon be asking for Lillian's hand in marriage. But Charlie had never given a definitive answer to Graham when he asked, and Graham hoped that perhaps Charlie might find someone else (despite his claims that he did, truly, love Lillian).

He eventually made his way back downstairs and happened upon his boss. Cornelius smiled and shook Graham's hand with vigor even though they had just seen each other at the office only yesterday. Graham immediately made out the slight smell of whiskey on Cornelius's breath.

"How'd you like the gifts up there?" Cornelius asked.

"Pretty spectacular," said Graham.

Cornelius nodded. Graham knew Cornelius well enough by now to know that the man's attention did not usually last long unless that person would further his own self-interest.

"Henry..." Cornelius took him by the elbow, pulling him aside so he could not be overheard. "When we're back in Manhattan, I want you to come with me to see someone. I have my eye on this beautiful little peach. You have to see her."

Graham laughed.

"No, no," said Cornelius. "This one's different. My friend Beckwith painted her a few times. I saw one of his paintings and decided I had to meet her. I'm trying to convince her that she should be an actress, but her mother's been giving me some resistance."

Graham didn't say anything.

"Well?"

"Well what?"

"Will you come along? I think the way to convince her mother is if she sees a younger man…might get her to thinking maybe her daughter can marry someone with a good income."

Graham laughed.

Cornelius was about to say something else when he spotted his wife glaring at him. He excused himself. "Damn. Must keep up appearances, Henry."

Someone rang a bell and Mr. Cornelius summoned the guests outside to announce that although the Count and Countess would reside primarily in Montenegro, he was bequeathing them Lindenhurst as their home in America.

A few audible gasps preceded a polite round of applause.

Henry walked around for a little while, feeling slightly lost. Mr. Cornelius stood outside smoking cigars with a group of men. Graham walked over and joined them.

Cornelius put his arm around Graham's shoulder. "This young man here, under my tutelage, has singlehandedly put my competitors on the defensive while bringing increasing profits to my business interests."

Graham smiled modestly, though it would be a lie to say that he didn't enjoy the praise. Someone handed him a cigar. Every now and then he'd add something witty; but the entire time that he stood there, his eyes searched for Lillian.

*

Lillian and her mother were caught in conversation with Mrs. Harriman. They'd only returned to America twice since leaving for Europe four years ago. The Harolds had stayed on under the guise that they preferred the old culture; but in truth they hoped that their daughter's nerves might be soothed. Whether it was thanks to the psycho-therapy, or because in the past four years their daughter had simply matured and grown—didn't really matter. She seemed fully whole. Composed. Only rarely did she fall into one of her darker moods.

Mrs. Harold was also beginning to grow bored with Europe. She felt Alice's wedding was a perfect excuse to return to America. Mrs. Harold (a shrewd politician in her own right) knew Mrs. Cornelius would always be grateful so long as she was given the impression that the sole purpose of their return home was in order to attend Alice's wedding.

Since their arrival in Manhattan, Mrs. Harold and Lillian had been bombarded with invitations for tea and dinners, leaving them both exhausted. They knew seeing old friends here at the wedding today would mean only more social commitments.

The weather that day was beautiful. The trees were just beginning to turn their autumnal colors and there was a slight nip in the air at night. The smell of cider and burning wood in the air. Lillian felt there was no better time to be in New York's Hudson Valley.

She was only a few yards from where Graham mingled with Cornelius and the other men, but they had not yet seen each other.

"I'm sure today is a dream come true for Alva," said Mrs. Harold.

The two women gossiped for some time. At one point Mrs. Harriman told Mrs. Harold about Alva's contacting a genealogist, a trend popular among the newer moneyed families of New York, all of whom were happy to learn (and never questioned) that they were of superior bloodline and once titled in Europe. This seemed a logical explanation for their rise above the rest of the chaff out there.

"And do you know who he traced her lineage to?" Mrs. Harriman chuckled.

"Shall I have a guess?"

"Charlemagne!" Lillian chimed in, laughing herself now.

Still amused, Mrs. Harriman looked at Lillian. "Why yes. So you've also heard." She looked at Mrs. Harold. "Apparently, this fellow traces every family's ancestry back to Charlemagne."

Mrs. Harold laughed. "Does he?

"He does. It makes the whole thing even more absurd, if you ask me. Did you know she's taken upon herself to use the rubber stamp of her letters to Charlemagne's code of arms?"

At this new revelation, Mrs. Harold laughed even harder. "Oh, that sad, poor woman."

"And despite her royal lineage, Mrs. Astor once again declined her invitation?"

"Oh she must have been livid. Absolutely livid."

Lillian smiled. "Mrs. Harriman, by any chance have you

seen Charlie?"

"Not since the ceremony. I'm sure you will bump into him at some point."

Lillian had seen Charlie from time to time in Vienna and Paris. He had come to Europe five times in the past four years, and each time came to call on her. She also saw him the two times her family had returned to New York. He was always caring and patient and swore to her he would wait until she felt better. Other than the closest members of her family, Charlie was the only one who knew about the inexplicable sadness that sometimes took her over and the treatment she was getting in Europe. Most men probably would have abandoned her. But they had shared so many secrets throughout the years that it seemed there was hardly anything they did not know about one another that could affect their feelings toward one another.

As Lillian looked again for Charlie she spotted a familiar looking man conversing with a group of older gentlemen. She put her hand on her mother's forearm. "Look. That's Henry Graham over there, talking with those men."

Mrs. Harold looked over. "Why, yes. It is."

"He looks quite well," said Lillian.

"Henry Graham? Oh, Andrew Cornelius has him working the Street," Mrs. Harriman explained very matter-of-factly.

Mrs. Harold frowned. "Oh. I imagine the poor man has had a hard time of it there."

"Quite the contrary. He's been doing extraordinarily well. The young man's proved himself to be remarkably bright."

Lillian kept her gaze on Graham. She was quite impressed as she listened to Mrs. Harriman.

"My husband says the young man has a great head for business. And he's done quite well for the Cornelius fortune. He and Charlie are very close friends now, though Alva is a little wary of their friendship."

Lillian felt sorry for him. It seemed unfair, but she knew that Alva, like many women who had only come into money later in life, was incredibly insecure. Alva Cornelius was the daughter of a Pittsburgh coal miner and seamstress. She had caught the eye of a younger Andrew Cornelius many years earlier when he visited one of his father's mills. At first, she showed little interest in the young man, which probably only increased Cornelius's interest in her. When the young man left, rejected and somewhat embarrassed, one of Alva's friends advised her that she had just snubbed the heir apparent of a vast family fortune. A week later, when Cornelius ran into Alva again, she was much more pleasant and agreeable to his advances.

Alva tried as best she could to distance herself from those she deemed as less superior much more than those of the old moneyed families did. But in the back of her mind she always suspected (sometimes rightfully so) that her past was gossiped about whenever she wasn't present. This insecurity of hers unfortunately was also sometimes taken out on her children.

Lillian found herself a little caught off guard seeing this new, more confident Henry Graham. Yes, she couldn't help but be impressed.

Mrs. Harold must have sensed something in the way Lillian watched him, because she suddenly said: "Shame though. Even in the best suit, the young man still has that wide, Ice Harvester's back."

Mrs. Harriman chuckled. Lillian shot her mother a look.

"I hear that Charlie Cornelius has started courting you in earnest now, Lillian?" Mrs. Harriman asked, changing the subject.

"I suppose his intentions remain to be seen. He hasn't proposed yet."

"Oh, please, Lillian! He'll ask you to marry him quite soon, I'm sure. What man in his right mind wouldn't?"

"Charlie isn't like most men, Mrs. Harriman. He's far too wrapped up in his adventures."

"Oh Lillian. He was hardly a man when we were last in America," Mrs. Harold said.

"He was nearly thirty. He was not a boy."

Mrs. Harriman excused herself as Mrs. Harold caught her daughter looking in Graham's direction again.

"Lillian," Mrs. Harold said, her voice a stern whisper. "I can read your mind."

Lillian gave a sheepish smile. "What?"

Mrs. Harold sighed. "Lillian, you have a tendency sometimes to not think of consequences. The last thing this family needs is any kind of scandal."

"Like the gardener scandal, you mean? Now an ice harvester."

Mrs. Harold looked shocked, but then broke into a quick

smile. "You put my heart into palpitations with your wild talk, Lillian. I swear you do."

*

A while later, Charlie Cornelius spotted Graham with his father and a few friends. He hurried over, took him by the arm and pulled him away from the conversation.

"My God, Pal, had I known the predicament you were in, I would've rescued you sooner. Let's get out of here. Grab some drinks, go upstairs and watch all the girls walk by."

A woman's voice called out as they were about to mount the stairs.

"Well, well, well. Aren't these two handsome specimens?"

Graham's heart sank as Charlie hurried over to Lillian and embraced her.

"Good Lord, Lillian!" He boomed through the main hall.

Lillian looked over Charlie's shoulder at Graham and shot him an amicable smile. "It's good to see you, too, Henry." She gave him a more reserved embrace. "You two look like you're up to no-good."

"Us?" Charlie said, beaming. "Have I told you that you look stunning, Lillian? Henry, isn't Lillian stunning?"

Graham hesitated. He wished he had Charlie's charm. While it was true that he had gained confidence as his success grew, he still could not find the courage to speak to her. Lillian had stopped writing him after that last letter. He could not understand why. After all, it was Lillian who began their correspondence and her letters always contained some element of flirtation. At least that's how they always came across to him. In fact, she had actually written: "*Every time I stroll alone in one of the parks of Vienna, I am reminded of our time together in Central Park and wish you were here to join me. It seems you made quite an impression on me that day, Henry Graham.*" As far as he was concerned, he was telling her what he thought she wanted to hear—his intentions. He considered her silence a pure rejection of him.

She could not look right at Graham. They were like complete strangers again. All those weeks of rehearsal were a waste. He couldn't remember a damned thing he'd planned on saying to her in the days leading up to this wedding.

They made small talk, Charlie and Lillian. Graham watched Lillian drop coy innuendos, playing with her hair as she listened with rapt attention to every word Charlie said.

Eventually, Charlie saw an old buddy pass by and made to excuse himself.

"I hope you're not going to stand me up again. Last time we were supposed to go for a walk you sent poor Henry over here as your substitute."

Charlie laughed. "I'll be right back, Lillian."

"I will not wait much longer, Charlie Cornelius."

"I won't be long. I promise."

"Very well, then," she said, giving the faintest smile at Henry. "And anyway, I can always go for another walk with Henry. He's fine company."

But Lillian and Graham struggled to make small talk.

Graham had opened his soul to her in that letter, made his intentions fully known—and she had cut off all communication. They both stood uneasily.

"So, Europe was nice?"

"Oh, beautiful. But it is good to finally be home."

"Do you usually stay overseas for that long of a time?"

"No. Not that long."

"What kept you this time?"

Lillian frowned. Hesitated. "I understand you're doing quite well working for Mr. Cornelius?"

He looked at her. "How'd you hear this?"

"You should know by now that there are a good number of us who have nothing better to do than gossip." She smiled. "Has Mr. Cornelius turned you into a Lech yet, Henry?"

Graham laughed sharply, relieved to see Charlie walking back across the parlor with two Gin Rickeys in his hands.

"May I steal Lillian from you, my friend?" Charlie asked, handing Graham one of the drinks.

"Of course." Graham stepped aside.

Lillian put her arm in Charlie's and the two of them went off together.

Graham stood alone outside the parlor room and drank his cocktail down in one fell swoop.

Glancing out the window at the mingling guests, he felt a wave of loneliness creep over him.

Suddenly, there was a clatter as a tray full of glasses fell to the ground behind him.

"I'm sorry, Sir," the waiter said, bending over to quickly

put everything right.

"That's quite all right," Graham said.

The waiter paused and looked again at Graham.

Graham turned, but he could feel the eyes of the waiter burning into his back.

"I don't believe it. Henry Flanagan?"

"I think you've mistaken me for someone else."

"No…it's you. I'd know you in a heartbeat. How the hell… I thought"—

Graham quickly faced the man, hoping no one heard him.

"It's me…" the waiter said. "It's me. Murph!"

"I know" Graham said, forcing a smile in recognition.

Murph grinned, obviously very amused to learn of his fellow workers' turn of fortune. "Well, well, well. Don't you look the dandy! How the hell'd this happen? We all figured you'd run off to Mexico and here you are living the good life! If that don't beat all."

"Shhh. You need to keep quiet." Graham looked around again. "You're working for Mr. Cornelius?"

"For the past year. I was a kitchen boy for the Rockefellers before this. I'm supposed to be staying out of sight of the guests. It's a good job and I don't want to lose it. Good thing it was just you in here."

Just me, thought Graham. "Good thing."

"Well, well. Looks like you've done real good for yourself, Flanagan." Murph paused. "Didn't see your name on the guest list. But I guess you changed your name. What do you go by now?"

Graham grimaced. Could he trust him? Murph was an old friend, but it had been a long time. *What if he tells someone else about seeing me?*

The idea of his past catching up to him was terrifying. Graham's anxiety increased by the second. Murph stood there, smiling at him.

"Who'd have thought! Who'd have thought the fates would've turned out the way they did for you, Henry."

Who'd have thought.

Murph filled him in on what he knew about some of the other men from their ice harvesting days. Once he caught him, there seemed nothing left for the two men to talk about. Although they were once friends, time had made them strangers to each other.

Just then a voice came from behind him. "Henry! What the hell are you doing in here? I didn't even know you'd arrived yet."

Graham turned around to find William Harold smirking in the doorway. After the incident at Rector's, Charlie had mediated. The two men had no other choice but to accept the others' existence. Since that time, they managed to form what to outsiders might seem like a kind of friendship; or at least an acquaintance. Still, Graham always felt tension when he was left alone with William. There was something Graham couldn't quite put his finger on, something about the way in which William still looked at him, as if each smile hid contempt.

William glanced at Murph and nodded. Murph smiled

and nodded back. "Afternoon, Sir," he said.

"I don't believe we've been introduced." William looked at Graham. "A friend of yours, Henry?"

"William Harold, may I introduce Tommy Murphy."

Murphy shook his hand. "Me and Henry here are old pals."

"Is that so?" William smiled. "I'm sure he was as fine a fellow when you knew him as he is now."

Graham tried to convince himself that perhaps it was all in his head—that the mockery behind William's words were all imagined.

"Do you work here at Lindenhurst, Tommy?" William asked.

"Yessir."

"Did Henry help you secure the job?"

"Nossir."

"No?" William looked at Graham. "What sort of friend are you?"

Graham chuckled to play along.

William put his arm around Graham's shoulder. "Come-on, Henry. I don't know about you, but I'm dying for a whiskey." He looked at Murph, nodded. "Nice to make your acquaintance, Tommy."

Murph returned the nod. "You, too, Sir." He looked at Graham. "Guess I'll be seeing you around."

"William, I'll catch up with you in a minute. I just need to talk to talk to Murph for a moment."

"Sure thing, Henry," said William. "I'll see you in a bit, then."

Henry looked around to make sure they were alone. ""I

wanted to find someone to say hello. One of the chambermaids. She took care of me when I was first brought here."

A knowing smile crept up on Murph's face, which Graham chose to ignore.

"What's her name?"

"Colleen. Colleen Callahan."

Murph went pale.

"What's wrong?"

"She's dead, Henry."

Graham hesitated. "How?"

"I didn't know her all that good. Happened not too long after I got here. The gossip downstairs is that she got herself pregnant by your friend Mr. Cornelius. He called in Madame Renoit to come down from Manhattan and *fix* the situation. But she got infected and died."

Graham felt sick. He glared at Murphy. "You should be very careful when you speak about Mr. Cornelius, Murph."

"I'm just repeating what I've heard downstairs. That's all."

"So that's how the help talks about him? The man who puts bread on their table?"

Murph stared at Henry. "I don't' see why you're taking offense, pal."

"You're slandering Mr. Cornelius. They're lucky I don't report every one of them."

Murph looked at Graham carefully. "Ah. I see how it is now." He squatted back down and put everything back on the tray before standing up. "If I was you...Mr. Graham...I'd be more concerned that one of them don't go and report you."

"What's that supposed to mean?"

"You tell me. Does Cornelius know who he's got working for him?"

"Careful, Murph."

"That a threat?"

"You can take it however you want."

Murph sneered. "There's coppers all outside the gates here, Henry. Seems they don't want any of the rabble rousers getting on the grounds. Little do they know one of the men they're protecting from the riff raff is the man they've been looking for these past few years." Murph laughed. "Can you imagine the looks on their faces if someone was to go out there and tell those idiots that you're here, living the life of Riley?"

"Listen, Murph--."

"One thousand dollars."

"One thousand dollars?"

"That's the reward they're offering for information regarding your capture. Did you know that?"

Graham looked at Murph. "Are you trying to blackmail me?"

"I'm just telling you what they're offering for your reward." He paused. "That's an awful lot of money. Maybe not to someone of your station, but for me that's more than I make a year."

"So is that what it's going to take, Murph? A thousand dollars for you to keep things quiet?"

"I ain't no snitch, Henry. You know that. I'm just thinking a nice little nest egg for your friend might be the right thing to do, seeing as how good life's been to you. Share the wealth, eh?"

Graham grit his teeth. "Very well. One thousand dollars it is."

"But I think a more agreeable number would be about three thousand."

Graham's eyes widened. "Three thousand?"

"Give me a nice head start. Maybe even put some of that money into investments and such...got any tips you can share?"

I can agree to this, and hope he never says a word. But can I trust him? Can I trust a man who is blackmailing me? Probably not. But what's the alternative? I can't lose everything and never see anyone again? No, I won't run.

And there will be no more killing. Not by me.

He will say something. At some point, I know that he will.

"Three thousand it is," Graham finally said. "I'll send it to you once I'm back in Manhattan. But if word ever gets out, I'll know where it came from."

"Like I said, I ain't no snitch."

Murph turned and strode out of the room. Down through the parlor, Graham could hear his footsteps drifting further away until there was only silence.

Graham walked back to the window. Mr. Cornelius was outside, still speaking jovially to a couple of guests. Murph's *insinuations* had put him in a foul mood. He decided he needed to go outside. Get some air. Find a place to be alone.

*

Lillian and Charlie walked further along. Past the tall oaks and Lindens, they looked for a secluded place. Eventually, they came to a small bench on the cliffs overlooking the Hudson and sat down.

Lillian breathed in the fresh fall air. She looked at Charlie and smiled. "This day has been so beautiful. I can't think of a better spot for your sister to get married."

Charlie smiled politely, but didn't speak.

"And the Count?" Lillian asked, turning to face Charlie. "Are you looking forward to him joining your family?"

"The Count is a scoundrel."

Lillian laughed.

"I'm serious. He's a scoundrel through and through. He's marrying my sister because his family is broke."

"Oh, Charlie. That's a terrible thing to say."

"I'm not saying anything against my sister, the poor girl. I suppose if she had her way she wouldn't be going through with this, either. But let's face it, she's not exactly beautiful. She's so damned quiet and mousy. It's my mother behind all this. She's so dead-set on getting our family a title."

"Maybe she thinks Mrs. Astor will finally attend one of her dinner parties." As soon as she spoke, Lillian wondered if she'd crossed the line. But Charlie laughed, much to her relief.

They sat watching the river flow.

"I hear you're thinking of going to Africa?" Lillian finally said.

Charlie's face turned sour and he scratched the back of his head. "I don't know. I suppose. I find summering in Newport a bore. But I suppose it's still better than working with my father. Still, I'm not sure how much longer I can avoid the business. I'm running out of excuses. I'll have to decide what

I want after I go on safari."

"The only thing you seem to love, Charlie, is adventure. Since we were small, you were always getting into things." She smiled at him. "I wish you could still bring me on your adventures, Charlie. I've never had as much fun as I had with you. Other than Gertrude Bell, I think I may be the only other woman who has climbed the Bernese Alps."

"You might be right on that, Lillian."

"I do so miss traveling with you. I know my mother forbids it…but once we are married—will you start taking me on your adventures again?"

"We'll see."

"Because once we are married, it won't matter what happens when we travel."

"I know."

"Are you bothered by what happened on Mont Blanc, Charlie? It's just that we were both just so happy and it seemed right. I was very young and I would never have been willing to do it, Charlie, if it wasn't with you."

"I know."

"It was just that one time, and I've never done anything since. I was drunk from the thin air. It was just because it was you."

"It's all right, Lillian. I know."

She gave him an anxious look. "Do you think I'm less of a woman because I was going to allow it? It should have been me who stopped it instead of you. It was so close, so close. You wanted to preserve my virtue and you stopped yourself. You are better than me, Charlie. That day on Mont Blanc proved it. But I was only willing to give myself in a way a woman would give to her husband, because it was you, Charlie." She waited for him to say something. "Is that why you no longer take me with you?"

"I no longer take you with me, because it's not considered appropriate for a woman to go to the places I go. Your mother forbid it years ago, probably worried that what had already almost happened might eventually happen."

"But I do so want to go, Charlie."

"We can go off again like that someday, Lillian. When you're no longer under your parents rule, and under mine." He smiled, teasing her.

She laughed. "I'd like to go to Persia and take part in one of the digs. I've read they've been discovering incredible ruins."

He smiled again, took her hand. "In the meantime, I'll bring you back a lion's head to mount on your wall."

"Do you really want to go all that way just to kill animals, Charlie? I just don't understand what it is with you men and your hunting."

"We're not fully evolved, Lillian. We still have a bit of the savage in us."

"I just don't see you as a killer, Charlie."

Charlie looked hurt.

"Are you offended? I certainly didn't mean that as an insult. Quite the contrary. You are good and kind."

He looked out across the river.

At times, Lillian found Charlie's thirst for adventure very attractive; but at the same time, it felt like his thrill seeking put a wedge between them. Lillian poked him in the ribs and smiled coyly until he smiled back.

"Do you still think about it, Charlie?"

"Think about what?"

"The peak at Mont Blanc?"

He laughed. "All the time, actually."

"It was fun, wasn't it?"

He looked at her. "Yes. Very much so."

"Very wrong; but oh so fun."

"Yes. Yes, it was."

"Do you think it will always be that much fun for us? Even when we are old?"

"I don't know. I hope so."

"I thought you would never want to see me again after that, let alone still marry me."

"There's very little you can do, Lillian Harold, that would make me not want to see you again."

She put her arm in the crook of his arm and rested her head on his shoulder. They looked out across the river again.

Charlie sighed. "You know he's quite smitten with you?"

She gave him a look. "Who?"

"Henry."

"Henry Graham? You can't be serious?"

"Don't pretend you don't know. It's obvious. Didn't you catch the pained look on his face when we went off by ourselves?"

"I think that's just your imagination, Charlie."

"Balderdash!"

"Well…"

"Well what?"

"Well, I suppose I may have sensed something once, but that was a number of years ago."

Charlie paused, looked into her eyes. "He was really quite upset when you stopped writing him."

"Are you just teasing me, Charlie?" Lillian smiled, but her heart started pounding. She did find Graham attractive, but she'd dismissed it as nothing more than a very minor crush, one of many. The truth was that she had always imagined herself with Charlie and no one else.

"Why would I tease, Lillian? I'm just telling you that Henry is fond of you."

Lillian sighed. He was pushing her away. "Well, he's a fool if he thinks the feeling will ever be reciprocated."

She looked down at her feet, thinking carefully. "Why are you telling me this, Charlie?"

"I thought it was only right." He reached into his pocket and pulled out a silver lighter and a pack of pre-rolled cigarettes.

"How do you mean?" She looked at the cigarette, wishing she could smoke. Charlie could be so progressive about some things and then so conservative about others.

Charlie lit his cigarette and blew a plume of smoke up toward the sky. "I just thought maybe you should take it easy in front of him."

"What do you mean?"

"The poor fellow looked like he was about to fall to pieces when you spoke of marrying me."

"It's all in good fun, Charlie. Are you saying you don't want me to talk about a future with you?"

"It's not that, it's just…he's a real good pal, Lillian. I don't like to see you hurt him, because it means I'm hurting him, too."

Lillian looked at the red embers of Charlie's cigarette. What was going on here? She'd planned on a nice quiet talk. It seemed to her that he was bringing up Henry as a way to ruin this moment on purpose.

"Well then. If you don't want me talking about marrying you, maybe we shouldn't get married. After all, if talking about it hurts Henry….just think what actually doing it will do to him."

"Don't be like that, Lillian."

She turned away from him.

"Then you'll tell him yourself? Tell him you love me and you want to marry me? So he won't have any more notions of anything ever happening between he and I? Because it's the truth."

"I think he already knows that."

"So then tell him just to be certain."

"Fine. I'll tell him."

She smiled, satisfied. "If you must know, Charlie, I've never loved anyone other than you. I don't think I could ever love anyone else."

"Neither could I, Lillian."

The blue sky above them was spotted with white wisps of clouds. A flurry of birds suddenly rose up from the horizon and flew against the silhouette of the sun as a soft fall breeze blew over the two of them.

Charlie smiled at her as they held each other's gaze.

"I'm afraid there's no way for us to escape our fate, Miss Harold. I'm afraid you're destined to be a Cornelius."

He leaned in closer.

"I suppose there are worse fates." Her voice was a breathy whisper.

She looked out of the corner of her eye to make sure they were still out of sight of all the guests. Then she let him kiss her.

*

Graham finally rejoined the party. He accidentally walked into a conversation that was going on between Alva and some of her friends.

"It's the Swedes that stir up all the trouble in Chicago."

"Not just the Swedes, it's all the foreigners," said Mrs. Harold.

The conversation might have continued had it not been for the fact that Alice Cornelius was spotted frowning, walking back from getting her photograph beside a Weeping European Birch Tree. The moment she spotted Graham, however, she broke into a grin.

"Henry, Henry, Henry!" She came hurrying toward him.

Mrs. Cornelius' voice rose. "Alice! This is your wedding.

Conduct yourself like a lady. You're married to a Count now."

Alice looked down at her feet. "Yes, Mother."

Mrs. Cornelius rolled her eyes. "Soon you'll be on your own, Alice. I won't be around to make up for your carelessness"

Alice put her arm in Graham's and brought him out of ear-shot. Ever since she'd first met him, Alice felt she had a certain kinship with Graham—one much stronger than with any members of her family. Maybe it was because, as much as they adored Charlie, they both felt as if they were always lost in his shadow.

"I'm not sure how I'm supposed to address you now. Countess?"

"God no! Just Alice."

"Countess Alice?"

"Just Alice."

Graham smiled.

"Why are you looking at me like that?" Alice asked.

"You look beautiful, Alice."

Alice's face turned crimson.

"How does it feel? To be married?" He asked.

Alice's eyes began to well with tears and her lip began to tremble. It took Graham by complete surprise and he quickly pulled her aside so her mother wouldn't see her.

"Jesus, Alice...are you all right?"

"I don't want to leave, Henry. I don't want to go to another country. I want to stay here. I want to stay home. I like it here."

"It'll be okay. I'm sure you'll like your new life. It might take some time to get used to, but you will."

She wiped her eyes with the palms of her hands.

Graham gave a wry smile. "And if you don't, I'm sure your mother can tell you that you're mistaken."

At this, Alice let out a loud, cackling laugh. The guests looked over with bewildered faces. Mrs. Cornelius glared at her before resuming her conversation.

*

Later that night, when most of the guests had left, the younger attendees went to the lower building along the river where Mr. Cornelius had built his private four lane bowling alley. Lillian, who had not had anything to drink during the reception, now snuck snips of Scotch and Whisky and became drunk. She stayed by Graham.

"I wish your father had been able to attend today. I would have liked very much to see him," Graham said.

Lillian forced a smile. "I wish he could have come, too. But his health…it's taken another turn."

"I'm sorry."

"Some days are better than others. But I do know he would have been happy to see you. You made quite an impression on him, you know."

A few lanes down, William looked at Graham suspiciously, a cigarette dangling out of the corner of his mouth as he got ready to bowl.

Meanwhile, Alice was alone in the far corner of the room, looking around and yawning. Graham pointed out Alice's husband to Lillian. "Have you noticed that the Count puts his face in very close when he talks?"

Lillian looked. She started laughing. "My God! It looks like they're about to kiss!" She swayed a bit. "I'm dizzy. Is Charlie looking over here?"

"No."

"Are you sure?"

"Yes."

"Good." Leaning in, she whispered: "I don't want him to see me in this state."

Graham smiled. "But it's okay for me?"

"Yes."

"Why's that?"

"I don't know it just is." She looked around. "Help me up would you, Henry? It's my turn to bowl."

Lillian took her turn. Both times she nearly stumbled and the ball went right into the gutter. They were both laughing. Graham took his turn and sat down.

"Did you see that?"

"No."

"In that case, it was a strike."

She hesitated a moment, and then realized it was a joke. She laughed. "Charlie said you were a hoot, Henry. But I never saw it before tonight."

Graham lit a cigarette.

She whispered in his ear: "Are you drunk, Henry?"

Graham shook his head, no.

"Like hell you're not!" She laughed, lightly smacking him

on the arm. "But unlike the rest of this clap trap here, you don't pass judgment on me. Everybody here has to live up to the mores of whatever. But with you…with you I feel like you only see me in the best light." She took his hand and gazed into his eyes.

Graham's heart was pounding in his chest. He leaned in to kiss her.

She pulled back with a start. "What are you doing?"

"I'm sorry." He stuttered, seeing the anger in her eyes. "I didn't mean"—

"What sort of woman do you think I am?" She looked around to make sure that no one had seen.

He put the cigarette out in the ashtray.

Lillian looked around once more and then turned to him with a kinder expression. "Henry, I really do think you are swell. Truly, I do. Maybe I gave you the wrong impression, but I don't see how that could've been possible. After that last letter you sent me…the last thing I want is to lead you on. I suppose it may be my fault. After all, I'm not a school girl anymore, and I suppose I give men the wrong impression when I'm friendly with them. I think you're a nice man. That's all. I don't think of you in any other way." She looked over at Charlie horsing around with her cousin and Henry Vanderbilt. "I love Charlie. I have always loved Charlie, and I have no doubt I always will."

At this, Graham nodded and rose, lighting another cigarette. "It's time for me to go to bed. I'm sorry for my behavior. It's been a pleasure seeing you again, Lillian."

Charlie and his other friends implored Graham to stay up with them a little longer; but he shook his head quietly and walked out of the bowling alley.

Touring the grounds, he felt humiliated. Between the letters and the way she looked at me in there—it's all just a game for her. She's played me for a fool. He wondered if he would be able to ever face her again. At some point, he stopped, leaned against a tree, lit another cigarette and blew the match out with a plume of smoke cursing that damned letter and his stupidity in writing it. "To blazes with her," he spat out, tossing his cigarette away.

He passed out for about an hour under a pine tree and woke up in the dark, cold and sick to his stomach. He walked back up the sloping property and returned to his room to get ready for bed.

He heard a knock on his door. Another knock.

Graham took a deep breath and opened it.

"Alice?"

"Hello, Henry," she said, pushing herself inside the room and taking a seat at the edge of his bed. She sat there looking around, unable to make eye contact with Graham.

"What are you doing here?"

"My new husband will not be much of a husband to me, Henry. It seems there's someone else who he finds more appealing."

"I'm sorry, Alice."

"He does like them handsome, I'll say that." She looked at Graham and chuckled. "It appears I'll be one of those wives,

Henry, whose husband is forced to live life in the shadows."

They were both quiet for a few moments.

"I saw what happened, Henry. Tonight. In the bowling alley."

Graham didn't speak.

"But why her? What else is there to her other than her looks? What is it that you men find so appealing? I mean I can understand the appeal to my brother. He's not a man given to much introspection, Henry. But you…I'd have expected you to be different."

"I don't know what you think you saw, Alice"—

"Don't play me for a fool, Henry. I saw it with my own two eyes. I am drunk now, yes. But not when I saw the two of you. She represents everything I despise. Fixated on her vanity. Her life is spent plotting how she can become my brother's wife while also getting every man to do her bidding. But you, Henry? You! You I would have expected more from. I would have thought you'd not fall under her spell."

She waited for him to say something. "Look at you. Look at what you've become. You told me that you turned down my father's offer of employment. Yet here you are. The same as the rest of them."

"That's enough, Alice."

"And why? For her? Have you turned away from your principles for that simpleton?"

"There's much more to it than you think, Alice."

"Like what? To become rich?"

He shook his head.

"No? Then how do you explain the betrayal of my brother

that I witnessed tonight?"

Graham looked down. "It was a mistake."

"Oh, Henry. I do care about you. I don't wish to be mean and horrid. I'm here as your friend and confidante. Listen to me when I say stay away from her, Henry. There is no way that this will work out well in the end."

"I know."

"Then you will? You'll stay away from her?"

"I don't think she'd allow it anyway."

"I know her, Henry. I've known her my whole life. She enjoys the attention. She will not write you off."

He didn't think Alice was being very fair to Lillian. But she was drunk and upset and he felt that arguing the point with her would only make matters worse.

"I'm not going to let that happen," Graham said. He smirked. "I've wised up."

Alice laid down on the bed. "Good," she said, closing her eyes. "I'm very glad to hear that, Henry. You've always been kind to me. I love you. I think you know that. I will never let you get hurt."

Graham was about to say something, but she'd started snoring.

He took his suit jacket and put it on the floor and laid on top of it. It had been years since he'd slept on the ground. He struggled to get comfortable.

The next morning he woke with a start. His head was pounding and he felt nauseous. Alice was standing over him with a concerned look.

"You were having a nightmare," she said.

He looked at her. The sleep still not yet out of his eyes.

"You kept yelling that you didn't mean to kill someone."

Graham sat up. Rubbed his eyes. "It was just a dream, Alice."

"You've never killed anyone, have you, Henry?"

"Of course not," he said. "You better get back to your room. There's liable to be gossip about the two of us."

She smiled. "There are much worse things that can be said about me. In fact, I might like that kind of gossip."

He smirked. "Go on. Get out."

She walked to the door, opened it and walked out.

Artois, France. October 1915

By October, Graham had recovered enough from his wounds to go back to the front and rejoin his battalion. As he limped down the trench, every face he saw was unfamiliar. The smell of gunpowder and the stench from the rotting corpses overwhelmed him. He identified himself to the sergeant who asked him to wait. "The Capitaine says he wanted to speak to you when you arrived," he said.

Graham waited. A few minutes passed, when he felt a hand on his shoulder.

Calloway stood there, grinning. "The dead have come back to life I see."

"They thought they were going to have to take my leg, but there was a nurse there who took care of me and brought me back to health."

"I bet she did, Graham."

Graham smiled, careful to keep his head below the trench, out of the aim of any German sharp shooters. He shook Calloway's hand, happy to see at least one familiar face. "It's good to see you."

"For me too. Too bad it has to be here."

"Where are all the others?"

"There are no others. Just you and me left. And the Capitaine." Calloway cleared his throat and invited Graham to come and join him down the trench a way for a bit of whiskey.

"I've been told to wait here. The Capitaine wants to see me."

Calloway frowned. He looked around, making sure no one was listening, and leaned toward Graham: "The Capitaine's been through quite a bit, gone over the top a few too many times, I think. Seemed as capable an officer as any when he first got here. But the war's gotten the better of his nerves, if you ask me. I don't think he's in command of all his senses. He keeps sending us on these night patrols. We keep losing men and we ain't coming back with nothing. But he tells Staff HQ that we're making progress, killing Germans and unsettling their nerves and all; so they think they're a fucking success. But each night ten guys go out, and we're lucky if eight come back."

"Do all the men feel the same?"

"All the ones that the Capitaine hasn't gotten killed yet."

"What about the Colonel? Maybe he'll listen."

Calloway shook his head. "The Lieutenant was going to talk to him, but he caught it last night on one of the fucking patrols." Calloway laughed. "Sorry, friend. If I don't laugh… you know, I gotta cry."

The Sergeant came out from the dugout and called Graham's name. He signaled for Graham to follow him down.

Graham descended into the back side of the trench, and came into a large single room. There were two officers sitting at a table looking at a map, illuminated by the light of a single candle, whose light flickered and cast moving shadows against the dirt walls. The room was dank and smelled of wet sawdust and spilled absinthe. A Corporal was standing at the other end of the room, staring off into space.

The Capitaine's back was turned to Graham, but the Colonel looked up from the map. Graham saluted. The Capitaine slowly turned around in his seat, rose from the table and came over with a grin spread across his face. Graham could see he had the wide eyes of a madman.

"So you live, Graham?" the Capitaine spoke in French, kissing him on either cheek.

"Yessir."

The Colonel looked up from the map again. "This is Graham?"

The Capitaine nodded. "He fought very bravely before he was wounded."

"I just tried to stay alive."

"You took it upon yourself to take command when all the other officers were killed and I had been knocked unconscious."

"I led them to the Canadians, that's when I found you."

"I heard before you did that, though, you ordered the men to throw their grenades to the area of trench the Germans had taken and drove them out."

Graham did not say anything.

"Just cut to the chase, Phillipe," barked the Colonel. He looked at Graham. "You've been promoted. You're a

Lieutenant now." The Colonel took a drink of his absinthe and signaled to the corner of the room with his chin. "There's your bunk."

Graham shook his head. "Sirs, with all due respect, I don't think I would make a good officer."

"Nonsense! You have quite the nerve, Graham. I'd say you'll be likely be up for the Croix de Guerre."

"It was all just a blur."

The Capitaine and the Colonel gave one another an odd look. The candle light flickered across their faces.

"I don't think you understand, Graham. You don't have any choice in the matter," said the Capitaine.

"Come sit down with us and have some Absinthe." The Colonel said.

Graham took a seat at the table. The Corporal came over and poured them some Absinthe. The Capitaine pointed at the map. "We're just planning our patrol for this evening. I don't know if anyone's told you, but we've had incredible success with them. We're driving the Germans mad. I suspect he's near the breaking point."

Graham glanced at the map. "How can you be sure?"

The Capitaine gave him an odd look. "Because it's been reported."

"By the men on the patrols?"

"By signs you probably wouldn't understand."

Graham noticed that the Capitaine blinked rapidly.

"Signs?" Graham repeated.

"In some cases I utilize hypnosis in order to ascertain the

locations and activities of the enemies. It is amazing what the subconscious can accomplish, Graham."

"The Capitaine also came up with the idea of placing flags in the enemy trenches," the Colonel said. "He's spotted any number of them behind enemy lines."

"Have you actually seen any of these flags, Colonel?"

"I myself haven't seen them, but my eyesight is not what it used to be. I take Phillipe's word for it, though."

Graham put his tin cup down. The Colonel signaled to the Corporal to refill the cup, and he did. Graham drank again.

A loud roar erupted followed by a huge blast. As the earth shook, the Corporal nearly fell over, spilling some of the absinthe on the map. Dust came falling down off the walls.

"By God they're at it again!" The Colonel called out.

Both officers rose from their seat and held their tin cups up in the air, singing "Ma Tete" in loud booming voices. As the shelling continued, they sang louder, until they were now shouting out the lyrics.

Graham watched them in horror. The Capitaine looked down, "come on, man. Get up and sing."

But Graham did not move.

"Are you disobeying an order? Stand up and sing."

"I don't know the words."

"That's all right," the Capitaine yelled as another shell came falling, the earth shaking and the dirt falling off the walls. "Just hum to the melody."

"Sing, Lieutenant! Stand up and sing or I shall write you up!" The Colonel yelled.

"Crucified! You shall be crucified on Gogol if you do not stand up and sing!" The Capitaine cried.

Graham stood up, held his tin cup and reluctantly joined them.

Fatal'ment je s'rai condamne
Car y s'ra prouve qu' j'assassine.
Faudra que j'attende, blame et vane
Jusqua c' qu' enfin on m' guillotine.
Alors un beau jour on m' dira:
"C'est pour ce matin…faites vot' toilette.
Je sortirai…la foule saluera
Ma tete!

Finally the shelling stopped.

They fell silent.

"You were a little off key in some spots, Capitaine," said the Colonel.

"Yes, well. I've had a bit of a cough …"

"Will that be all, sirs?" Graham said.

The officers looked at him.

"Sirs? May I be dismissed?" Graham asked again.

"Yes, yes. Go on, go on!"

When he came back out of the dugout, there were four dead bodies by the stairs. He stepped over them, and went looking for Calloway.

"Well?" Calloway asked.

"Don't bother going to the Colonel about the Capitaine."

"Why not?"

"Because they're both fucking out of their minds."

CHAPTER 24

New York, NY. July 1914

That year the winter and spring seemed to rush by. Suddenly it was summer. Alice and her new husband had returned to Montenegro, leaving Lindenhurst abandoned. The rest of the Cornelius family were in the process of spending their summer months up in Newport, like the other families of society.

As for Graham, he planned to remain in sweltering Manhattan, working hard for Cornelius. He'd twice been invited up to Newport, but refused the offers owing to some sticky union disputes. When he wasn't working for Cornelius, most of Graham's free time was spent planning his own business venture. He'd been keeping this venture a secret for nearly a year; but he was giving careful consideration to leaving Cornelius and starting his own company in what he thought might be a burgeoning industry coming out of Fort Lee, New Jersey: the moving pictures.

Graham had attempted to meet with Cornelius to discuss his plan on a number of occasions. He wanted to give him the opportunity to be an investor; it was the least he could do. But Cornelius never seemed to have the time to meet with him. However, once his wife was fully settled in at Newport and Charlie had gone off on safari in Africa, Cornelius returned to Manhattan.

Finally, he called Graham to his office.

Graham had been rehearsing this discussion for weeks; but he was still nervous about having to present it to Cornelius. Graham knew he expected absolute loyalty. He was known not to take it well when one of his employees decided to leave him.

Mr. Cornelius's secretary led Graham into Mr. Cornelius's office where he sat behind his large desk. He rose from his seat and met Graham halfway, shaking his hand.

Mr. Cornelius returned to his chair. He opened a small humidor on his desk and held it out toward Graham. "Cigar?"

"Thank you," Graham said, taking the cigar.

Cornelius tapped the newspaper sitting on his desk and frowned. "It appears the IWW has convinced those ignorant sons-of-bitches in Paterson to turn down the owners' compromise of one less hour a week."

"What are the demands?"

"Safer conditions and a forty hour work week." Mr. Cornelius guffawed. "A forty hour work week! Do they have any idea how much that will cut into production? The damned fools. Fine, I say. Let them strike. Let their children starve to death because they'd rather picket than work to earn a wage. They'll have no one to blame but themselves. I just hope the owners don't give in and the newspapers don't start playing on public sympathy for these ingrates."

Cornelius straightened his back. "Anyway. Enough on that. There's bigger news out there than Paterson. Have you heard there's now whispers that war may be coming to Europe? If it should happen, let's pray they're right when they say it won't last long. Did you know that lunatic son of mine is already talking about volunteering?"

"He did mention that to me, yes."

"And what was your response?"

"I told him to let Europe sort it out themselves."

Cornelius chuckled.

"He disagreed with me, of course. Said it was democracy and liberty at stake."

"The young man's a damned fool. He thinks it's all a game. I've never fought in a war, myself, mind you. But I imagine it's not pretty."

"No sir. I imagine not. If you ask me, it's none of our concern what goes on over there."

"Well, I have to disagree with you, on that point, Henry. It is our concern. Charlie might be on to something when he says liberty is at stake."

"Seems to me it's less about liberty and more about family quarrels between the European monarchy and elites."

"Every now and then, that socialist streak comes out, son. You do realize there's an awful lot of interest...a lot of our interest at stake. And there's no doubt there's always money to be made from war. A lot of money to be made."

"You say it like it's a good thing."

"Of course not. I was just stating a fact."

Cornelius sighed, and turned to Henry with a warm-hearted look in his eyes. "Henry, let's have out with it. There's been an eight hundred pound gorilla in the room for quite some time. We both know you're looking to move into your own business ventures."

Graham looked down at his hands.

"Did you really think anyone could make a move in this city without my knowing it? My question for you, though, is: why? Perhaps some men are interested in money for the sake of money alone; but I've never fully understood what their motivation was, nor could I ever really trust them. The truth is we're all animals of the basest sort, Henry. Everything most of us do has been done as means to attract members of the fairer sex. And it's no secret that pretty girls are like moths to the light, when it comes to money and power.

"You're a man of fine moral caliber, and I respect you for that, Henry. If I'd have been in your position, I probably wouldn't have come to tell my employer my plans. But you… you put it aside out of respect and honesty." Mr. Cornelius smiled affectionately at Graham. "I feel your potential in this company is limitless. But your honesty, which is a great strength in that people will trust you, can also be a weakness, Henry. And a good businessman knows how to exploit a weakness. There's still a lot for you to learn. If you never break the rules, Henry—you'll eventually get run over by those who do. I think I've told you about how my father once used his connections to cause such a panic that the stock market plummeted. The weak were wiped out and my father walked away with a profit. It was intellect and gall and ruthlessness. One must learn to always put themselves first. It's in our very nature and there's no escaping that, Henry."

Graham puffed on his cigar. Cornelius waited for him to speak, but he didn't.

"You're not yet able to separate what's necessary to survive versus what some might call unsavory practices. Your loyalty to my family, until now, has been unswerving. You've made me a lot of money, Henry. You have a good sense for business, unlike my own son. I don't need to tell you that Charlie is not a businessman; and I finally accepted that he'll never be one. I need someone to run my business when I'm gone, Henry. And as much as it saddens me to admit it—Charlie will not be that individual. The only one I trust fully is you. I'm telling you this now, because I don't want you running off and doing some damned fool thing like investing in these moving pictures."

"I disagree with you, Sir. I think that millions can be made."

"Balderdash!" He laughed. "Besides, even if it could bring in millions, it would still not be anywhere near the kind of money you would make should you stay on course with my guidance, Henry. Nowhere near as much. Your hard work will be paid in full and then some. You'll be millionaire someday. Just be patient, my boy."

Cornelius hesitated, his eyes glimmering. "Henry, let me be frank with you a moment. I think I know what's behind all this. Charlie's been a damned fool when it comes to Lillian. Alva wants nothing more than to have her as a daughter-in-law...but as far as I'm concerned, she and Charlie may not be best suited for one another, despite what they both might think. Still I will be perfectly frank with you, Henry. Lillian will never be with a man of your background, a man of simple, albeit very respectable, financial means. I tell you this not to be cruel; I tell you this, because I love you like a son and I don't want you to make a mistake you will live to regret. Lillian is one woman among billions. One woman with many faces. You think if you strike out on your own, your wealth will come quicker, perhaps...and then you might woo her. The only path toward that kind of wealth, Henry, is through me."

They were quiet for a few seconds as Graham let Cornelius' words sink in.

"Sir, I would never leave your employ without your blessing. That's why I wanted to speak with you first."

"I know that. And in that case, I can't in good conscious give you my blessing to pursue some foolish fad. But it's your decision, Henry. I'd like you to continue to learn the business. When the time comes, you'll be able to run it. For all intents and purposes, Henry, you're already a rich man."

"I don't know what to say, Mr. Cornelius. This is really so unexpected. I suppose I should take your advice."

"You deserve this, son. God rewards hard work."

Mr. Cornelius beamed. He walked over and embraced Graham. "This makes me happy, Henry. Knowing that you'll one day take over …it means that all the hard work and wealth my family has accumulated over the past sixty-four years will continue to grow.

As Graham went to the door, Cornelius called to him: "Henry?"

Graham stopped, his hand still on the doorknob.

"I had some visitors today," said Cornelius.

"Oh?"

"Detectives."

Graham turned pale.

"They were looking for a fella by the name of Henry Michael Flanagan." Cornelius cleared his throat. "Apparently, this fella killed that Pinkerton at the IWW rally years back. They had reason to believe he worked for me, if you can believe that. I asked where they'd heard such claptrap, and at first the two detectives didn't want to give me the source looking to cash in on the reward. But I insisted. Turns out it was some fool waiter I had working at Alice's wedding. I gave the two detectives some money for all their troubles. And I made sure that the fella who gave that information was fired and blacklisted up and down the eastern seaboard. They found three thousand dollar in his room. Not sure where he came up with that money, but I can only assume he must have stolen it."

Graham wasn't sure what to say.

"It's all right, son. I'm just trying to tell you you're safe. There's no one who's going to come looking for you now, so long as I have any say in the matter."

What was he to make of this? Graham stood there.

"You okay, Henry?"

"Yessir."

"I'm glad you came to me about your plans, Henry, rather than just setting out on your own," Cornelius said. His eyes suddenly went cold. "But remember this favor, Henry, if you're ever again tempted to be disloyal to me."

Graham's heart was pounding in his chest. He wanted to get out of there as quickly as possible. He was sweating, too, and his mouth was dry. "Yessir," he said. "You know you have my utmost loyalty."

"I hope so."

Cornelius excused him. Graham hurried out of his office. Someone said something to him, but he kept on moving. Outside, he hurried down the street and into an alley, leaned his back again the wall and tried to compose himself. It seemed his loyalty to Cornelius was no longer a choice.

CHAPTER 25

Midway through that summer, Lillian's father finally passed away. The funeral was held in New York City at the Woodlawn Cemetery in the Bronx. Graham offered himself up to Lillian and her mother for whatever help might be needed to get through this hard time. He even sent flowers a few times to Lillian in hopes of cheering her; but he only received a simple telegram expressing Lillian's thanks and appreciation for his thoughtfulness.

Soon after the funeral, Lillian's mother returned to Newport while Lillian insisted on staying back in New York City. She wanted to be alone with her grief.

A couple of weeks later she decided she would join her mother in Newport. She had the valet summon a cab so she could send a telegram to her mother.

The cab took her down 5th Avenue. The streets were clogged with delivery trucks and motor cars. Lillian adjusted her hat and her dress and looked out of the window.

Then she saw him.

He was walking by himself, dressed in a grey suit and wearing a white, straw boater hat. He seemed to glide along the sidewalk, his eyes pressed forward, focused and intense. For the first time since her father had passed, she felt the stirrings of an emotion other than grief. She tapped the driver lightly on the shoulder and asked him if she could get out.

He was about ten yards ahead, maybe more. She hurried after him, cursing the hat and gloves her station required, even in summer. She worried that by the time she reached him her face would be flush and sweaty. When she eventually felt she was within earshot she called out his name.

At first, he didn't seem to hear her. She said his name again, louder this time. A few people turned their heads and she put her gloved fingers to her mouth, embarrassed. Graham stopped and turned with a curious expression on his face. It took a moment for him to recognize her, but when he did he smiled.

She pretended to brush a strand of hair sticking out from under her hat, when in truth she was wiping away sweat.

"This is a most pleasant surprise," she said.

Graham nodded. "It's great to see you again, Lillian."

He noticed the black armband she was wearing.

"Once again, I'm terribly sorry for your loss, Lillian."

She lowered her gaze. "Thank you. I received the flowers you sent."

He nodded again. "Where are you headed? I'll walk you there, if you don't mind?"

"Actually, nowhere in particular. I was just going for a stroll."

"Do you mind if I join you?"

"I think I would like that."

They continued along the avenue, walking just on the outskirts of the park. She reminded him of the day they spent together the night after the party held in his honor.

"It seems so long ago now, doesn't it?"

"I suppose. I think I still have the photograph we took."

"I remembered I was a little surprised at how much I enjoyed your company."

He said nothing.

"Have you been up to Newport at all this season, Henry?"

"No. I've been too busy with work. It's a shock you even caught me outside."

"Well, you mustn't work so hard." She took a deep breath. "It's so good to see someone I know and like. The city is deserted this time of year."

He walked on with her, searching for the right words. Lillian felt there was something charming in the way Henry always acted toward her; his sincerity, and the way he looked at her—as if she were the only thing in the world that mattered. If only Charlie could be a bit more like Henry, she thought. But that would make things too easy. Life was meant to be complicated.

Still, she enjoyed having Henry as a friend. When she really thought about it, maybe Charlie had been right at Alice's wedding: that she was even being a little bit cruel with Henry, giving him the wrong idea.

Maybe it was cruel. But he enjoyed being near her—that was obvious. And she enjoyed the attention. So, what was the harm?

As they walked on, Lillian asked, "Do you have any plans this evening, Henry?"

"I suppose I'll just go home and have my dinner and read."

"Oh." She waited for him to ask her what her dinner plans were. "I was thinking I might like to dine away from my house tonight."

Graham did not catch on, so she quickly decided to prod the conversation in the right direction. "Unfortunately, there's no one around to dine with."

Graham couldn't seem to look right at her. He hesitated, seemed to think about something. "Would you like to join me for dinner? We could go to Del Monico's."

She smiled. "Actually, I think it would do me some good. Yes."

Much to her surprise, Graham appeared preoccupied. Out the corner of her eye, she spotted the Western Union sign across the street and decided then and there that she wouldn't send the telegram to her mother. Not just yet.

CHAPTER 26

That evening Henry Graham called on Lillian Harold at her brownstone. It was a beautiful summer night for their walk to Del Monicos.

A couple of blocks later, the streets were clogged with motor cars and delivery trucks and the summer heat made the bags of garbage on the sidewalk smell.

"I don't know how anyone could spend an entire summer in Manhattan," said Lillian.

They were given a table at the far end of the restaurant. Because it was the summer season, Lillian didn't recognize any of the patrons. And that was probably a good thing. There were some in her circles who had nothing better to do with their time than spread vicious rumors. She imagined the sight of her dining alone with Henry would cause a minor stir. Everyone would know it was, in all truth, innocent—but they'd still gossip about it as if it weren't.

"I can't tell you how happy I was to see you, Henry. I told my mother I wanted to stay on in the city to be alone. But there were times when I wanted to talk to someone other than one of the maids or valets. All of my friends are either in Europe or up in Newport."

"Do you plan on going up to Newport?"

"I suppose I probably will," she said. "But I just can't bear the thought of having to attend one of those dreadful balls, especially without Charlie there. He makes those things so much more bearable. Don't you agree?"

"I suppose he does. He's still a bit like a kid."

"You're right about that." Lillian chuckled. "Has he written to you from his safari?"

"I haven't received anything from him. Have you?"

"Not yet. I sent him a letter to tell him about my father. I don't know if he's even received it yet."

"Do you think he will leave Africa as soon as he hears?"

Lillian looked down. "I'm sure that he will."

They took a sip of their wine. A couple of seconds passed before Lillian continued, "But I am excited to hear about his adventures. I'm sure they'll be riveting. I think this is just the thing Charlie needed to get out of his system."

"You two have been close since you were kids?"

She smiled. "My whole life, actually. I used to travel with him on some of his adventures."

"But not anymore?"

She frowned and looked past him. "There are certain expectations in our circles, Henry. The last time I was permitted on an adventure with him was when I was sixteen. As a woman, that kind of thing is no longer acceptable."

"Do you miss it?"

"Yes. Very much. That's one of the things that forms this

special bond—we both love to travel the world and find adventure."

"Well, maybe you can have that again when you're married."

"Yes," she said, a lump forming in her throat. "Maybe some day."

"Yeah, well, Charlie's a swell guy," said Henry.

"And he does think very highly of you as well, Henry."

"Your brother on the other hand…I understand you're his sister and all. But why Charlie is friends with him, I do not know."

"I know you think William's wretched, Henry. But he is a good man. You don't know what he's been through."

Graham scoffed. " Been through? What the hell could that dandy have been through?"

"You think just because he's rich he can't suffer?"

"He has the money to soften the blow."

Lillian glared at him. "If you must know, he was engaged to be married seven years ago."

Graham smirked. "Oh? What happened? She didn't take to his winning personality?"

"She died."

Graham's heart sank. "I'm sorry."

"She was murdered actually. William and Elizabeth had been invited to Lindhenhurst. William arrived a few days earlier and Elizabeth, his fiancé, was scheduled to take the train up with her mother. It was winter and a horse-drawn sleigh met them at the train station so they could travel through the snow. There were some highwaymen waiting in the woods. They held up the sleigh. As you know, this wasn't entirely uncommon. In the past, though, they'd simply robbed people on the road. This time, though, they beat the driver and Elizabeth's mother unconscious. As for Elizabeth, they took her. We expected there would be a letter of ransom. But nothing ever came. There was no sign of her, despite a massive manhunt. Everyone combed through the woods, police searched every home in the area, it seemed there was not an inch that had not been scoured. Yet there was no sign. Then the thaw came. A boy was out walking his dog and he found her. She was under some leaves. Half naked. It appeared that they kept her alive long enough to do with her what they wanted to do and then they slit her throat."

"Jesus. I'm sorry," said Graham. "I had no idea. Did they catch them?"

Lillian shook her head. "At the time, there were a large number of strike agitators who'd come to town recently for a socialist rally. Upton Sinclair, Elizabeth Gurley Flynn, Carlo Tresca, they were all there. My brother thinks that Elizabeth wasn't simply a random passerby who they decided to rob. He believes they were targeting the rich and that the killing was part of a larger scale war being waged against the rich. You can't deny, Henry, that there aren't some radicals who want to overthrow the government and kill the rich."

She was right. He could not deny that.

"And so you see, as far as my brother is concerned—anyone from around there could be her killer. And that even includes you."

Graham felt pangs of guilt. "I'm sorry, Lillian. I had no idea."

"Charlie was in Europe when it happened. He came back as soon as he received the telegram. You haven't any idea the state my brother was in at the time. I've never seen a man in such a state of grief. Most of William's friends didn't know how to react. Some of them even began avoiding him because it was so difficult to know how one should behave. Charlie was the only friend who stuck by him. I'm not saying any of the others were wrong. It's just that they didn't know what to do. Charlie didn't know, either. He just stayed with him. With all of us, actually."

Graham looked down at his plate. He took a drink. They were quiet for some time, the two of them. Eventually, he decided to try and change the subject.

"I went to Mr. Cornelius to let him know I planned on leaving his employment," he said, finally.

"Leaving? Why? Did someone else offer you something?"

"No. It's just…I think there's something to these moving pictures, Lillian. I know they say they will pass into oblivion; but I don't agree."

"I didn't know you had an interest in show business, Henry."

"I don't. I just think there's money to be made."

"Do you think it might hurt Mr. Cornelius's theatre?"

Graham laughed. "Who knows."

"Have you been?"

"To his theatre? No, I'm afraid I haven't had a chance to view his little spectacle. He did have me meet with some young girl whose mother needed convincing to let her work on one of the productions. But I don't know how long I can put him off. He keeps asking me to attend that godawful show. Thankfully he's in Paris. I'm hoping the show closes before he gets back."

"What is the title again?"

"*Tahitian Safari.*"

They both laughed.

"Is it true he made the playwright put the young beauties in hula skirts for every scene?"

"Yes."

They both laughed even harder and the tension that earlier seemed insurmountable quickly faded away.

"And what did Mr. Cornelius say about you leaving?" Lillian asked.

"He talked me out of it. He felt I was better off under his tutelage for now."

"And do you agree with him?"

"I wouldn't have, but he told me he planned on having me take over his interests one day."

"All his interests?" She looked at him with a curious look. "Really?"

"Yes."

"What about Charlie?"

"I'm sure Charlie will be involved in some capacity, but Mr. Cornelius feels I'm better suited to run the business the way in which it should be run."

"I don't imagine Charlie will be happy to hear this."

"He told me he doesn't want anything to do with it."

"He's only been putting it off because it's inevitable."

"Please don't say a word about this, Lillian. I probably shouldn't have said anything. If you feel it's that important, I'll let Charlie know myself. I'm sure he'll always be seen as the man in charge. I'll just be behind the scenes. I don't know the specific capacity in which I'll be involved. All I know is that Cornelius assures me that someday I'll be a millionaire. So long as I continue on the path I'm on and I remain patient."

"There is more to life than acquiring riches, Henry."

"It's still better than being poor."

She was quiet for a moment. There was something different about him. More hardened. What had changed? Perhaps she had been nothing more than a minor crush and he had since moved on? *Am I losing my looks?* She smiled coyly at him. "I think seeing you, Henry, was the first time I felt any glimmers of happiness since my father passed. I thought that feeling had all but welled up and died inside of me, until I saw you walking down the street."

"The time certainly has gone by quickly," Graham said. "Shall I walk you home?"

The streets were nearly empty. A soft breeze blew, helping to cool things off. The night sky was clear and full of stars. As they walked, she did most of the talking. Small talk, mostly, of people they both knew.

"Do you think there will be war in Europe, Henry?"

"I doubt it will come to that. It's just sabre rattling."

"I agree."

A young couple was walking toward them. Graham tipped

the brim of his hat. Lillian caught the woman admiring Graham out of the corner of her eye as she passed.

"Are you holding court with anyone these days, Henry?"

Graham laughed. "I don't have time for women."

Lillian rolled her eyes. "Oh please. You probably do, but you just won't tell me."

Graham looked up at the sky. "Lots of stars out tonight, huh?"

She looked up, frowned. "I suppose."

Finally, they arrived at the Harold residence.

"I enjoyed my time with you tonight immensely, Henry."

"Me, too."

"I will be leaving for Newport next week."

"Please tell everyone I said, hello."

He was about to turn to go, when Lillian said: "Let's dine out again tomorrow night, shall we? Seeing as how we've had so much fun this evening?"

Graham hesitated. He looked around.

"I mean, only if you want to, of course," she said.

Finally, Graham smiled. "Shall I come by around the same time?"

"Yes," she said, smiling. "That will be wonderful."

CHAPTER 27

For the next six nights in a row, Henry and Lillian went to dinner.

Lillian avoided her mother's pleas that it would be good for her to come up to Newport. During the day, Graham would duck out of work and meet her on the street. They'd sit on a bench in Bowling Green Park and watch people as they walked by.

On Friday night they decided to attend a show at the Strand theatre on Broadway. Afterward, they headed to Café de Paris for a late dinner. The restaurant was filled with theatregoers, and there was a dance floor where people danced the tango.

They ate and they drank and they talked. Over the past few days, Lillian had realized that she felt a certain level of freedom with Graham, one which she didn't feel around most of the men in her circles. She knew that every one of her actions or comments wouldn't be judged against her. No, not in Henry's eyes. With Henry, she was free to be whatever she wanted to be.

"My mother's trying to convince me to come up to

Newport."

"And will you be going?"

"I'm having second thoughts."

"Second thoughts?"

"I'm having too much fun in New York."

Graham smiled. But once again, Lillian thought he seemed uneasy. He looked around the restaurant, as if he was checking to see if they were being watched.

"I would have thought you'd be happy to spend more time with me."

"Of course I am. But Charlie'll be arriving in Newport sometime soon, won't he?"

They hadn't mentioned Charlie all night. It was Lillian who always used to bring him up. But this time it was as if to remind Lillian of her place. She and Charlie were destined to be together. There was something in his tone, something suggesting her staying in New York could be problematic.

They finished another bottle of wine and ordered one more. Soon they were both very drunk.

She smiled at him. "Do you know how to dance the tango?"

"No."

"I learned in Paris. I'll teach you."

They walked out on the dance floor, hand in hand. She came in close, took his hand and placed it at the small of her back, pressing her body against his. He closed his eyes. He could smell the scent of lilac in her hair and worried that she might sense his arousal.

There was nothing he wanted more than to kiss her.

They stayed until closing and stumbled outside into the night air with her arm in the crook of his arm.

She rested her head against his arm. "Henry?"

He looked at her.

"Show me where you grew up."

Graham laughed.

"I'm serious. I want to see where you came from."

"It's dangerous this time of night."

"I'm not frightened."

"Another time."

"Please? I'm not ready to go home just yet."

"Why do we need to go there?"

"You should know by now that I'm the curious type."

He looked up and down the street.

"Do you think if I see where you lived I'll think less of you?" She said, reading his mind. "Please, Henry. I want to see. I would only think higher of you to see what you've overcome."

They took a streetcar from Broadway and headed a few blocks toward the tenements of Hell's Kitchen. There were still some peddlers out by their stands even at this late hour. Graham and Lillian walked down a quiet side street. A gang of men were on a stoop, smoking. They stopped speaking and stared as Graham and Lillian approached. Graham realized the way the two of them were dressed made them stand out and he felt Lillian tighten her grip on his forearm. Graham said nothing, not looking directly at the men nor looking away. The last thing he wanted this evening was a fight. A moment after they passed, the men began speaking to one another, apparently busy with something else.

They walked a couple of blocks before reaching a red brick tenement. Graham stopped.

"This is it."

She looked up at the building. Clotheslines hung from the windows and spread across the air shafts separating the buildings. Gray clothes hung out to dry like insects hanging from spider webs.

He tried to make out her expression, but her face appeared stoic in the moonlight.

"Do you want to go inside?"

She nodded.

It was very hot inside the building. A single electric bulb cast dim light in the stairwell and flickered, casting shadows against the walls.

They took the stairs. She was still holding onto his arm. The smell of fish and boiled cabbage and many of the doors were left open to create a cross breeze. They came to the apartment where he had lived. The door here was open, too. She gazed inside. There were about ten people inside. The sound of snores and coughs came from within. A middle-aged man with a dark beard and unkempt hair suddenly darted up from his sleep and stared at the young woman with a sleepy blank expression. Lillian jumped back with a start.

"Excuse us," Lillian said, taking a few steps backward.

Without a word, the man lay down again and went back to sleep.

"Let's leave now," Lillian whispered.

They managed to get a trolley car, and took it to the last stop. It was very late and the streets were nearly empty.

"It's going to be hard to find you a cab," Graham said.

"How far is your apartment from here?" She put her arm in the crook of his elbow again.

"Not that far."

"Let's go there, and I can call for a driver."

He gave her a look, stunned at her audacity. He managed to compose himself. "I can simply walk you back if you prefer."

"It's too far. It'll be sunrise by the time you get back. It will be quicker if I simply call for a driver at your apartment."

*

Henry turned on a light and lead Lillian inside.

Lillian looked around. The apartment was small, but charming. The living room was sparsely furnished, but Henry was a bachelor. Beside the hearth was an oak bookcase and she walked over and glanced at the titles. Most were classics, but there were some newer novels as well: Henry James, Edith Wharton, Theodore Dreiser, even. On the stand near the bookcase was an opened copy of Darwin's "Origin of the Species," a gift from Andrew Cornelius.

"Are these for show, or do you actually read them?"

"I try and read them. There isn't much else for me to do when I get home, so I usually have a drink and treat myself to a book before I go to sleep."

He looked at the phone sitting on a table beside a floral

patterned sofa. She hadn't mentioned anything yet about calling her driver.

She looked at the books again. "It must have been terrible to have grown up like that. In those tenements."

"I probably find it worse now that I've grown accustomed to this life. As a kid, you don't realize. You don't know any other life. But when you're an adult, and you have children to support... it can break a person."

"Your mother, you mean?"

Lillian more or less knew the story of his mother. He assumed it must have been her brother who told her about it. How William found out, he didn't know. He suspected, however, that Cornelius had investigators look into his background before formally making any offer of employment. Graham doubted, however, that they ever knew the whole story.

"My mother was a very pretty girl. She married a peddler, my father. When I was about two years old, my father died from consumption." He frowned. "She did what she had to do in order for us to survive."

Lillian looked at Henry, empathy in her eyes.

"That's simply where I came from, Lillian. It's not who I am. One can't help the station in life that they're born into. But through hard work, they can change it."

There was a silence.

"Henry, there's something you should know about me." She glanced at him a moment, unable to maintain eye contact. "That day...that day I went through the ice"—she hesitated, looked around. "It wasn't an accident."

"I know."

"I know you do."

A silence.

She walked softly past him, her shoulder just brushing up against his side. "I should call for a car now."

His heart was pounding against his chest. *Is it worth it? Is it worth risking everything?*

She went to take the telephone, but he grabbed her arm. Slowly, she turned to face him. Their eyes locked. He kissed her on the mouth. At first, she was taken aback. Then she began to kiss him back and whispered in his ear, "Take me to bed, Henry."

He slowly undid her hoop skirt. She took off his suit jacket. He was aching with desire, struggling with the fastenings of her corset. She reached back, unfastened the clasps and the corset fell to the floor. She took down her stockings and garters and she stood naked in front of him. He came to her, pressed his lips against hers. She clasped his hair and unfastened his belt. His pants fell to his ankles and she took him in her hand and made him quiver, their bodies trembling and their hearts racing.

She's done this before. There is no doubt.

They walked into the bedroom, still entwined. They fell to the bed and he positioned himself on top of her, kissing her, touching her all over her body until he made her moan with delight. When he put himself inside of her, they both let out a gasp and stared into one another's eyes as the dark blue of dawn fell outside his window. They pushed into one another in unison until finally his body trembled hard and he let out an ecstatic groan and collapsed on top of her.

They lay side by side. She stroked the back of his head and tried to catch her breath, kissed him again on the cheek, and then the mouth. He lay on his back and she came closer into him, resting her head on his chest. She could hear his heart beating wild. She smiled to herself, and then closed her eyes. She felt happy, safe; more so than she ever had in her life. Everything in the world seemed good and pure.

They rose just before noon. Slats of sunlight shone through the corners of the drawn shade and caught the particles of floating dust. They made love two more times before Lillian decided it was time for her to get dressed and return home. She sat down on the chaise lounge in the living room and began putting on her stockings.

"This is scandalous, Henry. Absolutely scandalous."

"It's only scandalous if someone finds out."

She looked at him. "Someone will find out, Henry. Someone always does."

"I suppose I'm a poor investment for your future."

"I don't care."

He stood behind her and helped fasten the corset.

He walked her downstairs. They passed a charwoman on her hands and knees cleaning the stairs. The woman glanced up at Henry and Lillian as they walked down, paused for a moment before nodding her head. "Afternoon, Misses. Sir."

Once outside, Lillian smiled at Henry.

"I'll walk home by myself for obvious reasons."

Graham smirked and bowed his head. He wanted to kiss her and it looked like she wanted to kiss him, too. They broke into mischievous smiles before saying good day.

CHAPTER 28

Like any new lovers, Henry and Lillian couldn't get enough of each another. They continued to meet during lunch, when Graham snuck away from work. His normal custom of staying later than everyone else had gone to the way side, and he now often watched the clock, impatiently waiting to leave so that he could see her again.

They'd go to dinner. They'd go dancing. They'd go to the theatre and the picture shows. Some nights they'd do nothing but lie in bed together.

Graham was still convinced that there was money to be made in moving pictures. Mr. Cornelius was wrong in his belief that they were simply a fad, a novelty that would soon pass. He feared if he didn't act soon it would be too late. Could he do it secretly? Build up a small fortune in secret? Enough to pay off anyone that Cornelius might send to come get him if they were to learn about Lillian and him? It would take years. Their secret would get out before then. He was kidding himself, he knew. Still, he was in such a state that it seemed that almost anything was possible.

While they were lying in bed, Graham turned and looked

at Lillian. "Do you think I'm making a mistake staying on with Cornelius? Maybe I should take the gamble and venture out on my own."

"You're so clever, Henry, I feel no matter which decision you make, you'll find your success."

"He'll try and ruin me. Especially if they find out about us."

She kissed him. "Don't worry," she said, stroking the side of his face. "Whatever scandal our affair causes—we'll overcome it with the power of our love."

He tried to smile and believe her words. Lillian rested her head on Graham's chest. "When we're married, Henry, I don't want it to be anything like my parents' marriage."

Graham said nothing. In the past couple of weeks, they'd begun confiding things to one another, things they never confided to anyone else.

"My mother could be wretched to my father. I resent her for the way she treated him. Sometimes I think she only worsened his condition."

"You're being too harsh."

"No, I'm not. You don't know, Henry. She was always belittleing him. Calling him weak. He was such a dear man. The kindest, most warm-hearted man one could ever meet."

"I know." Graham said sincerely.

"He always had time for our family. Unlike many other husbands. He always came home at a reasonable hour. My mother would accuse him of hovering over her. He could never do anything that could please her. I swear, Henry. I'll never be like that woman. Never."

"I know."

He kissed her and they made love.

Later, they decided to leave the apartment and go outside into the night air where it would be a little cooler.

The streets were clogged with traffic.

"It will take forever for a cab to get me home. Maybe we should go back inside and I'll stay the night again."

Graham pulled her close and they kissed in public. They no longer cared if they showed their affection even if it was considered poor etiquette. The truth was, they couldn't keep their hands off one another. Lillian pulled away from Henry's embrace, laughing. Then she looked toward the street and spotted an enclosed Cadillac limousine waiting out the traffic. Sitting in the back seat was an older woman staring out the window at them in shocked disapproval. Lillian recognized the woman right away and her heart sank in her chest.

The woman quickly turned her head, refusing to meet her gaze.

"Who is that?" Graham asked.

"Mary Astor," Lillian said, painfully.

Neither of them said a word. The traffic finally started to move and the Cadillac passed.

Graham looked at Lillian. "Maybe she won't say anything."

"If only that were possible, Henry." She took him by the arm and put her head against his chest. "But she will. I am certain of that."

CHAPTER 29

Two weeks passed. Both Lillian and Graham thought maybe Mrs. Astor had surprised them both and not said anything.

Their anxiety returned, however, on August 3rd, when a telegram came to Graham at his job; it was from Mrs. Cornelius, inviting him to come up to Newport first thing Tuesday morning. Tomorrow morning. He couldn't be certain but the wording in the telegram seemed to suggest this was less an invitation than an order he couldn't refuse.

That night, Lillian came to his apartment.

"My mother sent a telegram, Henry."

"What did it say?"

She handed him the telegram. "It says that I have to go up to Newport. She called me, too, and told me I was required to take the New York Central first thing Wednesday morning."

Graham looked at his telegram and then he looked at Lillian's. "Do you think this has anything to do with Mrs. Astor?"

"Of course it does."

"Maybe we're reading into it too much, Lilian."

"No. I don't think so. I asked my mother over the telephone why it was so important. She said the Vanderbilts are having a ball at the Breakers; but when I refused, she said I had no choice in the matter. She would come down to New York and drag me up there."

Graham lit a cigarette. Lillian signaled with her hand for him to share.

She looked anxious. "What do you think we should do?"

"I guess we go up there and deal with it. Tell your mother that Mrs. Astor did see us, but nothing scandalous took place."

Lillian was quiet for a moment. She took a drag of her cigarette, thinking about something. "No. I will tell her the truth. I'll tell her that I am in love with you, and that I can't help how I feel. If she can't accept that she'll have to learn to deal with it."

"Are you sure you want to do that?"

"Yes."

He hesitated. "You do know we'll have to run away."

"We don't have to run away. There's nothing for us to be ashamed of."

"It's not that, Lillian. Cornelius will come after me."

"You're not scared of him, are you?"

"He's a powerful man. We won't be able to stay here. Ever." He paused. He knew he had to tell her.

When she heard everything he had to say, she looked off into space. She didn't say anything for quite some time. "And the truth is that it was an accident?"

"I swear, Lillian. I never meant to kill that man. There's not a day I don't regret it. If I could do something, anything to go back to that night and set things right I would. I swear

I would."

"You're sure Cornelius knows?"

"Yes."

"It doesn't matter. We will find a way." Once again, she grew quiet. "Maybe Mrs. Astor hasn't even revealed our secret."

He smiled. "We can only hope."

Lillian sighed. "Even if she didn't say anything, I doubt we'll get a chance to see one another while we're in Newport. Most of my time will probably be spent at dinners and balls. It's unlikely that we'll have any time to be alone together.

"I have an ominous feeling, Henry. That these last few weeks, of the two of us being together completely, that we'll never have anything like them again."

"Don't talk like that."

"I know I shouldn't but..."

"It'll all work out in the end."

"Do you think, Henry?"

"It'll be difficult at first. But in the end. . .yes. It'll all work out."

"I hope so."

"It will."

They made love and then made plans for their imagined future. They promised one another that, no matter what might happen, it couldn't change how incredibly happy they were, the two of them, just to be near each other. Nothing else in the world mattered, as far as they were concerned. Nothing mattered at all except the two of them.

CHAPTER 30

Graham arrived in Newport late the next afternoon. His anxiety over his meeting with Alva Cornelius growing. He hoped that Mrs. Cornelius' requesting his presence at Newport was merely a coincidence. That no one was aware of what happened between he and Lillian. But he knew this was simply naïve and wishful thinking.

One of the Cornelius's Valets greeted him at the train station, brought him over to a car and took him to the Cornelius mansion on Belmont Avenue.

"I suppose you've already heard the news," the driver said as he drove.

"News?"

"From Europe."

Graham shook his head, no.

"The archduke of Austria was assassinated. It's war in Europe now for sure."

Henry was shocked. He and Lillian had been so enamored together that they forgot the world outside was hurtling forward at a terrible pace.

The driver spoke feverishly. "France is already on the

defensive from the Huns and Britain'll be entering the fight soon. Once Britain enters the fight, believe me, there will be plenty of American volunteers to help fight against the Hun invasion."

Graham chuckled. "What the hell for?"

"To help the British. To fight for liberty."

"Whose liberty?"

"Europe's liberty."

"Why should Europe's problems concern you?"

"Because eventually…eventually it could affect us right here in the States."

"Well, I doubt it'll ever come to that."

The driver drove him up Bellevue Avenue, past the great mansions built along the cliffs overlooking the Atlantic. Graham asked the driver if there had been any word on Charlie and when he might be returning from his Safari. The driver shook his head; all he had heard was that he would be arriving before the summer was finished.

They pulled into the drive of the Cornelius Estate. It was a large marble mansion, with Doric columns out front, like the Parthenon.

A couple of footmen came out of the mansion and met the car as they pulled up front. One of the footmen ran to the back of the car and took out Graham's suitcase, while the two other men hurried over and opened the car door. Graham breathed in the salty air.

The beauty of his surroundings, the lulling static of the ocean waves breaking on the rocks below was an odd juxtaposition against his unhappiness in being here.

He wondered how long it would be before he and Lillian could sneak back to New York City and be alone again.

Settled in his room, Graham found a note from Mrs. Cornelius on the nightstand beside his bed. His presence was requested at four o'clock in the drawing room.

At four o'clock, as directed, he went down to the Parlor. Mrs. Cornelius rose from her chair and smiled warmly at Graham before taking his hands and kissing him on both cheeks. He was relieved by her greeting—it appeared she'd heard nothing.

"Henry, it is so nice to see you!" She led him over to a chair and asked him to sit down. "Have you heard about the news in Europe?"

"The driver told me."

"I just don't want Charlie getting some mad idea in his head to join the fight. Some of his former classmates from Harvard are talking about going over to help. I hope it's just bluster."

"Maybe he'll return from Africa too tired for any more adventure."

"I do hope you're right, Henry."

For the first time, pangs of guilt were starting to creep in about his affair with Lillian. Having been away from the Cornelius family and Charlie for a time, his betrayal of his friend felt more like an abstraction; but now standing in Charlie's home with his mother…it was as real as flesh and bone.

"Charlie should have outgrown all of this by now, but

he still has the curse of youth that makes him think he's invincible."

A quiet, palpable tension came over the room.

"Henry, may I ask you a question?"

"Certainly."

"Is there something that any of us have ever done to give you offense?"

"Of course not. You and Mr. Cornelius have been incredibly kind to me. I'm forever in your debts."

Mrs. Cornelius gave him an odd look. "Is that truly how you feel, Henry?"

"Have I given you any other impression?"

"Charlie considers you one of his best friends. You do know that?"

"I know."

"And I've always thought you felt the same about him."

"Charlie's a swell guy, Mrs. Cornelius."

Mrs. Cornelius eyed Henry now with distrust. "Henry?"

He finally looked up.

"I suppose Charlie's confided to you his intentions with Lillian?"

"Well, I suppose there are some things a young man will only confide to his mother." She hesitated a moment. "It's time that Charlie settle down, Henry. He'll be returning from Africa any day. When he does, I am going to press him to propose to Lillian."

A silence.

"I'm worried with this war nonsense that he might put

off his engagement yet again. Especially if his friends start volunteering. But Lillian has waited long enough for him, and it is only fair..."

They said nothing for a moment or two, and then Mrs. Cornelius said, "should Charlie say he's not ready yet, I would like you to help me convince him."

"I don't see how I can convince him. Charlie does what Charlie wants to do."

There was no mistaking a dark spot of hurt in her eyes. He had no doubt about it now. Word had reached her about the two of them, Lillian and Henry.

"After all that we have done for you, are you saying you won't help me? You know that there's nothing that would make my heart gladder than to have Lillian as my daughter."

"I know."

Mrs. Cornelius' lips tightened at the corners of her mouth. "I've written Mr. Cornelius in Paris. I'm sure he'll agree with me that it's probably best if you left for New York tomorrow and return to work. Of course we both want your future to be as bright as can be, but a lot of that will depend on how nobly you handle this situation, Henry."

The way she looked at him now made Henry burn with shame. Not so much for what had transpired between Lillian and himself, but because of the obvious hurt he'd caused Mrs. Cornelius.

"A driver will take you to the station in the morning, Henry. Please don't try and make any contact with Lillian while she is here. Nor Charlie."

"I can't promise you that, Mrs. Cornelius."

His defiance surprised her. She brushed at the sides of her dress to appear composed. "You must realize that life can be made very hard for you, Henry, if you continue on this path."

"Charlie has never given Lillian the time and attention she deserves, Mrs. Cornelius."

"If you care at all about Lillian, you'll do what is best for her. And you will be vocal in your denials of anything between the two of you. There are many sharp tongued individuals who would like nothing better than to destroy Lillian's reputation. I hope I'm not mistaken that Lillian is anything less than a moral and virtuous young woman and that these vicious rumors that have begun to circulate about her are false. You must set it right, Henry. If you care at all for Lillian, you must."

He was silent. Lillian's reputation was something he hadn't considered until now. At first, he was unable to speak. He didn't care what his fate might be. But he did care about Lillian and the thoughts of anyone saying anything ill about her upset him immensely. Finally, he spoke: "If you want me to say that there's nothing between Lillian and me but the most innocent of friendships, Mrs. Cornelius. I will. And anyone who says anything otherwise is a damned fool."

"That's what I thought." She paused, forced a smile. "In the end, I know you'll do what is best. Not only for Lillian—but for yourself as well."

Without saying another word, Graham went to his bedroom and closed the door. Eventually, the sun rose and a chamber maid came to tell him that the driver was out front with a car waiting to take him to the train station.

As the train hurtled back to New York, Graham kept looking out the window, wondering if he might catch a glimpse of Lillian's train heading in the opposite direction. He started second-guessing his decision to lie about the nature of the relationship between Lillian and himself. After all, what did they care what people said? They knew the truth. He knew it was only a matter of hours before Lillian would tell her mother her intentions. It would be a terrible scandal, no doubt. He wasn't certain what the future would hold for them, or if their affair would have to continue in secret. He closed his eyes. *She'll be back in New York within a day, maybe two. Our future together is about to begin…*

He started to nod off.

A northbound train hurtled past, causing him to jump with a horrible start.

CHAPTER 31

The Berwinds had just finished their garden at their Newport mansion, the Elms. It had taken seven years to develop, so they were happy to have Mrs. Harold as their guest to enjoy it, even envy them a bit.

It was always a kind of embarrassment for Mrs. Harold that their family didn't have a summer home. They had to depend on one of the society families to extend an invitation to stay. This summer, it was the Berwinds. The year before the Stuyvesant-Fish family, the Vanderbilts the year before, the Cornelius' the year before and so on and so forth.

Despite the fact that Mrs. Harold complained incessantly of the humiliation she felt of having to always be a guest of a family in Newport, she always quickly accepted the invitation. Despite the poise and culture she exhibited in public, the circles she associated with made her feel inferior. She'd always felt embarrassed of her husband and his seeming lack of motivation to increase their wealth. She always felt as if everyone in her circles looked down on her with pity for the bad luck of marrying a man whose family fortune had run its course.

Mrs. Harold met Lillian at the train station when she arrived in Newport. It was an incredibly hot day with no breeze.

Lillian and her mother hardly spoke at all during the drive.

After she arrived at the Elms, Lillian was brought to the room where she would be staying. She found a gown hanging in her closet for her to wear tomorrow evening at the Vanderbilt's ball.

A light rapping sounded at her door. A chambermaid entered and told Lillian that her mother wanted to see her in the garden.

They walked together, Lillian and her mother, through the Berwinds' new sunken garden. Mrs. Harold tried to make small talk, but there was an awkward tension between them.

"You timed your visit perfectly, Lillian. The last two days have been quite rainy."

Lillian was quiet.

"I think it's good that you're here. It must have been very lonely for you in New York."

"I didn't feel lonely. I wish you would've let me stay in New York, Mother."

"What for? Was there even anyone back in New York to share the time with?"

She hesitated.

"Lillian?"

Lillian stopped beside a marble pavilion and glared at her mother. "Is there something you want to ask me, Mother? If there is, why don't you just come out and ask it."

Mrs. Harold looked about to make sure they were still alone. "I've heard some very disquieting talk about you, Lillian."

Lillian waited.

"And what did it concern, Mother?"

"I think you know."

"I would prefer it if you tell me."

Mrs. Harold's face tightened, her eyes narrowed. "You are a young and pretty woman, Lillian. Why must you go about destroying your own reputation?"

Lillian's face turned crimson. "What does that mean?"

"He's not suitable, Lillian!"

"Who's not suitable?"

"That…that ice harvester!"

"He's a fine gentleman!"

"He has nothing to offer you, Lillian. If only you knew the horrid things being said. There's talk that you were at his apartment. His apartment!"

"And what if I was?"

She glared at her daughter with venom. "Do you want to be known as a ruined woman, Lillian? Some kind of harlot? Is that what you want? Because that is what people are calling you."

Lillian was speechless. A harlot? The hurt was palpable. She knew there would be talk and gossip, but to hear it now—it was much worse than she had imagined.

"I'm sorry, Lillian. I shouldn't have said that."

"Is that what people are saying about me? That I am a harlot?"

"Lillian, please. I am only telling you this because I love you, and I want only what is best."

"What is best?" She chuckled. "May I ask what is it that you think is best, Mother?"

"I've already told you. He has nothing to offer you, Lillian."

"You mean money. You mean he doesn't have money to offer me."

"You make it sound so cold."

"And how do you think it should sound?"

Mrs. Harold said nothing.

"I did see Henry. If you must know. I saw him many times. And yes, I did go to his apartment."

"Oh, Lillian," Mrs. Harold cried. She rubbed her temples. "You simply can't imagine what it's like for me to hear the horrible rumors about you and that man."

"But they aren't rumors, Mother. If you must know, it's all true. I love Henry, and we will marry."

"No," Mrs. Harold moaned. "No, no, no. I will not allow this."

"Allow this?" Lillian let out a spiteful laugh. "Charlie has no interest in me, if you must know."

"That's ridiculous, Lillian. I thought you had reconciled with those notions about Charlie. It is all in your head."

"I tell you it isn't."

"Are you saying you no longer love him?"

"Of course not. But he is never around, Mother. Once he was, yes. But not anymore. I've always convinced myself that things will change once we are married but I think I've only been telling myself what I wanted to believe. When he's done with his adventures he'll be invisible to me because of his work. How many women are miserable because they thought the man they would marry might change? Is that what you want me to be mother? Henry cares about me. He loves me. And I love him. I'm a grown woman. You can't tell me what I am or am not allowed to do."

"I am your mother."

"Then you will accept my feelings for what they are and let me do what I wish to do and give me your blessing."

"You saw where he lives."

"What of it?"

"Can you live like that for the rest of your life? Do you think Mr. Cornelius can allow Henry to continue to work for him if you run off together? Mrs. Cornelius was beside herself with grief when she heard these scandalous rumors. Thank God she loves you like a daughter and refuses to believe what she's heard. She thinks that man has tried to put you under his spell. She has been adamantly defending your character and insists that nothing sordid occurred between you and that…that man."

"Sordid? How can you even say such a thing!"

"You're still young, Lillian. And I know you think that what you are feeling will last forever. But I know of no one who has had that kind of passion endure. When the bills begin to come in, your love will go out the window. You'll see."

"Just because you had a problem with father, doesn't mean"—

"Lillian, you think you're above this, but you're not. You've grown up accustomed to a certain lifestyle. Are you ready to give all of that up? Are you so absolutely certain that what you feel now you'll feel five years, ten years from now?"

"Henry is a clever man. I have no doubts he will make good!"

"That's what I always believed about your father, Lillian." Mrs. Harold slowly walked over and collapsed onto a marble bench beside a rose bush. She seemed lost in thought for a moment, as if she were trying to find the right words to use. Perhaps she could tell her she once was in a similar situation, many years ago. She, too, loved a boy. But she knew he could not provide the kind of life she was accustomed to. He was a groundskeeper. If he had asked her to run off and marry him, she most certainly would have. But it never came to that. He fell in love with someone else. A seamstress. Looking back, she knew it was for the best. Eventually, she fell in love with her husband, or at least she loved him enough to marry. After all, at the time she thought he had status and wealth. She looked up at her daughter, her eyes welling with tears. "We're broke, Lillian."

Lillian gave her mother a puzzled look. "What do you mean?"

"I mean, your father accrued too much debt. We'll have to sell everything. The house in Manhattan. Everything! The Corneliuses have been incredibly generous to us, Lillian. If it were not for them, we would have lost everything already."

"Surely that can't be true."

"It is. I wish it weren't. But we have nothing, Lillian. What's to become of us now? What's to become of us if you continue down this path?"

Her mother buried her face in her hands and started to

weep. Lillian stood there for a moment. She had never seen her mother this upset in her life. Lillian walked over to her mother and knelt down to hold her, whispering that everything was going to be okay.

Lillian looked past her mother. *How will we take care of her? How could the three of us survive, on the run? What do I do now?* How quickly everything could change in just a few moments. She had seemed so certain only moments ago—this latest news, however, cast everything in great doubt.

CHAPTER 32

Mrs. Stuyvesant Fish had planned the fete to raise money for the Red Cross and help with the war effort in Europe. It coincided with the close of the summer season in Newport. Early in the day, Lillian walked with her mother and Mrs. Belmont through a flower show in town, where she spotted Charlie from a distance. Their paths hadn't crossed yet at any of the tea parties and luncheons or aboard any number of yachts docked at the harbor. She wasn't certain when he had arrived and he had not come to call for her. Thanks to Alva Cornelius and her steadfast defense of Lillian's moral fiber as well as Lillian's own presence in Newport—the vicious rumors about Lillian had already largely been quelled, except by those who had the strongest dislike toward her. Still, she thought that maybe Charlie hadn't called on her because of those rumors.

Lillian didn't know what to make of her feelings when she saw Charlie that day. She hadn't expected to feel much when she saw him because of the love and passion she still felt toward Henry. But seeing Charlie again in person seemed to alleviate some of the grief and anxiety she felt earlier about her mother's adamant stance that whatever relationship she had with Henry should be dissolved.

Now, as she watched Charlie from this distance, she saw the handsome young man. A man who could save the Harold family from financial and moral ruin. She watched him as he moved through the crowd, tall and slim, stopping here and there to shake hands with a friend or an acquaintance, smiling and filled with confidence. *It would kill Henry if he knew what I was thinking right now.*

The plain truth was this: the sight of Charlie aroused feelings that she had thought Henry had eradicated. They must have only been lying dormant. That's not to say that she felt nothing for Henry. Her feelings toward him hadn't diminished. But she now found herself suddenly bewildered and confused.

She might be in love with two men at the same time.

Throughout the rest of the day, this question weighed heavy on her mind. A number of times, she found herself drifting off while conversing with other guests, making her seem aloof and distracted. At one point, she heard only half of something Mrs. Stuyvesant Fish was boasting about regarding the festivities. It wasn't until the woman repeated Lillian's name three times that she finally snapped back to reality and had to ask Mrs. Fish to repeat her question. Insulted, Mrs. Fish quickly excused herself and disappeared into the crowd.

Later that evening the festivities moved to the lawn of the Breakers, the Newport residence of Mrs. Vanderbilt. Colonel

Landers had sent a detail of troops to guard the Cliffs to prevent ordinary folks from getting anywhere near where the festivities were being held.

All in all, it was quite an event.

There were numerous exhibitions at the Breakers including the Duke of Manchester's daylight motion pictures. The entire New York cast of the "the Third Party" had come up to Newport to perform the entire production for the guests on an elaborate stage that had been constructed just in front of the cliff overlooking the Atlantic.

After the production was over, a full orchestra played on the yard.

Alva Cornelius took Lillian's hand and commented, "I'm so happy that dances have finally returned to Newport! It's been nearly ten years."

Lillian drifted in and out through the crowd. She was in the midst of conversations with Mrs. Emily Post, Mrs. Belmont and the Ex-Senator Nelson Aldrich and his daughter, when she felt a hand gently take her elbow.

Charlie was smiling. She embraced him.

"You look beautiful, Lillian."

She did look quite beautiful. She was dressed in a white gown with a white and pink hat, her white parasol folded now in the dimming twilight and held down by her side.

After some polite conversation, Charlie asked: "would you all mind if I take Lillian away?"

Charlie and Lillian walked into the Breakers. They strolled into the enormous dining room where Charlie's African

Hunt photographs were being exhibited.

"These photographs are amazing, Charlie. I do wish I could have been there with you."

"I will make good on my promise, Lillian. I gave it a lot of thought while I was away. You will accompany me on all my travels once we are married."

Lillian felt pangs of guilt that she tried very hard to conceal. She stopped and looked at a photograph. "Who are these men?"

"The white man was our guide in Nairobi. He led Teddy Roosevelt on his expedition. The natives in the picture were our porters. They carried our tents and supplies. They even carried us across the rivers."

Lillian laughed. "Are you serious?"

"Of course." He paused, led her to another photograph. This photo showed seventy Nandi Spearsman. They were almost naked and they held long spears and horns.

"The spearsmen were incredible, Lillian. I wish you could have seen them. They walked the long walk down the valley and through the thick grass and thorn trees. I don't even know how they did it, but they tracked down a male lion from about four hundred yards away. We followed closely behind on horses while the warriors gave chase. They actually surrounded the lion. He was an enormous, black-mane lion. There's a picture of the beast somewhere over there.

"The spearsmen formed a circle around the lion and began to close in. Meanwhile the lion is snarling and swishing his tail and starting to roar. I was a good distance away and thinking I might have to make a run for it! But these warriors crept even closer. They circled within twenty yards of him. The lion charged—but he stopped short every time. His mane was bristling and his roars grew more ferocious. So the lion charges the men again and stops short. The men don't even budge. Then he starts pacing. He'd stop every now and then to roar. But his attempts to strike fear into those warriors were fruitless.

"The warriors moved within ten yards of the lion. I could not believe what I was seeing.

"The guide looked at this fella from England, an absolute fool from a very old family and he tells him: 'Go on. It's now or never.'

"So the fella raises his rifle and fixes the lion in his sites, but for some reason he can't bring himself to pull the trigger.

"The lion charges at the line again but this time he pounces on one of the spearsmen. So I immediately raise my rifle. The lion at this point has dug his claws into the warrior. I fire just as the warriors hurl their spears. The spears are quivering in the lion's body just as my bullet hits him. He finally steps back. He seems almost drunk as he tries to keep standing. Finally his body falls back into a cloud of dust. The warriors were all dancing and celebrating around the fallen lion.

"And then that blue blooded idiot actually looks at me and says: 'Good show, eh?'

"I told him he was a fool. He could have gotten that man killed because of his hesitation. He didn't really seem all that bothered, though. He was shocked I was so upset. God, men like that make my blood boil, Lillian. They truly do."

Lillian was enraptured by his tale. She wished very badly that she could have been there with him to take part in the experience. They strolled along, looking at more pictures.

At some point he asked: "What are your thoughts on the war, Lillian?"

"I think the war is an affront on liberty. But I do agree with President Wilson that America's involvement in the war should be avoided at any cost."

Charlie vehemently disagreed. "Wilson's stand is one of cowardice, even socialism."

"Oh? And why do you say that?"

Charlie struggled to come up with an answer, at least one that Lillian felt was satisfactory.

"Even without America's involvement," Charlie said, "I think it's the duty of every able- bodied young man to volunteer and fight for liberty."

Lillian pressed him, but again he could not fully answer.

"Is that what you plan to do, Charlie? Volunteer to fight in the war?"

"Of course."

She said nothing at first. "Do you really feel that all of this nonsense is worth dying for, Charlie?"

"My God, Lillian, you sound like Henry!"

It felt as if her heart skipped a beat. She looked away for a moment.

"It's a shame he's not here tonight," Charlie said. "I know he's been working all summer, but I'd have thought he'd at least break away for the finale of the summer season."

Eventually, they walked back outside to join the other guests on the lawn.

"Did you know Alice is volunteering as a nurse at a Red Cross Hospital in Belgium? From the letter she had sent, it seems as if the experience has had quite a profound effect on her. She seems to have a newfound confidence in herself. Between you and me, Lillian, I think Alice's getting far away from my mother was probably the best thing for her."

For the remainder of the evening the two of them were inseparable, Charlie and Lillian.

"Do you remember when we took your father's motor car out for a ride?" he asked.

She started laughing. "Of course."

"How fast do you think our top speed was before we flipped over?"

"I don't know. Fast enough." She smiled. "My father wanted me to stay away from you for a while after that. He said you were too wild and that I shouldn't be alone unsupervised with you until after marriage."

"We must have been going at least forty miles per hour. I thought about it while I was in Nairobi."

"It's a miracle we weren't killed."

"You did have a nasty gash on your head, though."

"Yes, I remember. I was unconscious for two hours." They became quiet. She smiled to put him at ease. "We have had so much fun together, Charlie. There's no one who loves life the way that you do."

"And there's no one on earth I've had more fun with."

She put her arm in his as they walked on. Every now and then, the thought of Henry would still pop into her head, but she was so wrapped up in the moment that the vision of his face began to fade and soon devolved into no more than a passing guilty thought.

Charlie and Lillian were fully accepted here. After all, this was the life they'd always known. These throngs of guests in their fancy dress, the women with their pearls and hats—these were all their friends and relatives, the people they'd known since they were infants, the people who had watched them grow into the adults they now were. She thought about the loneliness she felt back in Manhattan a month ago. There was something comforting here, a revelation that so long as she followed the circles where the seasons took them, she would never be alone.

Later that evening, Charlie finally asked Lillian to dance. He put his hand on the small of her back. Lillian could smell the musky smell of Charlie's tonic. She felt a little sick with guilt now. She'd given herself to Charlie's friend in a way she'd once almost given herself to Charlie. *The way in which a woman would give of herself only to her husband*, she thought. *Perhaps in some ways that some might say is even unacceptable in marriage.* She suddenly saw it now from the outsider's perspective. To do such things and then go ahead and marry Charlie—well, it did appear sordid to her.

Her mind was racing so fast that she was almost oblivious to the music playing. She danced in a hypnotic state. It was obvious that Charlie had no idea about the rumors that had been swirling around about her. Or else he simply chose to ignore them. Charlie didn't burden himself with the goings on of anyone other than himself. She used to think it was a flaw, a kind of self-centeredness. But now, as she danced with him, she saw it differently, saw the flaw as a strength, an extension of his own confidence.

The more she thought about Charlie's strengths, the more it seemed to bring Henry's own faults further to light—the insecurities of his past and even his present station, the way he put her on a pedestal.

She was measuring the two men up in her mind now. One against the other. *Try to love the one who best serves your own interests,* she told herself. She didn't fully realize it at the time, but she was intentionally focusing more on Charlie's strengths, ignoring his flaws—not so much because she loved him more than Henry, but rather because she realized now that it might be true what her mother had said. All of these people around her—family and friends—would become strangers to her and the life she had always known would cease to exist. She would have no one to confide in and rely on other than Henry. She'd not been in touch with him since she came up to Newport. She tried to sneak him some letters, but she assumed they'd been intercepted, as would any attempts at contact from Henry. In fact, she was somewhat surprised that he did not make his way up here to try and see her in all the time they'd been apart. A dark thought crept into her mind—what if Henry's professions of love were all lies? What if he had only used her? What's more, used her and ruined her for Charlie? No, she thought. Henry is not that kind of man. But how did she know for sure?

On the other hand, marrying Charlie would solidify her character. To continue with Henry could only exacerbate the rumor mill that she was an immoral, ruined woman. To join the Cornelius family would erase her family debts and save her mother from humiliation.

What's more—she still did love Charlie.

She loved Henry, too. Of this there was no doubt.

The larger question was: would she feel that way forever? Was it true what her mother had said, that all love, no matter how strong, eventually fades? With Charlie, at least, there was this life she had known, the life she could fall back on.

The orchestra launched into "Home Sweet Home" and the crowd dancing on the lawn grew larger. This was the final dance of the evening. When the song was over, and the crowd began to dissipate, Charlie brought Lillian over to a quiet spot overlooking the ocean. They took a seat on a park bench and looked out, watching the waves break on the jagged rocks below.

"There's nothing I love more than the ocean. I think I may have been a sailor in a past life," he said.

She looked out; low clouds were far in the dark blue horizon.

"Today's fete was incredible," she said. "I wonder how much money they raised for the Red Cross."

"I'm going to volunteer."

"Charlie"—

"I know what you're thinking, but I'm going to volunteer as ambulance driver. I got to talking to that fellow from Yale who was here. It sounds like a damned fine adventure and it's for a good cause. Plus, I'll be saving lives rather than taking them."

"When do you plan on doing this?"

"As soon as possible. No one thinks this war will last very long. I need to get to Europe before it's over."

"I know there's not much I can say to stop you." She hesitated, then joked: "Maybe I should volunteer to become a nurse, like Alice. This way, if you're ever wounded, I could take care of you. Make sure you don't lose any limbs or *other* body parts you might need later on."

Charlie laughed.

Then he grew quiet, looking out at the breaking whitecaps. A soft breeze blew off the shore. "Suppose you don't volunteer to be a nurse. Will you wait for me if I go?"

She grew quiet, guilty. "Of course I will. Why would you even ask me that? "

He made a face. "I don't think I need to tell you that I've heard some disquieting rumors, Lillian."

She looked at him. "They're just malicious lies."

"Yes, but you seem to have more rumors about you than most." He frowned. "I suppose it might be my fault. You've been waiting to marry me for so long, and I have just been putting it off, taking advantage of your patience. I suppose at some point…a woman might start looking at other options."

"Charlie, surely you don't believe those horrid lies? Please tell me that you don't?"

"Maybe I've taken you for granted, Lillian."

"It's not true, Charlie! I swear they're not true." *This is it*, she thought. *He is ending it with me*. She thought about Graham, waiting for her back home in New York. *He is making the choice for me*.

He looked uneasy. He dug into his pocket and pulled out a small velvet box.

She looked at the box, her heart racing. "What is that?"

He smirked.

"Charlie? What is it?"

"Our paths have been running next to one another for a very long time, Lillian. And I think now it's time that they merge into one."

He didn't go down on one knee, as she'd always pictured in her head. But he did smile when he took her hand in his. He opened the box. She gazed at the ring, and then Charlie. She was shocked. She realized that despite hearing those rumors—they meant nothing to Charlie. The fact was that, despite the terrible things people had said about her, Charlie still loved her and wanted to marry her. All this time, she never realized it; but Charlie could only see her in the best light. And so the moment she had always dreamed of was now here. For years, she was convinced it would bring her utter joy. But now she felt a stinging melancholy. As much as she wanted to marry Charlie, her choice would also obviously signal the collapse of what she and Henry had just started to build.

She started to weep. Both tears of happiness at the realization that her dream had finally come and tears of sadness for what would now cease to exist.

"Is that a yes or a no?" Charlie's smile was becoming a little unsteady.

"Yes," she cried, reaching over to embrace him. "Of course it's a yes. Of course, of course, of course!"

CHAPTER 33

Graham dove into his work in a futile attempt to keep his mind off the fact that it was now mid-September and he still hadn't heard anything from Lillian.

The summer season was certainly over; but, as far as he knew, Lillian still hadn't returned to Manhattan from Newport, as she'd promised him she would last month. She had not responded to any of his letters and telegrams and his telephone calls to the Elms went unanswered. Graham tried to convince himself that her mother must have been keeping her away. Each day he'd wake and think: today is the day she returns.

Still…

When he came home to his apartment at night, he would check his mail, hoping to find something from Lillian, but nothing ever came.

No letters.

No phone calls.

No telegrams.

Finally, he'd had enough. No sooner had he bought the ticket up to Newport when he happened to run into a mutual friend of his and Charlie's by the name of Roger Harris outside of Grand Central Station.

"Henry, old Sport!" The two men shook hands. "Where are you heading?"

"I'm catching the New York Central up to Newport."

"Newport? This time of year?"

Graham shrugged.

"So I hear Charlie's final done it."

"Done what?"

"Become engaged to Lillian, you dope."

Graham tried hard to maintain his composure. "When did this happen?"

"Last month. At that fundraiser thrown by Mrs. Fish."

Graham said nothing, looking off for a moment to let it all sink in. *This can't be. He must be mistaken.*

"You didn't know?" Roger Harris seemed genuinely surprised.

Graham shook his head, no, stunned. "When is the wedding?"

"In the next couple of weeks. October sometime. They're rushing, because Charlie's planning on volunteering to join the Corps of Ambulance Volunteers and head overseas. He's worried that he won't get to Europe before the war is over. I say, Henry, I really am surprised you didn't know all of this already. I would've thought you'd be one of the first to be told."

"I suppose they were waiting to surprise me once they returned from Newport."

"Returned from Newport? Lillian and Charlie have been

back nearly three weeks, Henry. They've been making the rounds to all the families for tea."

Graham's heart sank. He quickly excused himself and left for the Harold's home on 5th Avenue.

He wasn't sure what seeing her might accomplish; but he felt he had to go to her right away. He had to know what had happened.

The butler came to the door and told Graham that Lillian wasn't home, but Graham forced his way inside, insisting that he'd wait for her to return. The butler hurried away and notified Mrs. Harold, who came downstairs ordering him to leave.

Henry refused. Voices were raised.

"I'll call the police, Henry!" Mrs. Harold threatened.

"Like hell you will!"

A larger confrontation seemed imminent; but then the front door opened and Lillian suddenly appeared.

Her face turned pale the moment she saw Henry.

They were both silent. Even now, despite his rage, seeing her face—there was nothing that he wanted more than to hold her and kiss her.

"Please Henry," she said, pointing toward the door to her right. "Let's go to the drawing room where we can speak alone."

Her mother stepped forward.

"Please, mother. I'd like to have some privacy with Henry."

Lillian closed the door behind her and showed Henry a seat, but he refused to sit.

"I suppose you finally heard?"

"So it's true then?"

She looked down and nodded her head, yes.

"After everything we talked about, after what you said to me, I thought"—

"Please, Henry. Don't make this any more difficult than it needs to be."

"More difficult?" Graham let out a spiteful laugh. "I apologize if this is *difficult* for you."

"Henry, I feel terrible. But..."

"You feel terrible?" the spite in his voice was unmistakable.

"It's all so complicated now, Henry. I should never have said those things to you. I suppose I was just lost in the moment. I was grieving...I guess I just didn't know what it was that I wanted."

"So are you saying that you really do want to marry Charlie?"

She was quiet.

"Do you, Lillian?"

"Yes."

He went silent for a moment or two. He felt like someone had punched him in his chest. His mouth went dry and his muscles went slack.

"What about all those things you said? The plans we were making together? Were those all lies?"

Lillian's eyes welled with tears. "When I said them, I thought they were the truth. But things have changed. I'm sorry if I've caused you any pain, Henry. The last thing I wanted was to hurt you in any way."

"Well, it's a little too late for that, isn't it?"

"Henry, please don't be like this."

"Do you love him?"

"Henry—"

"Do you love him Lillian? If you do, I will leave right now and never bother you again."

"Henry, you don't understand…we are broke! My family is drowning in debts."

Graham's anger suddenly subsided. Perhaps all was not lost. He came over toward her and he took her hand in his. "I can take care of you, Lillian. I can take care of you and your mother."

"With what, Henry? You don't have anywhere near enough to cover our debts. Do you expect my mother and I to both fit into your apartment?"

"Maybe I don't have enough right now. But someday I will."

"Don't be naïve, Henry. Do you think you'll be in charge of Cornelius's businesses after his sons' fiancé runs off with you? He may not care, but his wife will see to it that he punishes you. Besides, he only told you those things so you'll continue to work for him."

He gave her a look. "What do you mean?"

"That's what Mr. Cornelius does. He makes promises to people. Did you know that he was already heavily invested in the moving pictures when you told him you were leaving? Did he mention that when you came to him about your business venture? Of course he didn't. He didn't want you as a competitor."

Graham stood there. He had no reason to doubt Lillian's

words. Somewhere in the back of his mind, he probably had those very same suspicions; but he'd always managed to excuse them.

Finally, Graham spoke. "Do you still love me? Did you ever?"

She paused and looked around the room, her eyes still welling tears.

Graham glared at her. "Was that a lie, too?"

"Please, Henry. Stop this."

"I won't. I want you to say for yourself that you love Charlie more than me."

"Henry, if you love me, truly love me the way that you claim, you'll leave here"—her voice cracked now and it was too much for her to fight back her tears—"and you'll never let me see your face again."

Graham didn't say a word at first. Finally, he spoke in a voice that was not much more than a whisper, "Very well, Lillian. We will never see each other again."

He walked out of the room.

Lillian's mother was waiting just outside the drawing room. When she saw the anguished expression on Henry's face, she remembered of her own past heartbreak. Her animosity faded. She gently touched his arm.

"Henry," she said. "I'm so sorry this had to happen to you. Truly. I am."

He hurried out the door and into the crowded street. His heart ached more than he thought he could bear, and he avoided glances from every passerby.

When he arrived outside his apartment building, he

noticed that there was a light on in his apartment. Someone was moving inside. He stopped, walked further down the block and watched the entrance of his building. There was another man standing just outside the door, in a suit, smoking a cigarette. Graham suspected he was connected to the man he'd seen inside his building.

The man outside spotted Graham.

He's turned me over to the police. That son of a bitch!

Another man appeared from the other corner and started making his way toward him. Graham turned and ran as fast as he could, as the men chased him and ordered him to stop. But he did not stop. He ran into the darkness, into the arms of Hell's Kitchen alleyways and back doors that, once, he had once known so well.

CHAPTER 34

Night after night, Lillian did not sleep. She lost her appetite for food and started to lose weight as dark circles formed under her eyes. People around her were growing worried. There was only one week left before her wedding.

She couldn't bear the idea of losing Graham. She was starting to think that she loved one man more than the other—and it might be Henry, the thought of a life without him too much for her to bear. Despite the fact that she knew it meant she would lose everything, she sat down and composed a letter.

Dearest Henry:

I am writing to you under terrible duress. Day and night, I am haunted by the last time that I saw you. Earlier today, Mother and I had a rather nasty discussion. I will not go into the particulars, but suffice it to say, I have not been seen in the best light because of the rumors that circulated about you and I. In the past (even up until this moment) such rumors against me would have bothered me. But at this moment, I find I am no longer affected by such things.

Why? Because I comfort myself with the thought of you. Every step I take, everywhere I look, I see us. I cannot help but pass Central Park without smiling and then nearly break into sobs with the thought we might not have that time again.

Charlie is a fine man, and I know you agree. I was oftentimes confused as to my feelings between the two of you. However, the time I have spent away from you shown me where my heart truly lies. With you, Henry. Each day, the thought of you fills my head. At times I think I'll go mad if I don't see you again. I love you, I love, I love, you. I cannot say it enough.

Please come to me, Henry. Tell me you still feel the same. Let me know, and I will put an end to this marriage business. I know you are a loyal friend to Charlie, but you are my friend, too. Only more—you are my lover. This is a terrible decision for both of us, I know. But in the end, I know we will both be happy. So long as we are together.

I pray every night that when I awake in the morning I will see your handsome face.

With my deepest Love,

Lillian

The next morning, Lillian called for her maidservant and ushered her into her room. She handed her an envelope and ordered her to give it to Henry directly.

"No one is to know."

Lillian waited for what seemed like an eternity for the maid to return. She packed her bags, knowing that she and Henry would have to leave New York and live in exile. She was frightened, but also incredibly excited. The life she had always known would be lost to her forever, yes; but what good was this life if Henry wasn't part of it?

There was a knock on the door. Lillian bid the maid to enter.

"Well? Did you give him the letter?" Lillian's heart was pounding in her chest.

"No, maam." The maid handed the envelope back to Lillian. "He's gone, I'm afraid."

"Gone? Did you go to his office as well as his apartment?"

"Yes, ma'am."

"Why didn't you just wait for him until he returned?"

"He isn't returning."

A hollow feeling began to creep over Lillian. "Not returning? What do you mean?"

"He wasn't at his apartment, so I did like you asked and went to his office."

"Yes, yes…and?"

"And the fella there told me Mr. Graham's run off and left town. Said there was a couple detectives came looking for him; but nobody's seen him in at least a week. He's wanted for murder, Ma'am. Turns out Mr. Graham's a criminal. A murderer in fact. There's no way he's ever coming back."

"Never coming back?"

"Yes, Ma'am. That's what I was told. Shocking. I'd never have guess, Mr. Graham"—

"Please, go," Lillian said.

"Is there anything else you need, Ma'am?"

"Would you please just leave me be!" She waited for the girl to leave the room.

She crumpled the letter in her hands, as her mouth twisted. Her shoulders started to convulse as she collapsed to the floor, sobbing.

PART III

CHAPTER 35

Artois, France. November, 1915

Try as he might, Graham couldn't convince the Capitaine that the night patrols were pointless. Night after night, ten men would go out, all of them sure that some would not return. There were some nights, too, when none did. But the Capitaine always sent a report to the Colonel declaring any of the men who didn't return as deserters rather than casualties or prisoners.

The nerves of the men were frayed. It had been months since there had been any actual battles. Almost all of the casualties now came from artillery fire and the damned patrols. Graham sensed the men were at the point of mutiny, though he did not come right out and say this to the Capitaine nor the Colonel. Graham tried to convince his commanding officers of the futility of these patrols.

One night, however, Graham sensed he might have broken through to the Capitaine.

"So these patrols…you and the men truly believe they are

pointless?" The Capitaine's face grew solemn.

"Yessir."

"Very well, then. I will talk to the men."

It was early evening. All was quiet. The men stood beside the fire step at attention, rifles at their sides. The sergeant marched up and down, inspecting the troops. Graham emerged from the officer's dugout with the Capitaine.

"Men!" Shouted the Capitaine. "I understand from Lt Graham that there are some of you who feel that our little night missions are accomplishing very little. I don't expect you all to see things the way a trained officer might. Now, that said, you all have my ear. If there is one among you who feel that the night missions aren't helping us win this god-awful war, let him speak now and advise me."

A German zeppelin flew overhead on reconnaissance. Normally, the men would have started firing on the zeppelin, but right now they cast uncertain glances at one another, as the Capitaine ordered them to remain standing at attention.

"So am I to assume that the information the Lieutenant gave me is false?" The Capitaine called out when no one spoke.

Finally, Calloway stepped forward.

"You feel these missions aren't accomplishing anything, Calloway?"

"I gotta be honest with you, Sir. Every time we go out on one of these patrols, we lose a man. We gain little information, if any. I think we get just as much if not more in one of the listening posts than we do on these damned missions."

The Capitaine sneered. "I appreciate your courage in speaking what you feel is the truth, Calloway." The Captain looked around, up and down the line in the trench. "Is there anyone else who feels the same?"

At first, no one said anything. Then another one of the men raised his hand. He was soon joined by another and then another.

The Capitaine looked at each of them in turn. "All right. Will each man who has his hand raised please step forward."

The men hesitated but followed the order.

"I will no longer be asking for volunteers for these night missions."

The men looked at one another with relieved smiles.

"Because each of you who stepped forward, you are officially assigned Night Patrol Duty for the remainder of this war, or until I say otherwise. As for you, Calloway, you can rest assured I'll have you out in No Man's Land every night until this war is over. Treason will not go by unpunished, men. You are all cowards! I know these missions are dangerous. But war's a dangerous business. I shall crucify you! CRUCIFY you! Crucify you all on Gogol!"

"Sir," Graham said, stepping forward.

The Capitaine looked toward Graham with an annoyed look on his face. "Yes? What is it now, Lieutenant?"

"Sir, if these men are going to go out on night patrol—then I wish to join them, too."

He looked at the men, and pointed his finger at Graham. "You see this man? Do you? Do you see that this man willingly volunteers himself to go out? Therefore, I must deny him permission. He's a very brave man, and I don't want to lose my bravest men. But what about the rest of you? When I asked if you felt these missions were a waste, none of you raised your hand. So, either you were afraid to speak. Or else, you believe these patrols to be effective; yet didn't step forward as the Lt here has done to offer support for your fellow Legionaires. Therefore, each of you will be assigned, at my discretion, for rotating night patrols."

Graham felt his stomach tying in knots.

"Sir, my stepping forward has nothing to do with bravery. I simply can't ask the men to do something that I won't do."

"So you say, Lieutenant. But I know bravery when I see it." He glared at the others. "And I know cowardice when I see it, too!"

"But, Sir!" Graham said.

"That is all," the Capitaine ordered. He turned, clasped his wrists behind his back and walked back down into his dugout, humming a song to himself.

The Sergeant looked up and down the line, a worried, perplexed look on his face. "All right, men," he said softly. "Stand down."

The men stood, almost as if in shock. "He's fucking mad," someone muttered.

"He'll have us all killed if we don't do something."

Calloway walked toward Graham and stood shoulder to shoulder with him. "I suggest you stay out of your dugout after dark tonight, my friend."

Graham shot him a look of warning.

"What other choice do we have, Lt?" Calloway asked. "What other choice is there?" He walked away.

The sergeant came around when night fell, notifying the men for the night patrol. Another group of men were assigned, "fatigues", adding sand bags on the trench, and a third smaller group was called to go out and add more barbed wire to the front of the trench. The rest of the men were told they could grab a few hours of sleep, but would then relieve the men working the fatigues.

Graham walked down the trench, trying to get a communication off to the Colonel in a last ditch effort to reconsider and give the order to the Capitaine to cease the night patrols. But the lines had been cut. Graham hurried down the trench. He needed to send a runner with a letter. Suddenly, a small blast came from down in the officer's dugout. Black smoke billowed out of the hole. The men remained standing where they were in the trench, smoking cigarettes with total indifference, refusing to make eye contact.

Graham ran down into the dugout where he found the Capitaine's corpse. He was missing an arm and both his legs were nearly off, hanging by a few raw tendons. Graham looked around the room. The Capitaine's disembodied arm had landed on Graham's bunk. As Graham bent to pick it up, he realized the hand was still clutching a photograph. Graham knew very little about the Capitaine's life before the war. The picture was of the Capitaine in happier days with his pretty wife and small child…it was difficult to connect the man in the picture with the man whom the war warped. He would probably be unrecognizable to his former self.

Graham came up the stairs and into the trench. He ordered Calloway and a couple of the men to remove the Capitaine's body. The phone lines were still cut and communication with Headquarters was impossible. He chose Calloway as a runner to notify the Colonel that the Capitaine had been killed.

"What should I say killed him?"

"You can tell him the truth or you can think up something yourself. But I'll be damned if I'll face a firing squad."

"There was no other choice, Sir," Calloway tried to explain. "We'd have all been killed off one by one so long as he was here. You know that."

"Go and notify the Colonel that the Capitaine has been killed."

Calloway returned early the next morning and handed Graham a letter from the Colonel. Graham opened the envelope.

His heart sank.

"What's it say?" Calloway asked.

"It appears I've been promoted again. I'm now the new Capitaine."

CHAPTER 36

Lillian felt the baby kicking inside her. She suspected it would come any day. Most days were spent in preparation: decorating the nursery, buying clothing. This seemed to help keep her mind off the war her husband Charlie was now fighting. She pondered how odd it was that in a matter of days a stranger would come into her life who she knew she would love more than anyone else. She daydreamed about their lives together, of what the child would be like in each stage of its life. But these happier thoughts were often interrupted by a nagging anxiety that seemed to refuse to let go of her: that her husband might never return.

She sometimes paced uncontrollably back and forth with worry, praying that the baby would push Henry Graham out of her memory. It was bad enough having these thoughts while she was someone else's wife—but to have the thoughts of someone other than the father of her child seemed terribly sordid. She was certain the child belonged to Charlie. It had been nearly a month before their wedding night. Still…was it possible? Doubtful. *No. The child is Charlie's. It has to be. Lord have mercy, Lord have mercy, Lord have mercy on us all.*

A knock came from the door and made her jump with a start. A maid entered her room, holding a letter above her head. "It's from Mr. Cornelius," she said, smiling.

Lillian took the letter from the maid's hand, and saw that it was indeed from Blighty England.

"Would you excuse me, please?"

The maid's smile diminished. She nodded. "All right. I'll give you your privacy. But please do tell me everything he writes, won't you?"

Lillian cracked a smile. "I will."

When the maid left the room, Lillian tore open the envelope and started to read:

Dearest Lilian,

Things are going well here at officer training in Blighty England, though we are all getting a bit anxious to hurry things up so we can join the action before it's over. Nevertheless, we are learning quite a bit and we're all ready to teach the Huns a lesson. They haven't assigned any of us yet, so I'm afraid I can't tell you where I'll be in the next few weeks. But I hope it will be sooner rather than later.

As for the weather here, it is a typical rainy England day. I am hoping it will be sunnier in France or Belgium, or wherever it is they send me.

I hope that you're not still sore with me for

enlisting to fight rather than driving an ambulance as we had agreed. You have to understand that this is the good fight, and I believe it is the duty and responsibility of every well-abled man to join. Please tell everyone not to worry for me, as I will be fine.

Right now, the worst part of all of this business is that I miss seeing your beautiful face, and feeling the softness of your lips. I do love you so very much, Lillian that I often find it difficult to be so far away from you. I know I don't often express it well; but it is the truth. We will be together soon, you and I (and that little Cornelius in your belly). This is it, Lillian. My last adventure, I promise you. After this, we will be together. Forever. I love you, and I miss you very much. Please express my best wishes to your mother for me, and let everyone know that I am well.

Lovingly,

Charlie

Lillian folded the letter and put it back in its envelope. She rose from her chair and put it in a small oak box where she stored the rest of Charlie's letters. This note, she noticed, was dated March 15th—over a month ago. She knew Charlie's officer training was over by now. Hopefully, they had given him a staff position somewhere safe and far from all the fighting. Of course that would have been the last thing he wanted, but she didn't wish to become a young widow. She didn't want her child to grow up without a father. "Lord have mercy," she prayed. "Lord have mercy on us all."

Later on that evening, Mrs. Cornelius, Mrs. Belmont and Mrs. Fish were in the drawing room enjoying tea, when Lillian Harold Cornelius came rushing into the drawing room.

"My word, Lillian! You look like a woman possessed!" Mrs. Fish said.

"I received a letter from Charlie."

Mrs. Cornelius straightened in her rosewood armchair. "Is he all right?"

"Yes, yes. He's still waiting to be assigned. But I'm starting to feel some pain. I think the baby may be coming."

"Are you sure?" Mrs. Harold said.

"Oh God," Lillian winced and put her hand over her stomach.

"Lillian? Are you all right, my dear?"

Lillian grabbed the sides of the chair and clenched her teeth. "No.".

Mrs. Cornelius took a deep breath, looked at her tea cup and then gingerly took a sip. "Lillian, my Dear, let's go upstairs. I do think it's time."

CHAPTER 37

Alice Cornelius returned to New York in June of 1916 to act as a key speaker for a Red Cross benefit, held on the grounds of Lindenhurst on a blazingly hot and cloudy summer day.

Lillian sat in the crowd, swaddling her infant son Andrew, listening intently to her sister-in-law as she regaled the guests with the atrocities of war.

Alice was impressive to behold. She stood totally erect, poised and confident as she spoke, much to the surprise of everyone. She had grown into an eloquent public speaker.

She told the guests about the slow horrible deaths she witnessed of the men who had been gassed. Told the guest how the skin would turn blue and how the men would cough their lungs out. Many in the crowd wept as she spoke. She told of listening to these boys and men cry out in pain, and the helplessness she and the nurses felt because there was nothing anyone could do. In the end, she asked everyone to dig deep and be as charitable as possible to aid the Red Cross.

Later, Lillian, Mrs. Harold and Mrs. Cornelius all came over to congratulate her on a job well done.

"I think you should have mentioned the Huns crucifying

babies," Mrs. Cornelius said.

"I would if I knew it were true, mother. I reported what I saw. Those are the only truths of which I can be certain."

Mrs. Cornelius scowled at her daughter, but said nothing. Ever since she returned from Europe, her mother found her daughter had become snippy and arrogant. It seemed as if she'd lost control over her altogether.

Alice now turned her attention to Lillian and the baby and smiled. She tickled the baby's chin. Then she looked up. "I can't tell if he looks like you or Charlie."

"It's too early to tell. I'm sure he will begin to resemble one of us as he grows."

"I'm sure." Alice looked around. "Let's go for a walk so we can speak in private."

They headed toward Alice's rose garden. Lillian couldn't believe how much she had changed. *Charlie was right. Getting out of her mother's clutches seems to have really been the best thing to happen to her.*

"So, I understand you saw Charlie in Paris, Alice?"

"Only briefly. He stopped by in late March to see me while we were both on leave in France. He couldn't stay long because they were sending him to Flanders. He said the Canadians had a very nasty time of things and they were putting him with a brigade that had all of its officers killed."

Lillian covered her mouth.

Alice let out a sigh. "If you saw the things that I've seen, Lillian, you'd know this is a terrible war; I can only pray that Charlie doesn't see any action."

"We can only pray. That's all one can do, I suppose."

An uneasy silence came over them. Finally, Lillian said: "The last letter I received from Charlie was last March. Just around the time that you saw him. He hasn't responded to any of my letters since. Not even to the letter I wrote to him about Andrew's birth. I know he's terrible about these kinds of things, but even for Charlie.... I'm getting very worried, Alice."

Alice sighed. "Well, these letters take time. There's nothing to worry about, I'm sure."

Lillian could see the worry and doubt in her sister-in-law's eyes. It had been nearly four months now. Not knowing how he was, or where he was—it was all very unnerving.

Alice changed the subject. "I feel that I should tell you that I saw Henry."

Lillian's heart dropped. "Henry Graham?"

"Yes."

"He's joined the war?"

"He felt he had no choice, Lillian."

Lillian looked down at the baby. She said nothing.

"He was wounded in Ypres. His leg suffered from gangrene and for a time we thought he would not be able to keep it. But I nursed him back to health and the leg was saved."

"So the war's over for him then?"

"Oh no. They sent him back to the front." Alice sat back, looked up at the cloudless blue sky. "Henry was always very kind to me. Even when everyone else dismissed me, he always listened." Alice smiled. "I have always had very strong feelings for Henry. It was his principles. That's what attracted me to him. He has a lot to do with the woman that I've become. My devotion to causes."

Lillian said nothing, not wanting to talk about Henry. For some reason, it made her feel as if she were sneaking behind Charlie's back again. She had, by this time, somewhat convinced herself that what happened between she and Henry had happened when there was no firm relationship between she and Charlie. No real commitment. It was simply a matter of emotional indiscretion, a desire for comfort following the death of her father.

Truth be told, she still felt moments of great remorse now that she was married to Charlie. She still sometimes thought she saw him walking along the sidewalk or riding in a passing trolley car, only to realize a few moments later that she was mistaken. *He's gone, and should be no more than a fading memory to you now*, she'd tell herself. *There is no one else but Charlie. He is your husband and you will be happy and loyal to him for the rest of your life.*

Alice studied Lillian's face for a moment and then looked again at the infant. "Please don't take what I am going to say as rude, Lillian; but there is something I must get off my chest. I'd often observed you and Henry together. And I must be blunt: I couldn't help but suspect that you two had feelings for one another."

Lillian shifted in her seat. "Why would you ever say that?"

"Because your face lit up whenever he walked into a room."

"And it didn't Charlie?"

"You were that way with both of them."

Lillian's expression became bitter. "Well, obviously you were incorrect."

"I'm sorry if I've given you offense, Lillian. I'm not judging you in any way. My concern is for my brother. Since my return, I feel I must tell you…I've heard rumors. I take these rumors with a grain of salt, mind you. But I feel it is better for you to speak it to my brother if there is any truth to them, even if it means breaking his heart now and letting him have time to heal before he returns home. This way he'll be prepared if gossip eventually leads to…" Alice looked at the sleeping infant. "Lead to other suspicions."

Lillian scoffed. "I thank you for your concern, and your advice, Alice. But I'm aware of what's always been in my heart, and that is my husband."

Alice forced a smile. "Very well then. I am happy for you both."

Lillian picked a rose, closing her eyes for a moment. She took a deep, uneasy breath and held the flower in front of her lip so Alice wouldn't see it trembling.

"I thought by now those rumors would have faded, Alice, but it seems they've lingered. Other women have always had it out for me."

"If it's not true it shouldn't bother you, Lillian."

"But it does. And it's not true; but I…"

"But you what?"

"I wonder what others think of me, Alice? How is it that they see me?"

"It shouldn't matter how others see you. All that matters

is how you see yourself. That is how I live my life."

"I know. But it does bother me."

Alice pursed her lips and her tone turned dark. "Well, dear. If you really must know, I feel as I think most others feel as well: that you are arrogant and self-absorbed. That you have never been held accountable for anything. But the truth, Lillian, is that you're an incredibly insecure woman who cares little for anyone but herself."

Lillian looked like she was going to cry. "Surely, you don't really feel this way, Alice?"

Alice didn't answer.

"Alice?"

Alice looked out at the gardens. "I've seen very little depth, very little compassion from you Lillian, though I know you're more than capable of both. Whether anything happened between you and Henry doesn't matter in the end. Somehow or other you gave him the impression that you were fond of him. I could see it in his eyes whenever he was in the same room as you, whenever the two of you spoke. You already had Charlie. Wasn't Charlie enough for you? As I watched you with them, I always knew you would break one of their hearts. It turns out it was Henry. Did you think I should see nothing wrong because you chose my brother? There was never any question that you would choose Charlie, despite what you might have told yourself while you were playing your little games. Yet, you lead Henry to believe otherwise, while you seduced him to join you in sneaking around behind my brother's back. And now, because of you, Henry's run off and, even if he should live through this terrible conflict, we will probably never see him again."

Lillian's eyes began to well with tears. "These are horrible things you're saying to me, Alice. Dreadfully horrible."

"You asked me, Lillian. I told you. I told you for your own good. You can't continue on this path."

Lillian started to weep.

Alice stood up. "I'm sorry if this comes as a shock to you, Lillian. Do you remember that night when we spoke in the garden in Florence? You knew then that I was in love with Henry. You commented on it yourself. The moment you knew someone else was interested is the moment when you decided to pursue him."

"That's not true!"

"It was all just a game for you, Lillian."

Alice turned away. Lillian called and begged for her to stay. But Alice kept on walking.

Lillian held the baby close to her chest, distraught. "Does Henry blame me, Alice?" She called out. "Please tell me if he does. I just need to know."

Alice finally stopped and turned to face Lillian. "Blame you for what?"

"For having to run off and join the Legion?"

"I wouldn't know, Lillian. To be honest, your name never came up in any of our conversations."

At that, Alice turned her back to Lillian and walked away.

CHAPTER 38

Days, weeks, months and then nearly a year passed without any word from Charlie. Despite the horrible suspicion that he was very likely killed, there was also always the hope among friends and family that he was, in fact, still alive. By this time, horrible stories were circling that many of the dead were either never recovered or blown apart beyond recognition.

Mrs. Cornelius was filled with such an overwhelming sense of dread that, at times, she almost lost her senses. She often had to take potassium bromide to help sedate her frazzled nerves. The uncertainty was unbearable. On the few occasions when Mrs. Cornelius caught herself smiling, she'd quickly stop herself out of guilt. A letter from the Canadian Army said only that he was now listed as missing in action, which could mean any number of things. The Cornelius family was told they would probably not know of Charlie's fate until after the war ended.

Alva had recently resorted to the use of clairvoyants. They advised her that her son was alive and well, either captured by the Germans or lost in a forest. This filled Mrs. Cornelius with a temporary sense of relief and enabled her to continue her day-to-day life. Lillian, however, found the clairvoyants nothing short of magicians and shysters.

That evening, as she sat at the dining room table with the other guests, Lillian Harold Cornelius was quiet. She wasn't the charming and witty conversationalist she'd once been. Her mother and Mrs. Cornelius worried that she might be on the verge of another breakdown.

The truth was her conversation with Alice in the garden that past summer had left her in such a state of anxiety that she sometimes found herself unable to breathe. Eventually, she realized the rumors about her and Henry would probably never cease. And so, in those moments of great anguish she was struck by a sudden revelation—the only person who seemed genuinely interested in her for who she was, who passed no judgment against her and truly understood her was Henry Graham.

She glanced over at her mother, in the midst of conversation with Mrs. Belmont, and a growing resentment began to bubble in her stomach. Her mother cared for nothing more than wealth and status and she had projected her desires on her own daughter.

As for Mrs. Cornelius? Lillian wondered if her desire to merge their families lay in nothing more than the fact that her father's family were genuine American blue bloods. What difference was there then, in her meddling with Charlie's future as opposed to meddling in Alice's so that there might be a title in her family? The women in her circles were guided by incessant insecurities, she thought.

Still, would she be willing to give everything up? Was her mother right that it would eventually breed resentment toward Henry? Try as she might, she could not imagine it. Part of her now hoped that her infant son upstairs did come from Henry; because if that was the case and he grew to resemble Henry—her break from the Cornelius' and from this so-called "fashionable society" would be complete and forever.

How much wealth was enough? She asked herself. It seemed in their circles it was never enough. Henry was an incredibly clever man. She had no doubts he would one day acquire his own wealth. At least enough to live in what her mother often referred to as: comfortable poverty.

I have made a mistake, and I will pay for this the rest of my life, she thought to herself. *Henry was the one who would always make me happy. Why hadn't I seen this all along? Why hadn't I thought things through? I could have been with Henry right now. Instead of with all these... all these awful people.*

"Lillian?" Mrs. Morgan said, looking down the table. "Is everything all right, Dear? You haven't touched a bit of your food."

Lillian looked up. "I'm afraid I'm not feeling very well."

"Would you like to go and lie down?"

"I think it would be best if I returned home," said Lillian. She rose from her seat. "I do apologize."

She glanced at her mother, and noticed that she was looking suspiciously at her daughter.

She took a cab and retreated to her room.

There was a knock on her door.

"Not now," she called out.

"Ma'am," a maid's voice came through the door. "It's urgent."

She hesitated. "Very well. Come in."

The door opened. The maid entered.

"What is it?" Lillian asked, annoyed. The maid remained silent. Lillian looked up and saw the distraught look in the young woman's eyes. There was something in her hands. A telegram. Lillian's heart began to pound in her chest. She looked at the maid. She felt she already knew what the telegram said. *Why did I allow myself those thoughts at dinner tonight.?* She thought. *Those horrible, vile thoughts.* Lillian rose from her seat and came toward the maid. "What's wrong? What is that?"

She took the telegram from the maid, unfolded it and started to read.

"I'm sorry ma'am," the maid whispered. "I'm so, so sorry."

It took a moment or two for it all to sink in. Lillian stepped out of her bedroom and walked unsteadily down the hall in shock. She finally reached the telephone and dialed her mother at the Morgans. Right away, her mother heard the shakiness in her daughter's voice.

"Lillian? What is it?"

"I've received a telegram."

"Is everything all right?"

"..."

"Lillian?"

"..."

"Lillian? Is everything all right?"

"He's gone, Mother."

Her mother went silent.

"He's dead, Mother," Lillian's voice was trembling. She choked back a sob. "He's dead."

CHAPTER 39

The Somme Region, France. July 1st, 1916

A constant barrage of artillery ripped the earth apart. The sky was thick with black gun smoke. Graham told the men very little about the planned Franco-British offensive; but the battles and build-up had been quite unlike anything they'd ever witnessed. He was certain that the urgency of the artillery shells soaring past them and into the reserve trench of the enemy meant that an offensive was imminent.

Even at Ypres he'd seen nothing like this. Day after day, shell after shell pounded the earth, uprooting trees from their limbs so that all that remained of the earth was a gray and black charred moonscape. Piles of corpses formed hills across No Man's Land. Entire villages were demolished. The losses on both sides were well into the hundreds of thousands. Graham himself sensed his mind was not equipped to fathom such carnage. His mouth twitched. He stuttered. He had hallucinations of spirits walking through the trench, dragging their entrails. At times he lost control of his bladder and wet his pants in moments of absolute calm. Nevertheless, he managed to maintain at least enough of his sanity to be declared fit for battle…sane enough, he sometimes joked, to be part of the insanity.

He was uncertain when the offensive would come, but he knew he did not have much time. The offensive was originally intended to be led by the French; but the massive German onslaught in Verdun in February had made it impossible. The British were now going to lead in order to divert the Germans from Verdun.

Graham's regiment were among the French troops who were not redirected toVerdun. Currently, they were entrenched between a Canadian Company from Newfoundland and a British Company out of Newcastle. Once the bombardment ceased, their orders were to command their men to slowly walk, shoulder to shoulder, across No Man's Land. This would be followed by a Cavalry charge to finish off any remaining enemies. Graham was shocked. Here was a war unlike any other: machine guns, chemical gases, artillery, airplanes and now tanks—yet the British generals were implementing a strategy apropos of muskets and swords. Even if it were to succeed—what would be the cost?

It was four in the morning, Graham was sitting at the table in his dugout reviewing the map of the battle terrain. His men had assembled above in the trenches, preparing for battle. The Sergeant came down the stairs. He stood at attention and saluted.

"Sir, the Captain of the Canadian company would like to

see you."

Graham made a face. *What is it now? The British changing their minds?* "Send him down, Sergeant."

The Sergeant climbed the stairs. A moment later, Graham saw the boots of the Captain coming down the stairs and then the rest of the man's body before he set his eyes on his face. Graham's heart sank. *My God.*

"Hello, Henry," Captain Charlie Cornelius said, forcing an uneasy smile.

Without saying a word, Graham nodded, silently offering Charlie a seat. Charlie sat across from him. Graham held up the bottle of absinthe.

Charlie nodded. Henry poured him a drink in a tin cup.

"Alice had told me which regiment you were in. When I heard we were positioned next to you, I thought..."

Graham took a drink, wiped his mouth with his sleeve and then refilled his glass. There was an uneasy silence that lasted much longer than either one of them would have liked.

"I do love her, Henry," Charlie finally said. "I know you've always thought I didn't; but I always did. I suppose I took her for granted, in the past. I'll give you that. Thought she'd wait for me no matter what. So I do understand why you'd think she might have deserved someone else. That someone else being you, obviously."

Graham still did not speak. He took another drink.

"I've thought about it a lot...why you'd pursue her, considering we were pals. Hell, you know a lot of times in these trenches all you do is think. But I thought about it a lot,

Henry. In spite of it all, I still consider you my friend. I'd like to think if I told you how I really felt for her that you wouldn't have done what you did."

Graham stared at his empty cup, playing at the edges of it with his fingers. "I'd like to think if I knew how you really felt about her, that I wouldn't, too," he finally said. He rubbed his palm across his scruff. "But I can't really answer that with any certainty, Charlie. I'm sorry that I betrayed you. I suppose I told myself you didn't really care, because I couldn't help how I felt toward her. I tried. I did. Christ, sometimes I think life would have been a whole lot easier for me if I never had any feelings toward her. Either way, it really doesn't matter, though, does it? In the end..." He poured himself another drink. "She chose you."

Charlie signaled for Graham to refill his drink. They drank for a little while without speaking.

"I didn't mean for you to end up here, Henry. That was never my intention."

"No? So jail was your intention? The death penalty? Not much of a difference if you ask me."

"I just wanted you away from New York, away from us. If I'd known you'd wind up here, I figured you'd just go on the run and settle somewhere else."

"Oh? And what if they caught me, Charlie? What if I didn't notice them and walked right into that trap. I guess that somewhere else would have bars for windows, eh?"

"They weren't detectives, Henry."

Graham gave Charlie a questioning look.

"They were just some guys I hired to play the part so you'd go away." Charlie shook his head. "I put money in your bank account, too. So you'd have a nest egg for yourself wherever you might have landed. Have you even checked your bank account since any of this transpired? Don't get me wrong… there was a part of me that wanted revenge. The thought of you going to jail did cross my mind. But I knew if I did that, I'd probably come to regret it. And I don't know that Lillian would ever be able to forgive me if I did something like that."

Graham was quiet a moment. He looked down. A smile started to creep across his lips. He lifted his head and looked at Charlie. He started to chuckle and it soon evolved into laughter. He looked at Charlie.

"Looks like I made a big fucking mistake joining the Legion then, doesn't it?"

He laughed harder. Charlie started to laugh now, too.

Graham recomposed himself. "Don't feel bad, Charlie; I probably would have joined the Legion regardless. My head wasn't right at the time."

"I'd like to believe that, my friend. I would, but…"

"Trust me. Men'll go and do some pretty stupid things when it comes to a woman. You can't blame yourself for my own stupidity."

Charlie smirked, nodded his head.

A silence. It lasted for a while. Charlie clasped his hands. Something was tormenting him.

"I don't think I'm going to live through this, Henry."

"Jesus, Charlie. You know better than to talk like that"—

"It's okay. I've come to accept it."

"Nobody knows when they're going to catch it."

"I know. But this...the Germans have deep bunkers. If all of this artillery doesn't do the job...we'll be like lambs walking to the slaughter."

"I know," Graham agreed.

Charlie made a face. "I want you to go back to New York. I don't want Lillian remarrying some damned fool. The only one who won't have me turning in my grave is you, old sport."

"Listen to me. We're both going over the top together. We're both going to live through this war. Nobody can survive this kind of shelling. If the German's aren't all dead, they've retreated. No Man's Land is going to be so clear we'll be able to play a game of baseball on it. Take my word for it."

"Just promise me, you'll take care of Lillian."

Graham finally nodded. "Of course."

"You still do love her, right? The war hasn't changed that?"

Graham looked down at his hands. Then he poured himself another drink and drank it down in one fell swoop. He closed his eyes, cradling the tin cup in both hands, and nodded his head.

"It's time I go," Charlie said, as he rose from the table.

Graham stood up, too. For a few moments they just stood there, unsure what else there was to say other than goodbye. They shared a look of sadness and fear.

Charlie tried to muster a smile. "Good luck to you, Sport," he tried to say it, but he choked on the words.

"To you as well."

They shook hands and then Charlie turned to go.

The sun had now started to rise. Graham walked up and down the trench, urging his men to write their letters to their loved ones. He didn't have to tell them this would likely be their last chance.

Graham stopped at the far end of the trench now. Though he said nothing to Charlie about it, he sensed his death was imminent, too, and he'd come to accept his fate. He saw the war as something waged and declared by powerful men and fought by men and boys who, like himself, were foolish enough to allow the men in power determine their fates.

This sudden clarity filled him with an odd sense of calm the past few days. He had all this time been blaming suffering on God or the absence of God; but perhaps all along God's presence or absence was a moot point. After all, it was Graham who allowed himself to follow orders; it was he who put every ounce of his being into making money for Cornelius…perhaps his reasons were not for money alone, true; but his desire to possess Lillian was desire nonetheless and when he could not have her—he fell apart and volunteered. *The root of all my suffering has been desire.*

He walked down the line and offered some last comforts to his men. He stopped by a soldier he had come to like, a Frenchman from Beaujolais. Graham put his hand on the soldier's shoulder. The young man jumped with a tremendous start. His eyes were filled with tears, and he was clutching the letter he was writing home. "I just want to see my wife again, Sir. I just want to see my little boy grow up."

"You will," said Graham, trying as hard as he could to muster a comforting smile.

The man gulped, and nodded his head.

Graham walked up and down, patting each of the men on the back as if he were both offering encouragement and a final goodbye.

Even Calloway, who had seen more action than anyone else in the Brigade, was visibly shaken.

"We're in for a real shit storm," Calloway forced a smile. "If you don't mind me talking to you like equals, Capitaine?"

Graham smiled, extended a hand. "Good luck to you, Calloway."

"Maybe someday after the war we can meet for a drink. Maybe we'll even laugh at all this."

Graham nodded.

Calloway shook his hand again. "See you on the other side, Sir."

The shelling grew far worse and then just as suddenly it stopped. Graham called for the periscope. The land between them and the German lines had been destroyed. The piles of corpses that formed hills across No Man's land had been blown to pieces, and charred tree trunks rose here and there. If I die and go to hell, Henry thought, would I even realize it?

His thoughts were interrupted when the phone rang. The Lieutenant looked at Graham.

"Sir? The phone."

Graham nodded and slowly lifted the receiver.

At exactly 07:30am, zero hour, they were to go over the

top and attack. Graham didn't acknowledge the order. He simply hung up the phone.

When he turned around, the men could see the fear in his eyes.

"Fix bayonets, my Braves!" he shouted.

There was nothing but silence. Graham walked down the end of the line. "Finish your letters and stick them to the sides of the trench so they get to your loved ones."

He took the letter he'd written out of his pocket and was about to pin it to the side of the trench, then put it back into his breast pocket where he also kept the photo of Lillian and him. He patted his pocket, felt both the letter and the photograph. He looked at his watch. They had only ten minutes left before the attack. The moment he blew that whistle, he knew he'd be sending most of these men and boys to their deaths. He turned his back so that his men could not see his face.

He sensed that his death was imminent. His heart ached. He doubted that he would ever see her again. *Please,* he prayed silently. *Please let me live. Let us all live.*

A couple minutes later, he rubbed his face with the palm of his hand, regained his composure and checked his wristwatch. He put his whistle in his mouth, his eyes fixed on his wristwatch counting down the seconds one by one. The artillery firing stopped. There was silence everywhere except for muffled prayers and quiet weeping. There was no doubt that many of the men right before him would, in only a few seconds, cease to exist. They'd already lost nearly two hundred thousand men this summer alone. Yet, he had, somehow or other, managed to survive. He might have thought that he was predestined for some other purpose; but he'd seen far too much death and carnage in this war to believe anyone was spared for a reason. It was all left up to chance. Still, he wanted to believe he was wrong. He wanted to believe that he would live long enough to see her just one more time. He was about to leave his letter for her, to be sent should he die. But at the last minute decided against it. He'd written the letter a couple of months earlier, actually, but had never sent it, worried that should he make contact with her it might be his end. Considering the fact he was still alive, maybe there was something to it. He closed his pocket, patted it, felt the letter and photograph inside.

Graham raised his pistol in the air. He took a deep breath. Stared at his wristwatch.

The hand clicked back. Then it moved forward.

He blew his whistle.

The men let out a roar as they climbed over the trench into a terrible volley of rifle and machine gun fire.

An ocean away, Lillian Harold Cornelius awoke from her sleep with a terrible start.

EPILOGUE

April 1928. Somme Region, France

At first, Lillian was hesitant to take Alice up on her invitation to come to France. She did not think she could muster the strength to visit the field where Charlie had died; but she felt enough time had passed, and it was only fair that her son Andrew visit the place where his father's life had ended.

Andrew walked slowly, somberly across the fields. Small trees had now started to grow out of the crushed landscape and thousands of mounds had replaced the craters, a landscape forever changed by the war. Tall and lanky, Andrew looked more and more like his father with each passing day. In fact, every now and then, Lillian would find herself taken aback by a quick facial expression or movement of the boy that would show a startling likeness to Charlie, as if his ghost had paid a visit to her. It always elicited a bittersweet reaction within her. She watched him now as he stood in the open fields looking out. Her heart ached.

Alice walked up beside her; but she did not say a word.

Ever since the war ended, Lillian had become actively involved in many of Alice's social causes. She'd been an ardent Suffragist, and after women were given the vote she became enmeshed in a number of causes meant to help the plight of the poor. After Charlie's death, she'd distanced herself from the inner circles of "society" and became what some might call a recluse. Only recently had she started to make more appearances, but usually in hopes of raising money for one of her philanthropic endeavors.

She used the money from Charlie's trust and purchased Lindenhurst from Alice in 1923 for a bargain. She converted the conservatory into a business college for women, a place to learn a trade so that they could work in other outlets other than seamstress or domestic service. She had also donated a great deal of money to the arts and opened a private school for impoverished boys, hoping that those who attended her school had a chance to maybe one day become millionaires themselves.

She lived at Lindenhurst most of the year, rarely venturing into Manhattan unless it was absolutely necessary. She politely refused most dinner invitations that came her way. The gossip mills speculated that she would never be able to get over the death of Charlie, who, everyone commented sadly—was the one and only love of her life.

But the truth was that Lillian no longer cared what anyone said or thought about her. Time had made them more like strangers. The only exception was Alice Cornelius, who she wrote to regularly about their efforts.

They were both quiet for a very long time, Alice and Lillian. Finally, as if she could read Lillian's mind Alice said: "Henry's here as well."

Lillian looked at Alice.

"There was only one survivor from his battalion," Alice continued. "A man by the name of Calloway."

Lillian looked down and nodded.

"He apparently stayed in France," said Alice.

"And you've spoken with this man?" Lillian asked.

Alice shook her head. "I thought perhaps it would be better if you spoke with him."

"No," said Lillian. "I don't want to do that."

"It's time to bring the entire process to its end, Lillian. This may be the last piece you need to do so."

Lillian nodded her head. "I suppose you may be right, Alice."

A week later, Alice drove Lillian and Andrew to the hilly outskirts of Lyon, the rolling green pastures of grape vines, the car bouncing and jarring as it took the cobble stone roads up into an old village.

Alice parked the car outside of a small old stone cottage, purported to be the last address of this man Calloway.

Lillian remained seated, looking at her clasped hands in her lap.

Alice looked at her. "Do you want me to come in with you?"

Lillian shook her head, fiddling with her wedding ring. "Wait here with Andrew. I won't be long."

"Andrew and I can go for a walk in town and see if we can find a place to eat."

Lillian got out of the car and walked to the front door of the home. She knocked. A moment or two later, a rotund woman came to the door. "Yes? What is it?" the woman asked. She spoke fluent French, but there were the slightest traces of an accent; *Australian, maybe*, thought Lillian. Possibly, even, American. Nevertheless, the woman eyed Lillian up and down. "Is there something I can help you with?"

"My apologies for bothering you, Mademoiselle," Lillian spoke back to her in French. "I'm looking for a Mr. Calloway. Does he live here?"

The woman gave Lillian another questioning, perhaps even suspicious glance. Without moving her body away from the entrance, she called upstairs for her husband.

The woman showed Lillian inside, but she did not offer her a seat and went back to cooking dinner. Lillian stood there, looking around at the surroundings. The walls were stone, and a long pine dining table stood beside the hot kitchen where burnt pots and pans hung from the rafters of the low ceiling. The aroma of garlic, vegetables and simmering meat wafted throughout the small kitchen. Lillian spotted a young girl drawing pictures in the corner of the room. Lillian smiled and said hello. The girl smiled back, said hello, and went back to her drawing. Lillian heard footsteps coming slowly down the stairs.

Calloway appeared, balancing himself on his cane. The sleeve of his shirt was pinned at the shoulder where he was missing an arm, and from his reliance of his cane it was quite apparent his leg, too, had been greatly wounded during the war. His thick head of gray hair was messy and his beard, too, was gray and unkempt. As the man turned his head slightly to look toward his wife, Lillian realized the beard was meant to cover part of his face, which had been badly burnt on one side. Calloway looked at the stranger standing before him and came to a complete stop.

He did not speak a word. He looked closer as if he might recognize her.

"Mr. Calloway?"

Calloway nodded his head hesitantly.

"My name is Lillian Cornelius." She let out a nervous chuckle. "I imagine you're wondering why I'm here."

He stared at her, still without speaking a word.

She cleared her throat. "I understand you served under Henry Graham in the French Foreign Legion?"

Calloway eyed her now with even greater suspicion. "You a friend of Graham's?"

She made a face. "I suppose you could say that we were friends."

"How would someone like you come to be friends with an ice harvester?"

Lillian took Calloway's remark in. An ice harvester? Is that what he told his men?

Calloway frowned. "And I suppose you came here wanting to know how he died? That's what most folks come to see me about, so I'll just come right out and say it: It was quick and it was painless."

She frowned. "They always say that."

"Ain't much else to say."

This was not going as she planned. She looked at Calloway and then down at her feet. "I'm very sorry for bothering you and your family" she said, moving toward the door. "Good evening."

"Wait!" His tone was still gruff, but there was a trace of kindness to it. "You eaten?"

"Thank you. But I am fine," said Lillian. "I am meeting my sister-in-law and son."

"Here. Sit. Lucy is a wonderful cook." He looked at his wife and asked her to set a place at the table for their guest.

Lillian was hesitant at first; but she walked over to the table. Calloway grunted and took a seat across from her. He balanced the cane against the edge of the table. Lucy put the food down. She had the short, stubby hands of a peasant woman; but as Lillian looked closer she noticed that there were remnants of a remarkable past beauty. Calloway opened a bottle of wine, and poured a glass for his visitor and one for himself.

Lillian looked at the girl. "You have a very pretty daughter, there."

Calloway laughed. "Oh she ain't mine. God only knows who she belongs to." Calloway leaned across the table and spoke to Lillian in a hushed tone. "Lucy was real damaged goods by the time I met her, the poor girl. She was a heroin nut working in a brothel. I was pretty broken from the war and all, too. So I took her in. Her and her little girl. We're quite the pair, me and my Lucy."

Lillian said nothing, shocked by the brunt personal nature of these details.

"She had a rough life even before the war. That's what set her down the path of ruin." Calloway snorted. "She won't let no man touch her, if you know what I mean."

"Yet she's your wife?"

Calloway gave an ironic laugh. He took a gulp of his wine and wiped his mouth with his sleeve. "I'm harmless to her. My visible wounds are the least of my problem."

Lucy glared at Calloway. He cleared his throat and quickly changed the subject. "As for me, I just help out around here when I can, take care of the fields, act like a dad to the girl. I came into some money, which helps us out. I'm just thankful for the company and the conversation. After all, what other woman would be willing to take in the likes of me?" He laughed. "Besides, my little Sophie over there…she brings out the best in me. Helps me make up for all the bad things I done. She's an angel, that one. Reminds me and Lucy that there is some good in this world."

Lillian nodded.

"Graham…He was one of the finest officers I'd ever served under," Calloway suddenly said. "I ain't just saying that for your benefit neither."

She forced a smile. "That is not surprising to me at all."

They were quiet for a moment or two. Lucy finally took a seat with her daughter at the table and they began to eat, their eyes darting back and forth between Calloway and their visitor.

"So what did you really come here for, lady?" Calloway asked.

"I don't know, really. I suppose one of my greatest regrets of my life is that I was such a cad to Henry the last time I saw him."

"And you blame yourself for him joining the Legion?"

She nodded and looked down at her plate. She had hardly eaten any of her food.

"Yeah, well…if it's any consolation, I never heard him speak ill of you. Not a word. You probably think about it a lot more than he ever did."

Lillian stared at Calloway, observed the way he drank his wine in big gulps, his sloppy table manners.

He caught her observing him. "Funny, ain't it?"

"What is?"

"How the fates work?"

She gave him a questioning look.

"All those men with people who loved and cared about 'em; and me with nobody back home who'd ever shed a tear if I caught it—yet, they're all gone and here I am. Still alive."

"We never know the creator's divine plan for any of us. But you are the only one who did survive and I believe that surely there must have been a reason."

Calloway shrugged and laughed. "Well then he certainly does work in mysterious ways!"

Lillian frowned. "Thank you for your hospitality and your time," she said to both Calloway and his wife, as she made a move to get up. "But I must get going."

"Wait," said Calloway, grabbing her hand. Their eyes locked. "I have some things. Things that belonged to Graham." Calloway gestured for Sophie to go upstairs to his room. "Bring down the wooden box I keep in my top drawer."

A few minutes later, the girl returned with the wooden box. She put it on the table in front of Calloway. Calloway patted the girl on the head and smiled affectionately at her and, for the first time, Lillian noticed a gentle humanity in Calloway.

Calloway opened the small box. "These were Graham's belongings." He took out a couple of medals. Then he took out a photograph and handed it to her. "I think you know the woman in this photograph."

She gasped. It was the photograph they had taken in Central Park. The photograph was torn at the edges and stained with blood. She covered her mouth and choked back a sob. She quickly recomposed herself. She looked at the photograph again. A soft smile of nostalgia crept across her lips.

Calloway then handed her an envelope. It, too, was bloodstained. "This is the last letter he wrote. He kept it with him for whatever reason rather than leaving it behind to get sent. I never read it. But I'm guessing he meant this for you."

She took the envelope. She was about to open it, but he took her hand. "Maybe you should read it in private?"

She nodded.

Lillian thanked them for their time and rose from the table. Calloway walked her to the door.

"You need to stop blaming yourself," he said. "It was his own decision to volunteer and fight. Just because you pissed him off, don't mean you're responsible for him going off to war. He blamed it on his own stupidity. That picture you got there. He looked at it every day. It brought him a lot of comfort during some real bad times. Made him determined to try and stay alive."

"You are a kind man, Mr. Calloway," she said and kissed him on the cheek.

As Lillian was about to open the door, Lucy called to her. She spoke to her in English, an unmistakable New York accent: "The war's been over a long time, Miss. There really is no other choice for any of us other than to carry on now, is there?"

Lillian smiled just a bit and nodded. Then she walked outside.

Lillian saw that Alice and her son had not yet returned from their walk. She walked further up the road and found a quiet spot overlooking the vineyards. She found a large rock and leaned against it.

She took out the letter, opened it and started to read:

My dearest Lillian:

There are three possible fates for this letter. The first is that it will be lost and buried or blown to pieces with my body and never make its way to you. The other is that my body will be found intact and with my remains this letter will be found and mailed to you. Finally, the third is that by dumb luck I manage to come out of this madness unscathed and return to you, envelope in hand, and look at your pretty face as you read.

While the latter is the most appealing, I have seen enough of this war to know it is the least likely to happen. I suspect my death may be imminent, Lillian. Yet, at this moment, my thoughts all return to you. Like the damned fool that I am, I thought perhaps running off and joining the Legion might have rid me of your memory; but the truth is my love for you has never faded. Should I live through this, I will return to you so that we can be together every day from now until the end of days. I love you, I love you, I love you.

Moreover, I know in my heart that you feel the same for me.

If I am dead, I hope that eventually your grief will subside, Lillian, and you will have a happy life. I am thankful for having known you. Whenever I think back to the moments that have brought me any happiness in my life, they are all the ones I shared with you. In the end, I suppose that is all that really matters.

Know that we will love each other always. No matter what the fates may bring.

Henry

Lillian sat quietly for a few seconds. Her fingers traced the lines and curves of his handwriting. She stared at the bloodstained paper, and then she closed her eyes. *Poor Henry,* she thought. *Poor, poor Henry.*

She held the paper to her face and wept. When she was done, she looked out at the vast open spaces below.

Time had long ago made the decision for her. Time had revealed the truth. A truth that, for a little while, eluded her.

She truly loved them both. Charlie and Henry. In different ways, perhaps, and for very different reasons. But she did love them.

What other word could there be for what she felt other than love?

Both of them had, in their own ways, contributed to the woman she had become. For a while she had tried to convince herself that time would make Henry no more than a fleeting memory. That the love she felt for Henry was really one of passion and, with time, would eventually fade away, something she would look back on as no more than a distraction, a youthful whim.

But the truth was inescapable. The kind of love she felt toward Henry was the kind neither time nor death could ever fade.

Still, she was in love with two ghosts. She took the letter and the photograph and held onto them for a couple of minutes before letting them go. Carried by the breeze, she watched them drifting and dancing and falling further and further out to the fields.

Slowly, she rose and made her way back to the car. Alice and Andrew were coming up the road in the opposite direction. Andrew smiled from ear to ear and ran toward his mother, excitedly telling her about a castle he'd spotted in the distance. She smiled at him.

"Can we go, Mother?"

"I see no reason why we can't." She looked at her sister—in-law. "Is that agreeable with you, Alice?"

"Of course."

Andrew got in the car.

Alice came over to Lillian. She looked at her. "Will you be okay?"

Lillian nodded. Smiled. "I will be fine, Alice."

They got in the car. Alice drove while Lillian looked out at the great expanse of rolling hills and freshly blooming flowers. The leaves now green rustled on the trees. It was close to evening and the sky was turning into a palette of pink and red and orange. She glanced back at her son for a moment and smiled at him.

The grape leaves stirred on the branches and it seemed like the fields were alive and shimmering of green and gold like they could go on forever. She breathed deep and something in the air reminded her of the early spring breezes that rolled off the Hudson and up toward Lindenhurst, settling soft and warm, breeding the earth to birth the lilacs and lilies.

And so she looked out at the beauty all around her. She took it all in. Let the memories run right through her and settle inside of her like a river delta.

ABOUT THE AUTHOR

GP Johnston is a past recipient of the Claire R Woolrich Fellowship in Creative Writing at Columbia University and has published short stories, poems and essays in numerous small literary journals as well as the *New York Times* under a pseudonym.

GP is available for book clubs and events both in-person (dependent on location) as well as virtual and can be contacted directly at: gpjohnstheauthor@gmail.com

Made in the USA
Monee, IL
29 November 2023

47719535R00187